LIVE TO TELL

A Material Girls Novel

SOPHIA HENRY

Krasivo Creative

Live To Tell
Copyright © 2018 by Sophia Henry
All rights reserved
Published by Krasivo Creative
ISBN: 978-1-949786-03-3

Cover design: Amanda Shepard, Shepard Originals
Editing by: Kathy Bosman, Indie Editing Chick
Proofreading by: Jenn Wood, All About the Edits, Jackie Ferrell, & Julie Delva

"In the End, we will remember not the words of our enemies, but the silence of our friends." ~ Martin Luther King, Jr.

* * * * *

CONNECT with Sophia:
SophiaHenry.com

AMAZON // BOOKBUB

#BeKindLoveHard

Chapter One

MADDIE

When I attempt to open my eyes, the sunlight stings like Darth Vader's trying to pry my eyelids apart with his lightsaber, and I can only manage a squint. It feels like I've been trapped in darkness for years when it was probably only a few minutes.

Blinking through the pain, I make out a figure surrounded by a beautiful, shimmering, golden halo. I'm pretty confident I'm not dead, so it's not some angel in the religious sense. Erik Raines, our longtime landscaper, kneels beside me, rubbing his large, strong hands up and down my arms as if trying to warm me. That's when I realize I'm shivering uncontrollably.

The sudden, intense urge to puke takes over. I squeeze my eyes closed and roll onto my side, my body jerking as it expels water. My throat is on fire—raw and scratchy, like the morning after my college graduation when I downed way too many cinnamon-whiskey shots.

Erik's relieved whisper, "Oh, thank god!" brings me back to reality. Once the coughing fit lets up, I roll onto my back and take a deep breath.

"You're here? You're with me?" he asks. Water drips from the tip of his nose onto my chest.

I nod, wondering what happened.

"I'm going to lift you, okay? I'll carry you to the house and get some help."

"No!" I croak, grabbing the collar of his soaked, white T-shirt.

Terror fuels my panic as the memory of what happened and why I'm lying next to our pool, soaking wet with Erik next to me, floods my brain. I look from side to side quickly, frantically searching for Trent. My heart pounds so fast that I think it might explode.

"How could you do this to me, Madeline?"

I hear Trent before I see him—which is usually how it goes. His angry voice booms as he moves closer and closer. I grip the phone as every muscle in my body tenses up.

My sister, Liz, is on the other end; I should say something, but I've never told anyone how much Trent scares me. Instead, I wrack my brain, trying to figure out what I could have done to make him angry this time. It's always something.

"Maddie?" Liz asks. "Madeline?"

"How could you fucking do this to me?" He's next to me now. His dark brown eyes filled with rage and fixed on me.

My voice shakes when I answer, "Do what, Trent? I—"

"You're just like your whore mother—"

He raises his hand, and I cringe, cowering in fear as he bats the phone out of my hand. My heart races and tears spring to my eyes as it smashes against the wrought-iron table. The screen shatters before it bounces into the pool.

When I turn back to him, I can't meet his eyes.

I never can.

Looking at him when he's this angry is a direct challenge, and it never turns out good for me.

"I'm sick of you disrespecting me," he snarls. "I thought you were going to dinner with girlfriends last night?"

"I did."

"Then why did I get multiple phone calls saying you were out with another man?"

The muscles in my legs tighten as my flight response kicks in. Nothing I say will quell his rage—not even the truth.

"I went out with Lucy and Mary Hill, Trent. Lucy saw one of her colleagues

from the hospital and invited him over to talk. I knew him, too, so we all chatted for a few minutes, then he returned to his friends. That's it."

"Do you know how that looks for me? You openly flirting with other men?"

"I wasn't flirt—" I shake my head, denying his accusation. But Trent grabs me by the forearms, his fingers squeezing my skin, silencing me.

"I can't even begin to imagine how you conducted yourself when I lived in DC, but I'm here now, and it needs to stop," he says through clenched teeth. His eyebrows furrow, and he squeezes my arms even tighter. "I won't be publicly embarrassed because my girlfriend acts like a slut."

He shoves me hard. I pedal backward, losing my balance on the slippery tile, and fall into the pool. My head hits the edge, and everything goes black.

"YOU'RE OKAY NOW, Maddie. I'm here now. I've got you," Erik says, pulling me into his chest and clutching me tight.

Instinctively, I return the embrace and allow him to hold me until my heartbeat returns to normal speed. Outside of my father's, Erik's arms are the only ones I've ever felt safe in.

"You okay?" he asks.

I nod.

"Hold on," he commands, then lifts me and stands in one quick motion.

Good lord, he's strong! I don't know any weight-lifting terms, but he squat-lifted one hundred and thirty pounds.

Too exhausted to argue, I slide my arms around his neck and let him carry me. His heart beats rapidly against my cheek as he rushes me to the house.

He doesn't knock; he throws open the French doors to our sunroom and walks right in.

"Erik!" Mama snaps. She tosses a kitchen towel on the counter. Her angry tone changes to concern when she sees me in his arms. "What's going on? What happened?"

I didn't realize anyone else was home. I slipped into the backyard earlier to hang out by the pool without walking through the house. It had been a stressful day at work, and I wanted peace, quiet, and sunshine. Sunshine always recharges me.

"I fell—" I start to answer Mom, but Erik interrupts me.

"You didn't fall. Your boyfriend pushed you into the pool," he states firmly.

"Excuse me?" Mama turns to Erik, her eyes narrowing as if he'd said something outlandish.

It sure as heck *seemed* utterly outlandish.

"It was an accident," I correct him, lifting my head from his chest. "I lost my balance and fell into the pool. I was swimming back up when Erik jumped in. He was quick."

Erik tilts his head, his eyes practically bulging out of their sockets. It doesn't matter. No matter how large his eyes get, I'm not changing my story.

I'll never admit Trent pushed me. I've never told Mama about any other times he put his hands on me, and I'm not about to start now. I've learned to keep my mouth shut about things that could damage his reputation—and mine.

That's the interesting thing about memories. They can be manipulated easily. If you stick to a story about how things happened, it becomes reality.

"That's absolute bullshit!" Erik says.

"You are out of line right now," Mama says, giving him an icy glare. She points to the floor. "Now, put my daughter down."

I swallow back shame. I don't want to tell her the truth about the situation, but I also don't want her to be angry with Erik. He saved my life.

It wouldn't have been that bad if I had not hit my head on the pool's edge. I could have swum to the top and gotten myself out.

But that tiled edge did me in. Slippery when wet. Inflexible and unyielding when a skull smashes against it.

Once I hit that, I must've blacked out because I don't remember anything else except being on the ground next to the pool and seeing Erik's face when my eyes flashed open.

He leans over and gently places me down on the large, white, wicker sofa in our sunroom just off the kitchen. My back sinks into the soft cushions. I rest my pounding head gingerly against the back.

"Thank you," I whisper to him. "I'll never forget this."

"Meet me in thirty minutes." He stands but pauses to look directly into my eyes, murmuring, "And please tell your mother the truth."

I look away, unable to agree to either.

I know exactly where he wants me to meet him—under the massive black walnut tree in the backyard. The trunk is so vast we can sit practically unseen—at least, we could when we were younger. We're both significantly larger than we were then, but the tree will still conceal us. It helps that it's located in the back of the property, behind a maze of hedges, thanks to Mama's request that our yard resemble an English garden.

We've been meeting there since we were both thirteen. That's when Erik started working in his grandfather's landscaping crew. After a few weeks, we began an unusual friendship. He became my confidant —the person to whom I could tell anything.

Talking to him always feels safe since we don't have the same friends and have little contact outside of my parents' yard.

Instead of answering him, I twist my diamond solitaire pendant between my fingers. Trent gave me the necklace a few months ago during dinner with his family. Earlier that morning, he'd shoved me hard into one of the floor-to-ceiling windows that span my high-rise condo. When my forehead slammed against the glass, it busted open the skin at the hairline over my right eye, creating a nasty gash.

I've kept the memory repressed—locked away in the deepest corner of my mind. One I'd refused to open. Not only would no one believe me if I told them Trent hurt me, but also because there are far too many business ties between our families.

To accuse him of abuse would open up Pandora's box of problems for me. The victim is often blamed for bringing light to issues rather than the perpetrator being blamed for creating them. I'd lose my job— and that would only be the beginning.

But today, Erik opened the box, allowing the memories hidden in the depths of my mind to float to the surface. Now they're pounding to get out—literally. My head is killing me.

He gives me a long, hard look before he stands as if trying to convey how much he wants me to come clean. "I'll get back to work now," he says once upright.

"'Yes. Thank you," Mama says pointedly. Then, she lifts a finger as if remembering something and adds, "Oh, Erik! Let me walk out with you. I want to talk with you about the Darcey roses."

"Yes, Ma'am." He holds the door open, allowing Mama to exit before he does. I watch him walk out, the soaked T-shirt clinging to his muscular chest as he begins to close the French doors. He shifts his gaze to me as if he knows I'm watching him, then shakes his head in disappointment before shutting them completely.

I roll my eyes to the ceiling and take a deep breath, mentally chastising myself for not telling Mama the truth. This was my chance to let it all out. All the frustration, anger, and fear while dating Trent over the last few years. His temper—and subsequent physical reactions—have me constantly vigilant about who I hang out with and what events I attend. Constantly having to think about how I conduct myself in social situations, what I'm going to say, and how to say it before speaking has been exhausting.

I've always been strong-willed, independent, and active in the community. My sisters called me "Mayor Maddie" as a little girl because I'd talk to anyone breathing. I may seem flirty, but I'm just nice to everyone. I've always conducted myself with the utmost respect for who I'm dating, but with Trent, I've had to think about everything I do so as not to make him angry.

Today, I had a witness to him putting his hands on me. Today was the first time Trent slipped up in front of someone. Although, to be fair, he didn't know Erik was around.

But I knew Erik was watching. He's been keeping an eye on me for years.

How do I know? Because I've been watching him too.

Chapter Two

ERIK

"Erik, you've been with us for years, and we love your work," Cookie Commons says, cupping one of her prized flowers and taking a huge whiff.

The Darcey Bussell in her hand is a stunning, deep crimson rose created by renowned breeder David Austin and named after a former English ballerina. At least Cookie enjoys the flowers that cost her two hundred fifty dollars per bare root. They are the most gorgeous flowers I've ever worked with, but I have to admit having to successfully plant and maintain roses that expensive almost gave me a heart attack.

"Thank you, Mrs. Commons." A familiar feeling in the pit of my stomach tells me she didn't beckon me outside to talk about the rose in her hand or any other plant in this garden.

After more than ten years of working with her, I know Cookie's about to bust my balls for telling the truth. My account of what happened contradicts the bullshit story Maddie gave. She may not want to tell her mother the truth, but I have no problem doing it.

I can't stay silent when I witness abuse.

"I don't know what you think you saw—and quite honestly, I don't understand why you were watching my daughter by the pool in the first place." She gives me a smug, side-eye glance and drops her hand. "Trent Anderson is an upstanding young man. For you to barge into my home and spew lies about someone who will be our son-in-law soon is not only disrespectful, it's something I won't tolerate. Plenty of landscapers in Charlotte are qualified to care for our property."

Son-in-law? That must be an exaggeration because if Maddie were engaged, she'd proudly be sporting a huge-ass diamond ring. Not because she's vain or shallow but because she's vice president of something or other at their family business, Commons Department Stores, and she takes her job in fashion very seriously. Clothes and accessories are her life.

Typically, it's easy to ignore Cookie and brush off her anger or criticism. She loves to tell people how to do their jobs. I've heard her advice countless times since I started working here.

But I can't ignore her today. This isn't about my work as a landscape designer. This is about a human life. A human I care about like she's my own family.

I would want justice for anyone—but this is Maddie. And I've loved Maddie for years. Or, I mean, I have love *for* her. It's not *love*-love. We've been friends since we were kids.

"I understand you may think I was out of line, Mrs. Commons, but what I saw was horrific. It was a crime. And I won't keep my mouth shut when I see a man—any man—push a woman into a pool, watch her hit her head and sink under, and then walk away. Did you hear that part, Mrs. Commons? Instead of helping her, he *walked away*."

Cookie's gaze shoots straight through me. I continue anyway because her invisible eye lasers won't hurt me, and even though her fists are balled up at her sides, it's not like she'd ever hit me.

I can't keep quiet about the truth. I've been screwed over by enough people who didn't tell the truth, and I'm not about to make lying part of my life.

"Look, you don't have to believe that he pushed her. But why would he run, Mrs. Commons? Why wouldn't he jump in to help her?"

"I wouldn't dare assume I know anything about the motivations or actions of someone who isn't here to answer himself."

"Why isn't he here?" I look around the yard. "Even if Maddie fell into the pool on accident? Why wouldn't he help her out or stay to finish their discussion? Why would he leave abruptly?"

Cookie's icy gaze turns harder. "I believe I've already addressed that question. I cannot comment on Trent's motivations. He's a busy man. I can only assume he had plans that didn't include loafing around a pool with Madeline."

I scoff and try to tuck my hands in my pockets, but my jeans are soaked, and I can't shove a hand inside the wet denim.

Cookie continues, "This matter is not your business, and if you continue to act as if it were, you can pack up your equipment and never return to this house."

"I've said all I need to say." I lift my hand to tip my baseball hat and realize it's not there because I threw it to the ground when I ran to the pool. With no hat to tip, I end up giving her a weird salute and walk away.

There was no reason to argue with the woman of the house and lose my job. Though it wouldn't hurt me financially if I lost this job, I'd lose the precious few moments I get to see Maddie. That's worth more than money to me.

By the time I get back to work, my crew has finished the backyard. Instead of hopping on my mower to help them get started in the front, I walk to the far corner of the Commons' backyard and settle down beneath the shade of the enormous black walnut tree. Resting my back against the trunk, I stretch my legs, hoping that any minute Maddie will run out and spill her guts like she did when we were teenagers.

I long for those days again. Two kids, sitting shoulder to shoulder, talking about our lives as if we were each other's therapist—and best friend. A neutral third party to listen, without judgment, to whatever was happening in each other lives.

She helped me ace my first public speaking assignment in my first year of high school, giving me pointers on how to engage and charm my audience while making my point.

She talked me out of beating the shit out of the punk who keyed my truck in junior year. And she consoled me after my grandfather died suddenly of a massive heart attack.

That was the subject of our very last conversation under the black walnut. Two days before his funeral—the day she was supposed to leave for college in Savannah—I sat with her under our tree and broke down in sorrow and hopelessness. Other than my grandparents, she's the only person I've ever let see me cry.

Though I'd turned eighteen a month before and thought I should be strong and stoic in the face of tragedy, she didn't make me feel like less of a man. She didn't make me feel weak. She held me in her arms and let me sob. Then she told me her favorite stories about him.

Two days later, when I thought she'd be moving into her dorm, there she was, standing next to Cookie and Harris during my grandfather's funeral. That selfless support is the reason I've never been able to get Madeline Commons out of my mind—even after years of barely seeing each other.

Maybe our friendship was odd, but it was true.

Maddie would have drowned had no one else been around to see what happened. I don't consider myself a hero, but I'm relieved I was working at that moment. It's as if I was meant to be there.

Though the tree shades me from direct sunlight, there's still enough peeking through the branches to help dry me off. The water on my skin evaporates almost immediately. My T-shirt won't take very long to dry once I get back on my mower, but my jeans are soaked, and wet denim is one of the most uncomfortable things in the world.

But not as uncomfortable as seeing how quickly Maddie and Cookie swept what Trent did under the rug. I've had a suspicion he was abusive to her, just by the way I've heard him talk to her in those moments when I'm working in the yard and they're lying by the pool.

I try not to listen, but I catch a few things here and there.

I used to be able to monitor her better, but that's the thing about growing up and moving on. Maddie hasn't lived with her parents since she returned from college. We barely see each other or talk anymore, though I like to believe she drops by on Tuesdays because she knows I'll be here.

Maybe our childhood friendship ran its course, and I should stop expecting anything.

I have a feeling she's not coming out today. She could barely look at me, which I take as a huge red flag that this *wasn't* the first time he's done something this bad.

It's just the first time anyone saw it.

The longer I sit, the angrier I get. I want to beat the living shit out of that Trent guy. If I ever see him again...

Nope.

I can't let my brain travel down that road. No matter how much I'd like to, I can't. Over the last few years, I've had to be very careful to be the most law-abiding citizen who ever existed. I can't get so much as a speeding ticket.

For me, getting into trouble has worse consequences than others. Getting in trouble means I seal my fate of never seeing Maddie again.

Chapter Three

MADDIE

When Mama enters the house after talking to Erik, she's muttering something under her breath. I hear the words "the audacity" and immediately know she's talking about Erik's story that Trent pushed me into the pool.

I scramble to get off the couch because I don't want to face her, but as soon as I try to rise, I feel so lightheaded that I fall back into the cushions. There's a part of me that thinks, even if I did tell the truth, she wouldn't believe me or accept the truth.

Mama always describes Trent as "an upstanding man from a good family." No one would believe he'd done what Erik accused him of.

"You sit right back down, Madeline," she says, pointing to the couch. Normally, I'd do as I'm told. Sometimes, I miss the little things about living at home, like being taken care of by my parents when I'm ill or hurt. Knowing Mama will always wait on me makes me feel secure.

But even with a throbbing headache, I can't sit here and let Mama fuss over me while Erik waits under our tree. We have to talk about what happened. At the very least, I need to thank him.

"I'm fine, Mama. My head hurts a little, but it'll be okay," I lie, eyeing the small puddles of water from where Erik's soaking-wet frame dripped onto the floor. "I can clean up all that water."

"I'll get to that in a minute. Now let me take a look," she says, crossing the room to stand before me. "Where did you hit your head?"

"Right here." I point to the back.

She parts my wet hair and inspects the area. Then she moves her fingers along my scalp. "There's a bump right here. Does it hurt when I—"

"Ouch!" I yelp as she presses her fingers into the sensitive spot.

"I'll get a bag of peas."

"What am I supposed to do with a bag of peas, Mama?"

"Hold it against the lump to keep the swelling down." She shakes her head as she walks to the freezer, grabbing a green-and-white bag and bringing it to me. "It's like an ice pack."

I set it on the bump, wincing at the sharp sting against my scalp. As if another altercation with Trent wasn't enough to fray my nerves, now I'm sitting on a couch at my parents' house with wet, stringy hair and a bag of produce on my head. I'm mortified Erik saw me like this —minus the peas.

My body finally registers the assault of air conditioning, frozen vegetables, and my lack of clothing with an involuntary tremor. I curl my knees and hug them to my chest, trying to warm up. No such luck. It's time to change out of this bikini and warm up before I meet him. Maybe he'll forget about how hideous I looked when he dragged me from the pool.

Crap! My beach bag is outside. Hopefully, there's a random pair of shorts in a drawer in my room upstairs. They're probably from high school or college, but I haven't gained much weight since then, so they should still fit.

Heck, if they're a bit snug, it'll just make me more bootylicious.

But even booty shorts won't help if my hair looks like overcooked spaghetti noodles.

"Do you have a headache?" Mama asks, snapping me out of my thoughts.

"The bump is tender to the touch, but the ache isn't too bad." It is, but if I tell Mama the extent of the pain, she'll never let me leave the house. Instead, I make a mental note to grab ibuprofen when she's not looking.

"That's good." Mama returns to the sink, where she was standing before Erik burst through the doors with me in his arms. "You need to be more careful."

"I know. I'm going upstairs to dry off," I say, gingerly rising from the couch. Moving sucks, but I can lie down later. I don't think you're supposed to sleep with a head injury anyway.

Once in my room, I dig through my drawers, looking for anything to throw on. I can only find a pair of tight, black yoga shorts I used to wear for cheerleading practice. I remove my damp bathing suit bottoms and slide the shorts up. I can't go out with a rando bikini top, so I riffle through the drawer again, grab a pink tank top, and ease it over my head.

I'm unsure why I'm more concerned with my appearance than the situation, but everyone handles stress differently. When I can't quite process, I focus on the things I'm good at—pulling myself together and talking are two of those things.

Usually, my heart races when I'm around Erik because he's hot as hell. This time, it's fueled by fear and shame. No one has ever seen Trent hurt me before, so I've never had to talk about it. I could always push it back in the corner of my mind and ignore it.

But not this time. I have to face it this time because Erik won't let it go.

As much as admitting what Trent has been doing freaks me out, I know this is my chance to finally tell the truth and get the weight off my chest. I feel safe sharing with Erik.

I'd say he's the protective brother I never had, but I've always had a crush on him, so it's gross to think of him that way. I know he'll do whatever he can to help me. I never would have asked for it, but now that I have the chance, I'm going to use it.

It's a relief and nerve-wracking at the same time. Maybe this is my chance to stand up to Trent, to stop the cycle I've allowed for the entire time we've been together.

Before attempting the stairs, I pull my disheveled hair into a high ponytail. Then, I grip the rail tightly and take slow, deliberate strides.

My head pulses with every step, and I have to stop midway because I feel like I may pass out.

Dizziness and pain won't stop me. I have to get to Erik, no matter how much it hurts.

I breeze past Mama in the kitchen as if I'm fine and slip out the French doors into the backyard. Once my bare feet touch the silky grass, my heartbeat speeds up, and I want to run, but I know that's pushing it. I lift my hand to my head and hold the bump as if that will allow me to move faster. The pressure helps slightly, enough to increase my speed to match one of those fast walkers who do laps around the mall before it opens in the morning.

When I reach the black walnut, Erik isn't there.

Tears prickle in my eyes. Trekking across the yard was no small feat with a head injury. I close my eyes and take a deep breath, getting my bearings before scanning the area. My gaze ping-pongs to various parts of the yard, but no one is around.

Thankfully, I hear the sound of a mower coming from the front, so I know they haven't left yet. If only one of the guys left a riding mower back here. I could hop on and zoom to the front.

But they didn't, and I'm determined to reach Erik, so I grit my teeth and shuffle to the front yard. He's easy to spot as he zooms across the grass on his green-and-silver riding mower. He always looks like he's having a blast on it. Giant headphones cover his ears, head bobbing to whatever tunes fill his head.

I can only remember one time when Erik didn't look like he was enjoying life—earlier, when I opened my eyes to him kneeling next to me with sheer terror on his face. I never want to see him look at me like that again.

Wiping my sweaty palms on my shorts, I cut straight across the yard, zeroing in on my target. The target is moving, but I hope he sees and meets me somewhere in the middle. Exhaustion kicks in, making the yard seem almost as daunting as when I was a kid trying to cross it with short, stubby legs, but I refuse to let the pain get in my way. I have all evening to rest and one chance to get this done.

When Erik sees me coming, he stops the mower abruptly and jumps off. He pushes his headphones down so they hang around his neck. "Maddie, you look like you're about to pass out. You should go back inside."

A dirty, worn Real Madrid baseball cap covers his hair and hoods his eyes. He looks sexy as all get out.

There's a story behind that hat. When I noticed the tattered ball cap he always sported had gotten too small for his head, I got him a new one, and he's worn it ever since. I'm not saying that ever had anything to do with me.

Not gonna lie; I had to Google what Real Madrid was. Once I realized it was a soccer team—his favorite team—I pretended I knew the team and the game. Which is hilarious because the only reason I know the difference between a soccer ball and a basketball is because they're different colors.

"I'm fine," I lie, ignoring the pain as well as the itchiness already needling my ankles and shins. I've always been allergic to grass. That should have been a warning to keep my distance from Erik from the beginning.

But I couldn't stay away.

The mild irritation is a minor consequence for the chance to be with him again. Too much of a good thing can be bad for us, but it doesn't mean we stay away. It's like one of my favorite poems says— *even sunshine burns if you get too much.*

"Please let me explain what happened," I say.

The initial rush of panic subsides, and a flash of something—maybe relief—crosses his face. "No need, Ms. Commons." He dismisses me, like so many of my parents' employees have over the years.

Always agree with the Commons' daughters. Do what they want. Don't make waves.

But he's not just an employee; he's my friend—or he *was* my friend, and it kills me that he's talking to me like this. Maybe because we're out in the open rather than behind our tree. Maybe because Mama probably railed him. Maybe because he wants to be rid of me.

"Please look at me." I place my hand on his forearm to steady myself after a dizzy spell overtakes me. Erik's eyes shoot to mine. Surprised, yet cautious. Underneath my hand, his skin is already sweaty and warm. "You saved my life, Erik."

"You make what I did sound heroic, but it wasn't." He shakes his arm out from under my touch and crosses both over his chest. "It was human. What kind of person would let you drown?"

As soon as he says the words, his mouth straightens into a grim line. We both know exactly who would let me drown.

The same person who would push me into a pool in a fit of rage. Trent.

"I'm sorry. I didn't mean to say it like that."

"Don't be sorry. You're right."

"I know. But it's not my business. Nothing you do is my business anymore."

The words cut straight to my soul. Our friendship dwindled when I went to college. We still saw each other during the summer, but it was never the same as during middle and high school. He was my favorite person to talk to, even though we never met outside my backyard.

Being with him is a safe zone. No judgment. No worrying about biting my tongue or having my thoughts and opinions twisted into hurtful gossip.

Then his grandfather died—and a part of Erik did, too. During our last conversation under the black walnut, he poured out raw emotion he never shared with anyone else. I thought that was a turning point for our friendship. Maybe we would become closer. Talk more. See each other outside of my yard.

Instead, it had the opposite effect. The few times we crossed paths, in the summer when school was out and I wasn't out of state for an internship, our conversations were cordial, if they happened at all.

We never sat together under that black walnut again.

"Well, you're the one who made a big fuss today with Mama. Whether you like it or not, I just became your business again."

Erik shakes his head. "I'm here to work. I'm not after anything from you."

"I know that."

"Then let me get back to it." He glances over his shoulder at his mower like I'm keeping him. He never cared about that before. He's got an entire crew that can cover the parts he doesn't get to.

"I can't let it go that easily."

He takes a deep breath and swallows hard. "You need time to heal. To get your head right. What that guy did was fucked up. You shouldn't allow that, Maddie."

"It was an accident." It comes out in a whisper because we both know I'm lying.

I curse myself. My whole plan for coming out here was to tell the truth. Erik is the only person I can do that with. He's not part of my social network. He doesn't have any ties to Trent.

And I trust him.

"Are you kidding me?" He reaches for me as if he wants to shake me but stops, dropping his arms to his sides in defeat before making contact. "Do you honestly think what he did was an accident?"

I shrug, my gaze slipping to my toes, polished in pale pink glitter and softly sparkling in the sunlight.

"Are you thinking about staying with him, Madeline?"

The sound of my full name coming out of his mouth makes my stomach roll. He's the one who gave me the nickname Maddie. It caught on with my sisters and a few close friends.

My parents hate it and insist on calling me Madeline.

My given name is beautiful, but I also love the intimacy of a nickname, so I don't care either way. I like that the only people who use Maddie are those I genuinely care about. People who know there's another side of me than a flirty, flitty socialite.

"It's complicated, Erik."

"It's not. If someone gets so angry with you that he tries to kill you, I'd say that's a damn good reason to break up."

"He wasn't trying to kill me." I cross my arms and roll my eyes toward the clouds. Trent was trying to hurt me, but he wasn't trying to kill me.

At least, I don't think he was.

Why am I denying it? This is what I wanted when I decided to come out here and talk to him. I need someone to be on my side and help me escape Trent.

"He pushed you into a fucking pool and ran away. Whether he meant to or not, he almost did."

"I didn't come out here to be reprimanded. Don't you think I feel bad enough right now?" I snap.

I'm all business now because Erik is my only chance—the only person who can help me break away from Trent, once and for all. I came out here for help, and I refuse to walk away without at least asking. I don't have the strength to get away from Trent on my own. Our families are too connected. Even if they believed me, they'd sweep it under the rug. The only thing that matters to them is the illusion that Trent and I are a perfect couple. They've ignored the disrespectful ways he's talked to me and treated me for years.

He diverts his eyes to the grass. "I'm sorry. I was out of line." His stern tone softens slightly, but the softness doesn't sound as much like concern as it does defeat.

I reach out and touch his arm. His eyes shoot back to mine. "You're right, Erik. I need to focus on healing. Do you know what would help me heal?"

He looks up and tilts his head. I allow myself a second to get lost in the warmth of his soft hazel eyes. "What's that?"

"I need your help. I know I need to leave him, but I can't do it alone. I need you." Tears well up in my eyes from emotion and pain. "I'll do anything."

"Anything?" he asks with a humorless chuckle.

My heart sinks. While I've always loved flirting with him, I never pictured Erik as the type of guy to make a sexual innuendo at such an inappropriate moment. I thought I meant more to him than that. Though, I guess it proves we don't know each other anymore. I only know the fictional hero I created as a girl.

The one who saved me earlier.

His gaze moves from my face to someplace far behind me, and he shifts his weight from foot to foot as if he's ashamed to say something. "I could never ask you."

Maybe he wasn't being flirty before because his current demeanor screams embarrassment. "I'd do anything for you, Erik. Just ask."

"Would you marry me?"

Chapter Four

ERIK

"Wait. What?" Maddie asks. Her eyes are so big that they might pop straight out of her head. I wiggle my fingers, getting my hands ready to reach out and catch them.

"Never mind. It was just a joke." I probably should have given her a bit of background before I dropped such a bad line on her. But she needs to get away from Trent, and I need a way to stay in the country, so the ridiculous idea would serve both of us. That's probably why it popped into my mind.

"Erik, back up." Maddie closes her eyes and shakes her head as if trying to understand my outlandish request. "Where in the world did that come from?"

"It's nothing." I shift on my feet, uncomfortable that I even brought it up.

"It has to be something. No one drops a line like that out of the blue." The way she urges me to explain makes me think she wants there to be more to it. Maddie never could let things go. She's one of those girls who spills everything to her friends—and expects the same in return.

"Can I tell you something? In complete confidence?"

"Yes." She nods.

I can tell she's happy. I'm confiding in her because her eyes soften, and her shoulders drop ever so slightly. She's not on alert. She's genuine. But I've known that for years. She picked up many of her parents' qualities, but being insincere isn't one of them.

"I'm going to be sent to the Czech Republic."

"Wait. What? I don't understand. Who would send you to the Czech Republic? And why?"

"I'm going to lose my work permit in about"—I remove my hat and run a hand through my thick hair, soaked with sweat from the blistering sun and rising temperatures—"I don't know, six months, I guess."

"Why? How? What work permit?" Maddie asks, confusion twisting her lips and pulling her eyebrows together.

The more I say, the more puzzled she becomes. She doesn't know anything about me or my life. Despite our relationship as teenagers, I never once mentioned my dirty secret. Once I found out, I couldn't tell anyone.

Sweat drips from her neck and trails down the valley between her breasts. The long-running fantasy I have of wrapping her legs around me and fucking her against the black walnut in the backyard flashes through my head.

It's ridiculous to think about fucking her when we're having such a serious conversation, but I can't help it. After dragging her out of the pool and seeing her lying there lifeless, all I can think of is making her mine. I will protect her at all times.

"It's a bunch of political bullshit." I shake my head to dismiss both the conversation and the fantasy that's making my dick hard. "Forget I said anything."

I gotta get back to work. Standing here with her so close has me frustrated and angry. She's not mine. She'll never be mine.

I slap the ball cap back on my head and turn toward my mower. But Maddie reaches out and touches my shoulder.

Fuck me.

Can she feel the electricity like I can? The zap? The sizzle? The warmth?

She used to have a crush on me. I knew it by the way she would spy on me from behind trees and through windows when I first started working here with my grandfather. She tried to be slick at first, but once I caught her and asked her why she kept staring at me. She dismissed the question with a nonchalant shrug, handed me a bottle of ice-cold water, and all was forgotten.

"Please tell me, Erik," she pleads. "I want to help."

"I don't think you *can* help, Maddie."

She puts her hands on her hips, tilts her head, and gives me the prettiest pout I've ever seen. Her eyes are as big as saucers, imploring me to give in—a perfect imitation of that Puss in Boots character from the *Shrek* movies. The purse of her pretty, pink lips could bring a man to his knees.

I groan and lift my eyes to the sky. I've never been able to keep my mouth shut around her. "I'm unable to renew my work permit because a program that allowed me to stay in America, set up by one administration, is being revoked."

"What does that mean, 'allow you to stay here'? Why wouldn't you be able to stay here?"

I pause, reluctant to reveal my deepest, darkest secret after years of having to stay silent. But it doesn't matter now. "I'm not a U.S. citizen."

"You aren't?" Her face twists in confusion.

"Nope."

"How?"

"It's complicated," I say, hoping it shuts her questioning down.

"I'm not leaving here until you explain yourself, Erik. You're the one who brought it up."

I should have known she wouldn't let it go. Maddie's always had a huge heart. She's the girl who brings home stray cats—and stray people—because she genuinely wants to help everyone she meets.

She's also nosy as fuck. I used to like that part. It made me feel important and interesting when she asked questions about me. And let's be honest—I was a thirteen-year-old ruled by hormones, and Maddie has been hot since the day I met her. I'd do anything to get to hang out with her behind a big-ass tree.

Even though I'm embarrassed to admit that (technically) I'm an illegal immigrant, she's right—I do want to talk about it. I haven't had anyone to talk to because I don't tell anyone. The only people who know my immigration status are Harris Commons, who helped my grandfather find a lawyer, and my grandmother. Telling someone I'm illegal sounds so sordid like I snuck into the country or something. It wasn't anything like that.

"You know you can talk to me, don't you, sugar?"

I know "sugar" is a term of endearment that Southern ladies use frequently, but hearing her use it to address me in that soft, sweet drawl fills me with warmth and comfort. I know she'd never betray my trust, but I also told her father I would never tell anyone about my status.

I sigh with resignation. "Yes, I know I can talk to you." I glance back at my mower. "But this isn't the time. And we have a bigger problem to talk about than my citizenship."

She looks around the yard, feigning ignorance at the more significant issue at hand—Trent.

"Has he put his hands on you before?" I ask carefully but firmly.

She nods, but her eyes still won't meet mine.

"You know you need to get away from him, right?"

She nods again.

"Are you ready to do that?"

Silence. No nod. Nothing.

"You know that I'll help you, right?" I reach out and lift her chin with my fingers. "I'd do anything for you," I say, repeating the words she said to me just moments ago.

Her eyes fill with tears. "I didn't want to admit how bad it was to anyone. But you saw—" When she closes her eyes, the tears tumble out, spilling over her cheek.

I immediately grab her, pull her into my arms, and hold her tight. Her body shakes as she sobs. I tighten my grip and kiss the top of her head. "It's okay, Maddie. I'm here."

After a few moments in my arms, her shaking subsides. She pulls back, wiping her eyes quickly. "I want to get away from him, but I don't know how. Last time I tried to break up with him—" She stops.

My body tenses. Anger rips through me, making my blood boil under my skin.

I already knew he fucked with her head. Today, I saw him push her. Now I wonder just how many times he's hurt her physically.

If Maddie weren't right here, I would be in my truck on my way to find Trent and rip his heart out through his throat.

I'm going to be deported no matter what, so why not go out with a bang?

"He's never going to hurt you again," I say, looking her straight in the eye, hoping that helps her understand she can trust me completely. "I'm never going to let that happen. Do you understand?"

The tears are back, but at least she nods this time. Then she sniffs once, straightens her back, and stands taller. She hasn't had a chance to process what happened today. She's already pushing it aside and ready to get back to business.

She's not ready, but I'll let her have this moment. She needs to feel in control—even if it's a facade.

"I'm no pro at marriage or anything, but it would look a little fishy if we just announced it," she says, sniffing again. I wish I had a hand-kerchief or tissue to hand her. Offering her the bottom of my dirty, damp T-shirt doesn't seem appropriate. "Especially when everyone knows that I've been with Trent for years, but—"

Her entire demeanor changes as she processes the idea. Her eyes light up, and her lips curve into a half-smile.

I can't even believe she's talking this out. I was joking when I mentioned marriage. It was outlandish. Ridiculous. Risky.

And illegal. Completely illegal.

"But if *we* started dating, no one would bat an eye," she finishes her thought. "You saved my life. We fell in love. It's easy and believable."

"Excuse me?" I ask. It doesn't sound believable at all. "Everyone we know *would* bat an eye."

And probably my skull.

"Maybe we could start the fake dating process while we try to find other options to keep you here. Then, if we *do* have to get married, it wouldn't look so suspicious."

"Stop talking." I close my eyes and rub the bridge of my nose.

"What?" she asks. "Why?"

"You can't be serious."

"Why can't I? You saved my life, Erik. Maybe I can save yours, too."

"*Oh my god!* Stop. Talking!" I say louder. This girl is off her damn rocker. Maybe she lost brain cells when she was dying.

Maddie folds her arms across her chest, mirroring my earlier stance. "Well, that was rude."

"It's...I...I'm not trying to be rude. I'm putting an end to this crazy talk."

"May I remind you that you started this crazy talk?"

"Yeah, I know. It was a joke."

"Well, it wasn't a very good one." Maddie unravels her arms to brush her ponytail behind her shoulder. If my other clients did that, I'd label it the quintessential huffy, rich-girl move. But Maddie is different. Maddie has made my heart speed up since the first time I noticed her peek at me out of the narrow windows on each side of the front door of the Commons' mansion.

Today is different. My breath brought her to life again. If that doesn't make a man feel like a fucking god, I don't know what would. My eyes drop to her collarbone, where sweat beads on her creamy skin.

"I see that now." I shake my head, trying to regain control of my roving eyes and imagination. Because I know precisely which fantasy my imagination leads to.

"Were you being honest? Will you be forced to leave the country?"

"When the authorities come knocking, yes."

"Then let's do it."

"You can't be serious." How is she so easily agreeable to something so ridiculous?

"I'm dead serious," she says. "It can't hurt, right? It gives us a dating history, and if getting married is a way to keep you here, then we'll be covered. It won't seem out of the blue or forced."

"You do know that this plan is completely illegal, right?"

"Dating is illegal?"

"The intention behind our dating is."

"What other options do you have?" she asks.

"None."

Maddie smirks. It's as infuriating as it is sexy.

"What about Trent?" I ask.

The smirk slips from her lips. "I reckon this gives me my out."

"I'm happy to be your out if this is what finally gets you out. But I also want you to realize that you deserve better than that piece of shit. And you need to tell your family the truth about him."

She lifts her hand to her forehead, then slides it around to the back. I reach out and feel the raised bump under my fingers.

"Well, our families are intertwined in multiple aspects of our business, so I have to be very careful in how I approach the situation." Maddie bites her lip. "Can we give dating a try? It'll help you as much as it'll help me." Her voice is low, and she's less confident than a few seconds ago.

I have no clue what she's going through. I've always seen Maddie as this hurricane of happiness—a larger-than-life, confident, energetic force. The last time I saw her insecure, vulnerable side was years ago when we used to talk behind our tree. It makes her even more real. The urge to protect her from that asshole rises inside of me.

Even though starting a fake relationship is not a good idea, I can't help but agree because it'll allow me to get close to her. I can keep Trent away from her if I'm close to her. Maybe I can help her heal from the trauma he's put her through. She deserves to be as confident on the inside as she portrays on the outside.

"You sure you want to start this? Are you ready for the backlash?" I ask.

She hasn't had time to think about what she's getting herself into, but I can see the train wreck already. I know what her friends will say. I know what her mother will say.

Fuck. Her dad is gonna rail me as soon as he finds out. Not only could Harris pull his business from me, but I could also lose multiple clients because of this.

Maddie, who's always so quick with her comebacks, pauses. Then she looks me dead in the eye and says, "I'm ready to fight for your life like you fought for mine."

Someone help me.

As if her words didn't shock me enough, Maddie lifts her hand to my cheek and leans closer, lips hovering next to mine. The scent of bubble gum wafts under my nose. She always chews bubble gum. I've seen her walk out of the house in a power suit, five-inch heels, and a huge-ass, pink bubble protruding from her lips.

It's silly and sexy. Completely Maddie.

"This is for the neighbors. So everyone can see that we've started this passionate fling," she says without a hint of humor.

"How passionate?" I tease, calling her bluff by grabbing her hips and pulling her against me. Chest to chest, I feel her heart speed up. Our mouths are inches away, but neither has leaned in to seal this deranged agreement.

"We've gotta make this look real, don't we?" she asks, her breath warm on my face.

Having Maddie in my arms feels right, like our bodies were made to be molded together. I've wanted to do this for years. Ever since a silly crush turned into raging teenage hormones and, most recently, an intense, unstoppable longing.

It may be a fake relationship, but it won't stop me from treating her like the girl I've loved for years.

I wonder how I'll be able to keep my feelings for her out of this.

Because the truth of the matter is that I will have to leave the country. Unless laws change in the next six months, there's no way around it.

I don't need to tell her that right now. I need her to think there's a chance—or there's not even a reason to start this charade. It'll give me a better opportunity to return to the country if we both put our all into it.

"You came up with this idea pretty quickly. Almost like you've been planning a way to date me," I tease. She seems unaffected by the feel of my erection pressing against her stomach. I've dreamed about being this close—and doing these things—for over ten years.

"You'll never know." Instead of meeting my lips with hers, she rises onto her tiptoes and quickly kisses my forehead. "To be continued," she says in a breathy whisper.

After a few backward strides, she spins around and heads toward the house. My eyes linger on her perfect ass, hanging out of tiny, black shorts. I send a silent thank you to whoever created women's workout gear.

Tearing my eyes away from Maddie's ass is difficult but necessary. I replace my headphones and jump back onto my lawn mower.

Is she serious about this crazy plan or suffering side effects from minor brain trauma? If she wasn't, why would she put the thought in my head and start the charade in the front yard? We both know someone in this neighborhood is always watching.

With how much these Southern ladies love to gossip, I'd bet there's already a community email about our almost-kiss seconds ago.

Why would she lie? The short answer is that she's Harris Commons' daughter and had to have inherited some of his qualities.

Lying is as easy for Harris Commons as breathing. But that's a shitty thought to have about the girl who just selflessly offered to do something illegal to help me stay in the country.

It's incredibly shitty because the Commons have done so much for me and my family. Despite that, I'm confident he'd stab me in the back the minute I crossed him, so I take his kindness with a grain of salt.

Harris does things to have power over people, not out of the goodness of his heart. When he does you a favor, you owe him a favor. It's a simple rule I know all too well.

I may have warned Maddie about the backlash she'll face, but I'm bracing for a bit of my own. If any of the neighbors saw our interaction and it got back to him before we told him our reasoning, he would not be happy.

Cookie's gonna have a conniption when she finds out Maddie ditched Trent and started "dating" me. Despite how rough that will be on Maddie, it makes me laugh. I can't wait to see Cookie's face when she sees us together—watching her pasted smile grow more prominent as she tries to hold back a biting comment.

Maddie's mom threatened my job today simply because I told her the truth about what happened at the pool. I imagine she'll do the same when we tell her we're dating.

When my grandfather owned the company, losing the Commons' business would have been devastating because he relied on Harris and his referrals. Grandpa's ideal business model was fewer clients at a higher rate, based on the size of their property and the amount of work that went into each one. He prided himself on personally working on every client's property.

While I think it's a great model, I had other plans for the business —expansion. After he passed, I kept the high-end clients and the relationships my grandfather built. I work on all of their properties, just as he did.

However, I focused on building the business by bringing on other clients. Since then, I've built a good-sized base and have various crews running seven days a week.

Over the last six years, I've built a company that can withstand losing a few clients to the backlash of Maddie and my decision. It'll be a hit at first, but I can make up for it by taking on more clients whose yards I can complete quicker.

I can handle myself, but I hope Maddie knows what she's getting into.

Chapter Five

MADDIE

I've just come inside from talking to Erik when the front door slams into my back and knocks me forward onto the floor. My chin hits the hardwood, and I curse. When I woke up this morning, I certainly didn't expect to have to withstand multiple head traumas.

"Where's Maddie?" my older sister, Liz, yells as she rushes into the house, tripping in haste and falling right on top of me. Thankfully, her boyfriend, Austin, screeches to a halt behind her.

"Geez, oh Pete, Liz!" My hand flies to my side, where her foot kicked me as she fell. Then I arch my back and buck her off. The big-ass Michael Kors pocketbook I bought her for Christmas last year knocks into me, almost sending me to the floor again.

"Oh my gosh!" Liz pops onto her knees with lightning speed and places a hand on my forehead like I'm a child with a fever. Good lord— her reflexes are quick in an emergency. "What are you doing on the ground? Did Trent do this?"

"No. You did." I bat her hand away and get up slowly.

She glances between the door and me as the realization of what happened crosses her face. "Oh, crap. Sorry, Mads." Austin holds out his hand to help her back to her feet.

"What are you doing here? I thought you just got into town?" I walk toward the kitchen slowly, ready to down ibuprofen and a massive glass of water. Being outside in the scorching heat didn't help my dizziness.

Liz and Austin follow me.

"I heard Trent yelling at you, and the conversation cut off abruptly. Did you think I could ignore that?"

Liz and Austin recently returned from a three-month trip traveling around the country. He's a singer in a rock band, and she went with him on tour. Despite being seemingly opposite in every way, Austin has been exactly what Liz needed in her life.

After being in a car accident a little over a year ago, she lost complete use of her hand—which meant she could no longer continue her career as a surgeon.

I know it was difficult for her to face the end of a career she had worked so hard for. I can't even imagine something so devastating. But she met Austin during that low point, and he helped her get back on track. He helped her see that she could do anything, not just our parents' path. It had to be hard on her, but I think it was the change she needed. She starts her residency in family medicine in a few weeks.

"It was nothing."

"It didn't sound like nothing," Liz says. "I think we need to talk about it."

"Elizabeth? Is that you?" Mama calls from the kitchen.

"Yeah, Mama! I'm talking to Madeline."

Austin stops abruptly and grabs Liz's arm. "I seriously can't handle your mom right now." The circles under his bloodshot eyes are deep purple, and he looks like he's going to pass out on his feet. I feel terrible that he and Liz rushed over here for no reason.

"Very true. You're way too exhausted to deal with her," Liz agrees. "Why don't you go up to my room and lie down? I'll be up to get you in a little bit."

I guess we're all hanging out at Mama and Daddy's today.

Liz and I watch Austin fly up the steps, taking two steps at a time. His relationship with my parents got off to a rocky start, mainly because Liz kept him a secret from them. Mama hasn't gotten to know him yet because he and Liz have been gone for three months.

Not that time matters. I doubt she'll ever get used to him—or truly like him.

He's the sweetest guy and treats Liz like gold, but Mama will never get past his tattoos. She hates them. I'm not the biggest fan, but I don't think people who have them are inherently bad or anything.

Tattoos alone don't say anything about a person's character. Sadly, Mama uses that particular form of self-expression to judge people without knowing anything about them.

Commons Department Stores, our family business, revolves around personal style. We built our brand around "the common man," and we want—or should want—customers who identify themselves by their unique fashion and outward expression. This is ingrained in everything we do and all of our campaigns.

After giving my sister a once-over, I say, "You two look like death warmed over. Why don't you go back home?"

"Absolutely not! I'm not leaving until you tell me what the hell happened!" Liz isn't going to let it go.

Nobody in the Commons family lets anything go.

We wander to the kitchen.

It's my business. I'm handling it—with Erik's help—but still, it's being taken care of. Liz and I have always been close; she can tell when I'm holding back. Usually, I'm not good at keeping things to myself. I'm the one who tells everyone's business all the time. It's not malicious. Everything spills out when I open my mouth.

"It was nothing. Trent was being"—I pause—"Trent. He was upset over something, and we started arguing. I took a step backward and fell into the pool. I didn't realize how close I was to the edge."

"You expect me to believe that?"

"Why wouldn't you believe that?" I ask, lifting my eyes to hers, despite my fear they'll betray my calm demeanor. Thankfully, I had a chance to speak with Erik already. Otherwise, I don't know if I'd be this calm with Liz.

The situation with Erik has my insides flipping. A fake relationship leading to a phony engagement excites me more than it should.

"I could hear how angry he was. It was scary. We drove here

because we were worried, Maddie. And I know this isn't the first time he's been like that with you."

Ignoring my sister's concerns, I open the fridge and inspect my parents' food supply. Mama must be getting ready to host a gathering, as there are stacks of pre-made food containers, loads of fruit, and multiple blocks of cheese.

"You can talk to me, Mads. You know that, right?" Liz asks. Her voice is soft.

I know I can trust her, not just because she's my sister and I love her with all my heart, but also because she knows what it feels like to go against the grain in our family. She knows what it's like to choose a man your parents don't want you to be with.

I grab a lemon-flavored sparkling water and shut the fridge. "Everything is fine. What Trent did was shitty. It confirmed what I was already thinking. We're not a good match. I'm going to break up with him."

"What was that?" Mama asks. She's wiping her hands on a kitchen towel as she crosses the room.

Ugh. My stomach rolls, knowing Mama won't be happy about my decision. But it has to happen. The quicker I break things off, the faster I can start the plan with Erik. I trust Erik to help me and protect me.

"I'm breaking up with Trent," I say, popping the top on the can. "He came at me again, accusing me of cheating because I said hello to a guy who used to work with Liz." I shake my head. "He's constantly getting angry at me for no reason."

"Is that what today was about?" Mama asks.

I need to be honest with her, even if it's not completely honest. "Yes. He gets angry and mean. I can't deal with it anymore. I could handle his temper when he was at Georgetown, but now—" I pause. "He scares me, Mama."

"I didn't realize it was that bad." She folds the towel and places it on the counter.

"You've heard how he talks to me."

"I've never noticed anything out of the ordinary."

"Because being an arrogant, misogynistic dickbag isn't out of the ordinary in our world," Liz says.

Mama scowls and gives Liz a cold gaze. "Was that necessary, Elizabeth?"

"Sorry."

"He's always been harsh and disrespectful, Mama."

Though Liz and I said the same thing, my phrasing is more pleasing to Mama's ears. There's always a civil way to say something.

"It's your choice, Madeline. But I think this is all very odd and out of the blue. You've never mentioned any of this before."

I never had the courage to—because no one ever witnessed his abuse before.

"It's been going on since we first started dating, but it's gotten worse now that we're around each other more often. It's not a healthy relationship."

Mama pauses before she speaks, which means she's contemplating how to make me rethink my decision. "Just remember that our families work very closely together. And with this new mall, there's much more at stake now. We all need to be on good terms, which could prove very difficult if you choose to end your relationship with Trent."

And there it is—Mama tying the business directly to my personal life.

Sometimes, I wish I weren't the daughter who chose to work in the family business. It's not just a job—it's politics.

Usually, I'm all for making deals and forming alliances with other families and companies because it's all business, but this time, my safety is on the line. And having that tied to our business makes me very uncomfortable.

"I've always made choices in the best interest of Commons Stores, Mama. This won't be any different."

"Maybe so," she says firmly. Then she yanks the soiled kitchen towel from the counter and stalks toward me. She looks at me directly before saying, "I trust you know enough to hush your mouth about what happened today. It'll ruin that man's reputation—and yours."

Mama, the woman who taught me to throw my shoulders back, fix my lipstick, and move forward with my head high in even the most uncomfortable situations, storms out of the room. She's probably itching to call Daddy to relay the news. They've got to start planning their strategy for dealing with their daughter breaking up with an attorney who works with the firm that handles all of our legal matters. Not to mention that Trent is the son of Alfred Anderson, the architect who designs our stores.

Mama cares more about Trent's reputation and our business ties than my near-death experience.

It's the Commons family in a nutshell.

"Has he ever hurt you, Maddie?" Liz asks once Mama is out of sight.

"Nothing I couldn't handle." I glance at the doorway before crossing the room and opening the cabinet above the sink where Daddy keeps bottles of ibuprofen and antacids.

Liz's gaze shoots through me. She doesn't believe me any more than I believe myself.

"If you need someone, I'm here. I'm ready to stick up for you. I'll stand by your side."

"I'm fine, Liz. Trent's behavior today was the last straw, and I'm doing something about it. You heard me tell Mama." I shake a few pills into my palm.

"It sounds that way, but I wonder if you understand how serious this is. You know she and Daddy will try to talk you out of it, right?"

"I'm sure they will. The future of Commons rests solely on my shoulders," I say dryly before tossing the medicine into my mouth and washing it down with sparkling water.

"I'm proud of you for speaking up. I'm sorry he's hurt you. He doesn't get to treat you like this. I thought something was happening between you two, but I never saw anything, and you never said anything."

"You're reading too much into all of this."

"I should have voiced my concerns before it got to this point, Madeline. I'm sorry I didn't. It took me some time, but I see things—and people—differently now."

"Differently doesn't mean correctly."

"Sometimes it does," she says.

"I appreciate your concern, seriously. I'm good right now. After I break up with Trent, I'll need your support. I don't think he's going to take it well. As Mama said, Trent's family and ours have important ties. I'm worried about the reaction from all sides."

"Don't worry about that. Just focus on what makes you happy and keeps you safe."

It's easy to say for someone who doesn't have the weight of the family business on her shoulders. But working for Daddy was my choice, so I can't be upset.

Liz talks like she knows what's going on. Part of me feels like she does, without me even having to say anything. But how could that be possible? No one in my family could ever know the extent of what was going on in the relationship.

"I will," I say. "I am."

"What were you and Erik talking about outside? You were standing pretty close."

"The roses."

"You sound like Mama!" She grabs an orange from the overflowing fruit basket in front of her and throws it at me. It bounces off my thigh and onto the floor.

"Shut up!" I say, stooping to pick it up. The fruit has a significant dent, but I return it to the bowl anyway. If I put it dent down, Daddy —the only one who ever eats oranges—won't even notice.

"Well, I'm not trying to be a jerk, but you need to be careful, Maddie. It might have been nothing, but you were in the front yard, where anyone—including Trent—could have seen. And if he already accuses you of cheating and gets angry about it, actions like that will fuel his fire."

"I know." I nibble my bottom lip, contemplating if I should tell Liz about what Erik and I discussed. My older sister is one of my best friends, and I value her opinion over almost everyone.

I need to tell someone without revealing the exact details yet. It's up to Erik to let me know when I can say anything. Especially since I'm not sure if he's agreed to the scheme yet.

"Call me if you need me," Liz says, walking toward the door closest to the stairway.

"Erik wants to help me get away from Trent," I call out, but not too loud, because I don't want Mama to overhear. "That's what we were talking about outside."

Liz turns around slowly. "How does he want to help?"

I hesitate because Erik was right—the idea sounds ridiculous now that I'm telling someone else. "By starting a fake relationship with each other," I squeak out.

"A fake re—" Liz repeats as knitted brows of confusion quickly turn to raised brows of surprise. "I think that's a brilliant idea." Though she won't let it reach her lips, I can tell she's holding back a smile. It's in her eyes. As quickly as it came, it's gone. "But don't hurt that boy's heart, Madeline. He may act the part, shaking hands and sharing a laugh with his clients, but he's not in Daddy's Boys' Club."

I nod. She's right. I wasn't thinking clearly. The conversation with Erik and the exciting possibilities that accompany it had me overly confident that the situation could be resolved easily.

I know that won't happen, but Erik is putting his neck on the line by helping me, especially knowing Trent's temper and the family backing him.

He's counting on me as much as I'm counting on him, and I don't plan on going back on my word.

ONCE I'M HOME, I feel lighter, as if I can finally breathe again now that I'm in my own space. I kick off my shoes at the door and drop my bag on the floor beside them. As I move through the house, all I can think of is jumping in the shower. At least the ibuprofen I'd taken at Mama and Daddy's helped ease the throbbing.

Despite nearing the end of summer, the temperature outside is still in the mid-nineties, but the air conditioning has been running full blast all day in here. Goosebumps break out on my arms, so I turn the dial to the hottest temperature I can stand. When I step into the shower, the water feels fantastic as it pelts my skin, but I notice that I'm shivering—and the goose bumps won't go away.

Suddenly, the reality of what happened at my parents' house hits me, smacking me like a wrecking ball. My knees buckle, and I brace myself against the wall to keep myself up. Tears burst from my ducts, seemingly falling as hard as the stream of water coming from the shower head, and I almost can't tell which is which.

Trent almost killed me today.

I squeeze my eyes shut and run my hands through my hair.

If Erik hadn't seen what happened, I would be dead.

My heart pounds against my chest as panic, fear, and anger take control.

At Mama and Daddy's, I went straight into crisis mode. I'm good at thinking on my feet, no matter what problems arise.

Assess the situation, develop a plan, and carry out the plan.

I brushed off the severity of the situation, convinced everyone I had it under control, and lied about Trent's intentions.

Granted, I still don't think he meant to kill me, but whether he meant to or not—that's what almost happened.

It was a freak accident.

When he pushed me, he didn't know I'd fall into the pool. And when I did, he thought I'd swim back to the top and life would go on as usual.

Trent didn't know I hit my head on the edge. At least, that's what I kept telling myself, even as I drove home. The alternative is unthinkable.

But now, under the stream of scorching water, the lies wash away, swirling down the drain. I clutch my hair in my hands as I sink to my knees. The shower floor is covered with a beautiful mosaic of pebble tiles, which I had specially installed because I love the feel of the tiny stones massaging my feet.

But kneeling on it feels like punishment—like I'm being tortured for keeping secrets and telling lies.

Has he ever put his hands on you?

Yes.

Has he ever hurt you?

Yes.

Why didn't you say anything?

I fear answering that question because of the broad range of answers. Some reasons are the same as any woman in the same situation: fear of not being believed or what Trent would do if he found out I said anything. But other reasons are mine and mine alone.

How could I "tell" on someone who has so many ties with my family? Mama made it very clear. If I say something about Trent, it damages his reputation—if it even gets out. I'm sure it would never come to that—as our families would keep the situation under a tight wrap.

But even if everything was handled behind closed doors, saying something would damage my reputation irreparably. I'd be blackballed —kicked out of and excluded from business and social networks my family has been a part of for years. And if I were blackballed, that would almost certainly trickle down through my family.

People would stop doing business with my father because he has a daughter who doesn't know her place, who doesn't keep her mouth shut, and who accused one of the Anderson boys of something unspeakable.

Even if everyone knew Trent was indeed abusing me, there's always a way to excuse his actions—or cover them up. *My* integrity and credibility would be questioned, not his.

Who would believe me, a female SCAD—Savannah College of Arts and Design—Fashion Marketing and Management major, over a man who graduated with honors from Duke University and Georgetown Law?

And even if they did—they'd lie for him anyway.

I learned that early.

No matter how accomplished and successful I become, Trent will always be worth more than me in the eyes of men who run everything —from the city level straight up to the entire country.

That's the way the wealthy Boys' Club works. I know because I'm in the midst of it. The Commons family is one of Charlotte's founding families. My father, Harris Commons, is one of the city's wealthiest, most powerful men, and I'm the heiress to his business—and maybe even some of that power.

I know my role as Harris's daughter and as an executive in the family business. I'm a modern-day Southern belle who can charm her way into people's hearts with a wink, a smile, and a sharp eye for business.

It's not fake, but I know what I'm doing. I play the game. Hell, Mama groomed me for this game.

It's the only way to swim in an ocean of sharks.

Play by their rules. *Smile.*

Make allies. *Smile.*

Don't rock the boat. *Smile.*

Despite being a woman, I've been my father's "right-hand man" for years. I've seen what goes on behind the scenes, and I've chosen my battles wisely.

Which is why I've never said anything about Trent.

Telling the truth is an uphill battle I'm not equipped to fight. It's better to push it aside. I'll walk away as if it's a typical breakup and move on with my life.

Truth be told, I'm terrified of how Trent will react, but it's a risk I'm willing to take with Erik by my side.

Chapter Six

ERIK

My long legs shake, banging the too-short table with every nervous bounce. I grab my coffee cup to keep it from spilling. Caffeine probably isn't helping at this time of night, but I wasn't thinking straight when I ordered, so I went with my usual.

I'm waiting for Maddie at Amelia's, a French bakery near my apartment complex. It's a funky little place with delicious pastries, great food, and a ton of specialty drinks. I stop here to grab a medium-roast coffee almost every morning.

My palms are sweaty as I grip my coffee cup tonight. Maddie texted me about an hour ago, asking me to meet her at eight p.m. A follow-up text said she was breaking up with Trent and needed someone to meet up with to help her keep up her strength. Though she never responded when I asked for more information, I rushed home, showered, and changed quickly to make it in time.

And here I sit, on edge, hoping Maddie is okay. Since I received her texts, a million unanswered questions have run through my mind.

I hope she's doing it here—or somewhere in public. I don't expect her telling him it's over to go well. He doesn't seem to let things go easily, but I strongly suspect Trent wouldn't do anything crazy in public. He's a behind-closed-doors guy. He'd never risk ruining his impeccable reputation by letting someone see his true colors.

It's only been about five minutes since I sat down, but it seems like hours when I hear heels tapping on the concrete floors with purpose. Maddie strides toward me, wearing a black pantsuit that makes her look incredibly lean, sexy, and powerful. Her hair is tied back in a low ponytail that shows off her beautiful, delicate neck. She is sexy as fuck. Seeing her in her executive element has my dick jumping to attention, ready to salute her when I stand.

I rise to greet her. "Everything okay?"

She nods and smiles, but it's tired and doesn't reach her eyes. I immediately pull out a chair for her. She hangs her purse over the back before lowering herself into the seat. When she sits, I do, as well.

"How are you doing?" I ask gently.

She leans forward, placing her elbows on the table and holding her head in her hands. Then she closes her eyes for a moment, taking a mental break. When she opens her eyes, her gaze is locked on the table. "I feel lighter than I have in a long time. Like a huge weight has been lifted."

"You sure you're okay?"

She nods.

When I take one of her hands in mine, she looks up at me. "Promise?"

"I promise," she whispers. Then she straightens her shoulders and sits up straight in her chair. The brief moment of weakness is over, and the facade of strength and control is back. Because of her appearance, I'm almost tricked into believing it.

"Thank you so much for meeting me here. The thought of going straight home after that made me nervous."

The weight of her words hits me hard. This is the same woman who, just a few days ago, would barely admit that Trent pushed her into the pool. Telling me she fears going home by herself is a huge step.

"I'm glad you asked me. Do you think he would go to your place?"

"Honestly?" She lifts her weary eyes to mine. "Yes. He doesn't let things go easily. He's chased me and followed me. Waited outside buildings and restaurants before. It's like he wanted to catch me doing something."

"Jesus, that's fucked up." My words come out with an exhale. "You must have been terrified."

"I got used to it." She glances over her shoulder when a woman squeezing by our table bumps her unintentionally.

"You got used to being stalked by your boyfriend?"

Maddie shrugs and sips her drink. "It's how he was. He got angry and violent if I confronted him, so I just ignored it. Pretended everything was fine. Pretended I was surprised to see him."

"You don't have to take it anymore. I'm here for you. Whatever you need."

"Thank you. I appreciate that. You're the only one I could call. The only one I trust right now." She pauses and sets her cup down. For some reason, it feels like coffee with a friend suddenly transformed into a business meeting. "We need to talk about what we discussed."

"What did we discuss?"

"Getting into a relationship—a fake relationship, of course."

"Maddie." I sigh. "I told you I was joking. It was a ridiculous request."

"Maybe you were, but I need you right now, and the scenario we discussed would benefit both of us."

Her words sear like a stake straight through my heart. She needs me—but it's all business.

"I'd like to hear more about your situation, Erik. I've told you my truth. Now I want to hear yours."

"My truth? I don't know what that is," I say, leaning back in my chair and looking up at the clear plastic teardrops hanging from the wrought iron chandelier above the table.

Multiple chandeliers in all colors, shapes, and sizes hang from the ceilings in each room at Amelia's. The interesting decor—a difficult-to-describe mishmash of bohemian, French-inspired, eclectic pieces—is one of the things that draws people to the various locations.

How often do you see a replica of the Mona Lisa with sunglasses stuck over her eyes or a painting of Napoleon with a word bubble coming out of his mouth, asking for a salted caramel brownie?

"What do you want it to be?" Maddie asks.

"That's the magic question. Truth can be manipulated. Isn't that right? A week ago, the truth was that you and Trent were one of Charlotte's power couples. Today's truth is a bit different."

"That's not truth, that's perception." Maddie's cool, blue eyes don't waver.

"What's the difference?" I ask.

Our conversation took a turn, but it's okay because I want to get into her head. As much as I thought I knew about her, I realize I knew Maddie as a child, and we've both changed. Old Maddie was a sweet, bubbly teenager with grand philanthropic plans. She once told me she wanted to start a program where Commons would donate an article of clothing to someone in need for each article of clothing sold—sort of like the TOMS shoe model.

But that was before Harris started grooming her as his predecessor for the family business. I'm not insinuating she doesn't have the same ideals—or that she doesn't have those same world-changing plans.

The fact is—I don't know. Maybe I'm holding on to the image of an idealistic teenage girl who no longer exists.

"Perception is how people see something. Truth is what you know as a fact."

"Think about that statement, Maddie. How do you know something is fact? What if the only source you got your information presented their narrative as truth?"

Her eyebrows veer together. "I perceived that you were a U.S. citizen, but I know now that is not the truth."

"Touché." I tip my coffee cup to her before taking a sip.

"So, let's start over." She sighs and leans back. "Some people may have had a perception of my relationship with Trent. Their perception may be their reality, but it isn't mine. Now tell me your story."

Damn, it's sexy when she tells me what to do. The demand prickles the hair on the back of my neck. It makes other parts tingle, too. But I'm not going down that road right now.

I nod to her drink. "You need a refill before I start this?"

Maddie peers into her cup. "Mine's full, thank you." She reaches around, grabbing her ponytail and tugging on the elastic band tying her hair back. Shaking the loose strands through her fingers before letting it tumble over her shoulders shouldn't turn me on as much as it does. But she's got those big, bouncy waves that make her look like she just stepped off the runway at a Victoria's Secret fashion show.

I should agree to the fake relationship to see if she'll model the Commons lingerie line for me.

"The truth is," I begin, focusing my attention back on the story, "I didn't even know I wasn't a citizen until my senior year of high school. A few buddies and I were planning a trip for Spring Break, and I needed a passport. When I started gathering the documents, I asked my grandfather for my birth certificate. That's when he told me the real story of my childhood."

"What do you mean, the real story?"

I take a deep breath. I can tell the truth without revealing every detail of the story. "I always thought my parents broke up after I was born, and my father couldn't handle a kid, so he sent me to live with his parents, my grandparents."

"Oh, Erik. I'm so sorry. I didn't realize—"

"Promise me something?" I interrupt her.

"What?"

"Never feel sorry for me. I am more than my family's choices." The last thing I want from her—or anyone—is pity.

Maddie nods. "I know. I promise."

"My grandfather told me that my mom was from the Czech Republic. She met my father while he was traveling in Europe. He went back to the U.S. despite knowing she was pregnant. When I was a year old, she brought me to Chicago to meet him. He didn't want anything to do with either of us. Before we went home, she met the man I believed was my dad. She stayed in the country for two years after her Visa expired. When I was three, they broke up. She went back without me. Fake Dad wasn't about life with kids, so he sent me here for his parents to raise."

The guy wasn't my birth father, but she left me here with him anyway. I still can't fully comprehend that, but I don't remember. Maybe she did have my best interests in mind. I'm not ready to reveal much more about my mom because the entire truth about her is more than I want to admit right now.

"Wait, so the people who raised you aren't related to you?"

"Correct."

"Why would they do that?" Maddie blurts out. Then her eyes get wide, and she starts to backtrack. "I'm sorry, I didn't mean that as rude as it came out."

I'm not hurt or offended. I get it.

"I asked my grandfather that same question. He said it was because it was the right thing to do. The guy I thought was my dad was into drugs. It's sort of how he and my mom met. My grandparents knew their son didn't have the means or desire to take care of me. So, they offered to raise me."

My family here is not my own, but they're all I've ever known.

They've loved me as though I'm a blood relation. Hell, the man I call my grandfather left *me* his business.

Maybe he was trying to right the wrong of my mother abandoning me. Though we never talked about the why, they always made it clear they loved me and never regretted the decision.

Growing up with unconditional love was all the explanation I needed. With their unwavering support, I didn't need to question my mother's decisions or her lifestyle, which led to those choices.

I've never heard from my mother since she left. I didn't even think about her until recently when the reality of my situation hit me. I will have to go to a country I never remember being in. I don't know a soul in the Czech Republic. I've never had contact with anyone there. I don't even know my birth mother's name.

It doesn't matter. The only thing that does is that I was brought here illegally, and I didn't even know until I was seventeen. I've lived my entire life as an American citizen.

Once I found out my situation, my brain went into overdrive. I asked why they never adopted me—to make me legal. They said they were scared it would bring up immigration issues. They couldn't risk me being sent to the Czech Republic before I was old enough to fend for myself.

Unsure of what to do, my grandfather confided in Harris

Commons, hoping someone with his wealth and influence could help. Harris referred him to—and paid for—an immigration lawyer to handle my case. The lawyer processed my application for a Deferred Action program for people who had been brought to America illegally as children.

But I won't tell Maddie that part. I don't want her to know her father has been aware of my status for years.

"That was selfless of them," she says.

"It was." I nod. "I'm lucky to have been raised by amazing people. I'm grateful for them and the opportunities they gave me."

Maddie's lips slide into a sincere smile that makes the skin around her eyes crinkle. Her defined cheekbones glow with a stunning, pale pink blush. She's a gorgeous woman. Even as a teenager, she always has been when her cheeks and hips were a bit more round. She lost some curves as she got taller, but I'm not complaining. She's a fucking ten in anyone's book.

"Okay, technically, you weren't born here, but you've been here almost your entire life. You were a baby. Can't you apply for citizenship or something?"

"I wish it worked that way. There are all these rules for people who are in the U.S. illegally—even if we were brought here as children. I'd have to leave the country, and the chances of me being able to re-enter would be next to none."

"It doesn't make any sense." She shakes her head, trying to wrap her head around how ridiculous it is. "You didn't do anything wrong. You were brought here as a child. You didn't *decide* to break the law."

"I know."

I've screamed everything she's saying to the sky multiple times as I've tried to figure this out and find a way to stay.

"You're as much of an American as I am."

"In theory." I smile. "You have birthright."

"You're a business owner. You pay taxes."

"Yup."

Technically, I don't own my business. Her father does, but she doesn't know that. It's more of a technicality than anything.

We have signed documents stating that Harris has no control over my business. After my grandfather passed away, he agreed to put it in his name. I didn't feel comfortable because of my immigrant status, but it made sense since Harris is a successful business owner. I trusted he would be true to his word, and we've never had any issues.

Secrets. Lies. The kind of webs I never wanted to weave because of how many I've been caught in.

When I chose to apply for the Deferred Action for Childhood Arrivals (DACA) program at seventeen, I thought making the government aware of me and admitting I knew my situation was the correct course of action. I thought showing I wasn't trying to hide or sneak around was acting in good faith.

It was until there was a change in the people who run the government. Now, the new administration wants to crack down on illegal immigrants. It doesn't matter if they are boosting the U.S. economy, have families, or are law-abiding citizens.

Or that they were left here as a baby and had no choice.

All that matters is the word "illegal."

Illegal paints us as people who knowingly and willingly break the law. Illegal means they can say what they want about us, and people will believe it.

Countless politicians have called me a criminal, a murderer, even a rapist.

Simply because I am here illegally.

Crime data shows that illegal immigrants commit a very low number of violent crimes, but people believe in fear over facts.

If someone hears something enough times, they believe it. The number of people who think the lies is disheartening.

In six months, my work permit will expire with no chance for renewal—and I might be deported to a country I have no family ties or loyalty to because I tried to do the right thing when I found out my situation.

At first, I was confused and mad as hell.

By applying for Deferred Action, I didn't save myself; I secured a one-way ticket to the Czech Republic.

"Aren't you angry?"

"Of course I am, Maddie. I'm reeling inside. I'm heartbroken. I'm appalled. I'm furious. I've been trying to figure out what to do. How to stay."

My fingers clench around my cup. I've already been through the stages of grief, and, for the most part, I've accepted that I'll be required to leave the country when my work permit expires. Over the last few months, I've focused on tying up loose ends here when I'm forced to leave.

Still, talking about the situation gets me worked up.

"How are you so calm?"

Calm?

My eyes fall to my crushed cup, and I chuckle. "Because, despite all my fears and the fact that my entire life is falling apart, I have to focus on what I can control. And the only thing I can control is work. Money. Taking care of my grandmother while I'm here and able to pay for her care."

Maddie bites her lip, and I immediately feel like a dickbag. I wasn't trying to be mean or sound so snarky. I'm just stating the facts—my truth, as she calls it.

"I'm sorry," I say quickly, slumping in my chair. "I don't know what will happen to her when I leave. And it scares the shit out of me."

Though I know she's getting the best care I can afford, the thought of leaving my grandmother has haunted my thoughts—even in my sleep.

A few good friends from high school assured me they'd visit her and ensure she has what she needs. As much as I love them and know they're stand-up guys who would be true to their word, I don't think it would last long.

It's easy to forget to visit when it's not your loved one. Once people walk into a nursing home, the shabby decor, bleak rooms, and sour stench in the air are a complete assault on the senses and emotions. It's not a place you're rushing to get back to.

Then there's the other reason that leaving scares the shit out of me —leaving Maddie here with Trent. I don't know what else he's done, but I know he's hurt her. Now that we've formed a bond, I can't stand the thought of not being around to protect her.

"You won't be deported," Maddie says firmly.

"How can you be so sure?"

"I won't let that happen. I'm not letting someone send you away to a country you haven't been in since you were a baby."

"Well, it's not someone, Maddie. It's the Department of Homeland Security."

"I don't care, Erik. I'm going to fight this. It's absolutely ridiculous. Do you have a lawyer?"

"My grandfather and I spoke to someone when I applied for Deferred Action. That's the agreement keeping me here for the time being," I say. "That's what the lawyer advised me to do once I learned I wasn't a citizen."

"Okay, so you did the right thing."

"Was it?" I ask. It's a bit of a rhetorical question since I'm throwing Maddie into a situation she has no knowledge of or control over. "Signing up meant I admitted I was illegal. It means I'm on record. When it's time, they can track me down and kick me out. Maybe I should have stayed under the radar and let them find me the hard way."

"You did what you thought was right at the time," Maddie says. "I'm not letting you do this alone, Erik. We're going to figure this out. If we have to get married, we get married."

She's serious about this. I should have realized that she'd never let it go once she had an idea. I never imagined I'd be directly involved in one of her crazy ideas.

"I'm awed at how adamant you are about helping me."

"I care about you, Erik. I don't want you to be forced to move to a country you've never lived in. A place you have no ties to."

The silence between us is thick and heavy.

"You care about me?" I repeat. My heart races as I scoot over a little more, trying to get as close to her as possible in this clunky, old dining chair with arms.

"I always have."

"Tell me more about that." I can't keep the smile off my face. It's probably smug, but deep down, I always knew she liked me.

"Oh, come on! I've had a crush on you since we were kids. You had to have known that." She leans back as if she's embarrassed. Her cheeks flush a deeper pink that makes my dick twitch. "I made sure I was always home after school on Tuesdays. No matter what was going on. Practices, things with friends or family. I had to be home after school on Tuesdays."

Damn! She had it all planned out. "I knew you had a crush on me, but I didn't know you went to that extent."

"Oh, totally. I was completely boy crazy—and you were the object of my affection." She covers her face with her hand as if embarrassed to reveal a silly teenage secret.

"Affection or obsession?" I tease.

"Oh, hush! I thought you were so hot. I couldn't wait to catch a glimpse of you."

My gaze drops to her chest quickly, but I bring it back up just as fast. Hearing her admit she thinks I'm attractive and that she used to watch me turns me on. Every fantasy I've ever had about her pops into my head. That's when I decide I'm going to have some fun with this fake relationship, even if it's just getting to see her all hot and bothered.

"*Thought* I was hot? Past tense?"

Her chest heaves when she takes a deep breath. Her tongue flicks out to moisten her lips before she answers. "Present tense. You're absolutely gorgeous, Erik."

I reach out, sliding my palm across her cheek and into her silky blonde curls.

Suddenly, a loud commotion coming from the front of the bakery pulls me out of the moment. I peer over her head as people in line start calling out.

"That was rude."

"*Excuse me*."

"What an ass."

Maddie is about to turn around when Trent barrels through, pushing past tables like an elephant in a coffee shop.

"What the hell is going on?" he roars.

Maddie and I both jump out of our chairs. I place my body in front of hers, so Trent has to go through me before he can reach her. Several other people get out of their seats and move toward our table, and I'm instantly grateful to have supportive strangers willing to help.

Trent isn't a giant—on the contrary, he's pretty short—but he's a stocky dude with broad shoulders and a thick neck like he goes hard at a CrossFit cult multiple times a week.

His face is red with rage. A patch of light brown hair flops over his forehead, but it doesn't cover his beady eyes darting from me to Maddie. "I knew it! I knew you were cheating on me," he yells, pointing a fat finger at Maddie.

Adrenaline charges through my veins. My fists curl at my sides, but I keep my composure. "Dude, you need to chill out," I tell him through clenched teeth. Hopefully, he doesn't mistake my calm demeanor for being passive. I want to punch this guy so hard.

His head snaps back to me. His menacing grimace looks natural as if he gets this angry so often that his face is used to morphing into the evil version of the incredible Hulk.

"You fucking whore!" he spits out.

Fuck no. He's not going to talk to Maddie like that. Not on my watch.

I'm a split-second from punching him when an Amelia's employee grabs his shoulder and pulls him backward. "You've gotta leave, man. Right now," he says, tightening his grip and spinning Trent around.

Maddie grabs the back of my T-shirt and holds on tight. She's shaking so much that her knuckles knock against my back.

Trent shuffles backward, staring at me as if memorizing my face. I smile.

Take a long look, you piece of shit-motherfucker. Next time you pull something like this, I won't be so civil.

I swallow back the words I'm thinking. There's no need to aggravate the situation or make Maddie more frightened than she already is. Usually, I wouldn't even think of doing something that would get me in trouble, but I'd take on an army of Trents for Maddie.

"Thanks," I say to the people around us who got up to help as they slowly move back to their seats.

"What a fucking psycho," one of the guys whispers.

When Maddie releases my shirt, I spin around and take her in my arms. Her heart pounds against my chest, and I feel it straight to my toes.

Instinctively, I press my lips on her head and squeeze her tighter. In this moment, I vow to do everything I can to ensure she never feels this kind of fear again.

I dip my head to her ear and ask, "You wanna get out of here?"

As much as I love Amelia's, we need a vibe change right now. My favorite brewery in town happens to be right across the street. Maybe she's game to head over there for a minute. Give us both time to compose ourselves.

Maddie stiffens in my arms. "He might be outside. He might be waiting." Her voice is a wavering whisper.

"It's okay. We'll wait a few minutes. And I'll be right here with you. You're not leaving me to fend for myself, and I'm not doing that to you, either. From now on, we're joined at the hip, okay?"

Maddie leans back, looking up to meet my gaze. Her blue eyes enchanted me the first time I saw them, but this time is entirely differ-ent. This isn't the giggling teenager peering at me from behind her parents' front door. This time, she's begging for trust, protection, and commitment. I can give her those things—for the next few months.

"Promise?" she whispers.

"Promise." I intertwine my fingers with hers and squeeze her hand. "Finish your drink. I'll be right back."

Before Maddie and I head out to the parking lot, I check with the employee who escorted Trent away from us. He assured me he watched Trent get in his car and drive off.

Still, I'm concerned he's out there somewhere, waiting as Maddie feared. My other concern is that he went to Maddie's place. I don't want to worry her—or make her paranoid, but I know one thing—I'm not leaving her alone tonight.

I can't guarantee what will happen when I'm gone, but I will protect her while I'm here.

Chapter Seven

MADDIE

I'm shaken up.

Completely, and quite literally. I haven't stopped trembling since Trent showed up at Amelia's. I met him at a restaurant because I wanted to break up with him in public, somewhere I felt comfortable. He left before I did but must have waited and followed me.

I feel like he's watching me right now.

And what he's seeing is pissing him off.

Erik and I walk across Amelia's parking lot to the brewery across the street. Honestly, I didn't even realize there was a brewery around here. I don't hang out in the NoDa neighborhood very often.

I chose a restaurant near Amelia's to meet Trent because it's not one of our usual hangouts, so there was less chance someone who knew us would be there.

Trent wouldn't be happy with me breaking up with him, let alone in a place where he could be embarrassed in front of colleagues or friends. I know the owner, so I felt comfortable if Trent pulled anything shady like he did at Amelia's.

When my heel catches in the rocks of Home on the Range Brewing's parking lot, Erik immediately tightens his grip to keep me from falling.

"Whoa! I got you." Instead of letting me go right away, he holds onto me until I regain my balance. I appreciate that extra moment. The safety in stability. "You all right?"

"Yeah, I'm good. Should've changed my shoes before we went off-roading," I quip.

Erik chuckles. "I should have warned you of the rough terrain."

We've never spent time together outside my parents' yard, yet it feels so easy being with him. I didn't expect anything different since we always got along, but it's refreshing to be out with someone with whom I feel comfortable and free to say anything.

It's easy to have surface relationships. I know thousands of people in a friendly, acquaintance way, but when Erik opened up, I knew I could do the same. He's trusting me with the most important secret of his life. Having that level of trust, after years of not being able to talk about certain aspects of my life, is scary and a relief at the same time.

Erik guides me up a few stairs to the entrance of the brewery. His touch is warm and comforting—and familiar. Like we've been intimate before.

We never have. In all those years sitting together, with our backs against the vast black walnut in Mama and Daddy's yard, we never did anything other than talk. We've never so much as held hands.

Now, with his hand on my back and the feeling zinging around in my core that his touch brings, I realize it was a huge shame—all those lost opportunities. Erik could have been my first kiss. He could have been the first of a lot of things.

As enticing as it sounds now, I appreciate how innocent it was. I didn't need to move any faster than I did. And honestly, I don't need the sweet memory of our time together tainted by hormones and forbidden love. I can only imagine what kind of torment I would have gone through if any of my friends found out I'd kissed the lawn boy.

And yet, here I am. And all I can think about is mauling the lawn guy.

Erik is more of a friend than just the "help." But still. That's what Erik meant when he said there would be backlash.

Someone in my group of friends, someone I work with, or someone my parents know will comment. And when those comments come, they won't be very nice. They'll give me fake smiles or "Bless your hearts" to my face, but the claws will come out behind my back. I know because I've been on that side.

I've been the girl who judges someone for who they're dating or what they're wearing. I'm not proud of it, but I won't deny it. Erik saved my life, and if I can help him, I will. It's up to me to figure out how I'll handle the snark.

Honestly, it doesn't bother me as much now as it would have back when I was a teenager. I put too much stock in what people thought about me then. I wanted—no, needed—their acceptance. I needed their approval. I took the criticism to heart and made changes to return to their good graces.

Thankfully, I was one of the leaders in my group of friends, so it didn't take much to smooth things over. I've always been loud, outgoing, and willing to put myself out there—the one who made mistakes and asked for forgiveness instead of permission.

Erik puts his hand on the small of my back and leads me up a set of stairs to a large brick building. The front has an extended patio with multiple metal picnic tables. We enter through a rolled-up garage door. After passing a roped-off section, where several colossal brewing tanks stand, we arrive at the corner of a long U-shaped bar.

I love how open and airy the space is. It has a clean, rustic, modern vibe. Behind the bar, the words "Home on the Range" scroll over a white-tile backsplash fashioned from black mosaic tiles. Below the phrase, there's a row of wooden taps.

"Hey, Paul!" Erik nods to the bartender. Paul smiles and waves. Then he says something to the patron he was talking to and raps his knuckles against the bar before coming to greet us.

"Erik! How's it going, man?" They fist bump across the bar.

"It's hotter than two squirrels fucking in a wool sock out there, but business is steady, so I can't complain."

Paul shakes his head and laughs. "I have never heard that one before."

"One of my clients said it yesterday. Thought I'd try it out."

"Was that Mr. Farthington?" I ask.

"It was."

"That man is something else. He doesn't have a lick of sense, but he's funny as all get out," I say without taking my eyes off the chalkboard on the wall behind the bar that lists the beers on tap.

Erik puts his hand on my back. "Paul, this is Maddie."

"Hi, Maddie. First time here?" Paul asks.

"Is it that obvious?" I ask, shifting my eyes to the bartender.

"You have that deer-in-the-headlights look of someone who's never been here before. Take a look at the list, and let me know if there's something you want to try. I'll pour you a sample."

"Aren't you the sweetest thing! Thanks, Paul."

"I *am* the sweetest thing, but I don't think Erik likes hearing that." Paul winks. "Let me grab a pint for Rob. I'll be right back."

He leaves us to pour a goblet of something beautiful and amber for another patron. I scan the descriptions under each beer name, wondering which ones they are.

I set my hand on Erik's arm. "Which one is your favorite?"

He leans into me slightly. "Their options change quite a bit. I think the one that's always here is the top one, the pilsner. My favorite right now is the brown ale. It's chocolatey with a hint of coffee. It's dark but not heavy."

"I think I'll try that."

"Do you like beer? I'm sorry, Maddie. I didn't even ask before we came here."

"I like one every now and again. I prefer bourbon, but I've never turned down a nice, cold beer with a handsome gentleman."

"Bourbon?" Erik asks.

My mind floods with wonderful memories highlighted by bourbon drinks.

The yearly tradition of delicious Mint Juleps at the Kentucky Derby with my family and friends.

The Old Fashioned Daddy made me in a crystal highball glass to celebrate my promotion to Vice President of Feminine Apparel and Cosmetics at Commons.

The countless batches of Mississippi Punch with my friends and debs over the years.

In those moments, I felt on top of the world. I had a successful career, the most loyal and loving friends and family, and a seemingly bright future with Trent.

The thought of Trent mars the memories, and I push them out of my mind.

"Why do you sound so surprised, Erik? You were raised right here in the South."

He grins. "I was, but my grandparents are from Chicago originally. Southern traditions elude me."

"Well, you're officially dating a Southern belle. So, you best get used to the tradition. You'll need to know me inside and out if we're to get married in six months." I nudge his arm with my shoulder.

"Yeah, Maddie, about that." He turns so we're facing each other. "It was a silly idea. You could get in a lot of trouble, and I don't want to put you in that position."

"I'm not going to get into trouble, Erik. It won't go that far. We make it look real until we figure out a plan to keep you here. Heck, by then, laws may have changed. You never know in these crazy times. Seems like things are changing every day."

He stiffens. "I couldn't live with myself if you got in trouble."

"Sugar, this is *not* your decision. It's mine. I'm not doing anything illegal right now. We have an arrangement that suits both of us. You are helping me break free of Trent, and I'm helping you stay in the country. Easy peasy." I wave my hand as if the entire situation is light and easy. It's not. The fear of what Trent might do next is at the forefront of my mind. "You better start acting smitten with me if we want anyone to believe this."

"I won't have any trouble acting smitten with you." His lips slide into an irresistible smile. "Can you say the same?"

I push my hair behind my shoulder and stand up straight. "I'm a good actress. I starred in the Christmas pageant two years in a row."

"You landed the Virgin Mary role twice? That's impressive."

"Are you some kind of heathen?" I stare at him. Maybe he's not religious. I never even asked. That would be a hiccup in the plan. Not a deal breaker, but—

What in the world am I thinking? It's all fake. I don't have to worry about taking him to church on Sunday.

"Everyone knows the Virgin Mary isn't the star. I played the Baby Jesus right up until I grew out of that manger," I say, lifting my gaze to the beer list. "I was a tiny thing." I can feel Erik staring at me. "What?"

"You are something else, Madeline Commons."

"You're just realizing that now? After all these years?"

"You're serious about our arrangement?"

"As a heart attack."

When Paul returns, I request a sample of the brown ale Erik mentioned and the amber ale I watched him pour. After tasting, we both decide on a pint of the brown.

Erik follows me back outside to the front porch. Fall is closing in, and though it'll stay warm well into October, I relish every minute I get to be outside. Lots of people complain about the heat and humidity, but summer in the South is my favorite time of year.

I set my beer and pocketbook on a rustic, red picnic table.

The chatter around us calms my mind. I can see coming up here with friends. Except for four years in Savannah for college and two summer internships in New York and London, I've lived in Charlotte my entire life.

I'm familiar with neighborhoods, but since this one isn't where I usually hang out, I wasn't sure what the clientele would be like. It's got a great laid-back vibe—not pretentious or trendy. It's relaxing, which I need after the intense conversation with Trent.

A nagging voice tells me things are not over with Trent. I don't want to be with him, but I know he won't let our relationship go that easily—and neither will our families.

Or he'll make my life hell for dumping him.

I had already committed one of the most significant crimes I possibly could—I gave up on someone. If I've learned anything in my family, it's to be loyal. We work out our differences with the people we have relationships with—personal and business. You don't just cut someone off.

We were supposed to get married. He hadn't proposed yet, but that was the unspoken plan. Everyone thought our future union was a sure thing. It was only a matter of time after he moved home from Georgetown before he proposed.

No one will understand why I broke up with Trent, and it's my fault for keeping his treatment a secret. But that's the other part of being loyal. I had to keep his behavior under wraps. I'd be accused of trying to smear his reputation if I said anything.

Mama's gonna be pissed. So unbelievably pissed.

"To our unconventional arrangement." Erik raises his glass, pulling me out of my thoughts.

I grab my glass and lift it, clinking. "Fake it till you make it."

We both take a sip of our beers. I set my glass down.

"You look beautiful tonight," he says.

"Thank you." I'm not sure if he's saying it to establish the fake relationship or if he's being serious, but either way, it's sweet and makes me smile. "You clean up pretty well yourself."

"Are you okay?" He reaches across the table and places his hand on top of mine. The touch brings both warmth and comfort. I lift my eyes to his. There's a crease in his forehead between his eyebrows. This might be an arrangement, but Erik cares about my well-being. He's seen Trent's temper twice now.

"Honestly? I'm still shaken up." I take a deep breath and glance around the patio.

I'm not looking for Trent—I'm looking for sane. Like the three people at the table behind Erik, chatting happily about their night. Or the group behind me playing a lively round of UNO.

"You can talk to me, Maddie. We may be doing this for specific reasons, but please know you can talk to me."

I bring my gaze back to him and give him a half-smile. "Thank you. I don't have anyone to talk to."

"You don't have anyone you can confide in?"

"I can't tell anyone, Erik. My entire life would be ruined if I said anything. Not his—mine. Not that anyone would believe me anyway. They'd brush it off. They'd harass me until I let it go."

I'd seen it before. Hell, I'd been one of the people on the firing squad. Loyalty is fierce and strong even if it's not always correct—or what's right.

How do I expect anyone to believe me—or stand up for me—if I never did that for others? I'm too woven into the fabric of following along with the masses—of what would serve me and my interests.

Maybe it's time to go against the grain. Why did it have to take something happening to me before realizing that?

"That's fucked up, Maddie."

"Yes, but that's the way it is." I rub my finger over a patch on the table where the red paint has chipped away.

"When did you realize things with Trent weren't right?" Erik asks.

"It was slow at first. I've known Trent for a long time. His sister, Suzanne, and I are very good friends. We went through debutante together."

"Excuse me?" Erik interrupts. He leans in and blinks as if trying to hear or understand. "You met how?"

"Suzanne and I came out into society together," I explain. He tilts his head in confusion. "You have no idea what I'm talking about, do you?"

He shifts on the bench. "I've heard of debutantes and coming out, but I didn't think it was still a thing."

"Yes, Erik, debutante is still a thing! It's a grand tradition! Mama told me stories about hers ever since I was a little girl. All her photos burned up in a house fire." I close my eyes at the memory of waltzing the night away with sweaty-handed boys at various parties and my beautiful white dress that costs more than some women spend on a wedding gown.

"Did your sisters participate?" Erik asks, pulling me out of my daydream.

When I open my eyes, he's smiling at me. People think it's silly and outdated, but I enjoyed every minute. "No. I'm the only one that came out. I met so many vibrant, outgoing ladies. I still have lunch with a few of them once a month."

"It sounds like you enjoyed it."

"Absolutely. I'd do it again in a heartbeat. I learned so much. Not just about etiquette, dancing, and poise but also about presenting myself in a strong, confident way. I can hold my own in any situation."

"I have no doubt." Erik's lips slide into a smile. He takes another drink.

"I'm charming the pants right off you now, aren't I?"

"Hey now! Save that for the second date."

I laugh. "That's second-date talk?"

"Well, we can skip straight to marriage if it helps. Colors? Locations?" He winks.

"Slow and steady wins the race."

"Well, we've known each other for ten years; I'd say we've taken it very slowly."

"And look, it's about to get steady again," I say.

Is that why being with him is so easy? Is it because we already have an established relationship? After seeing each other almost every week during all four years of high school, maybe we're just picking up where we left off, muddling through the gap years we missed in between.

"Did you meet Trent through Suzanne?" Erik asks, bringing our conversation back.

I nod. "Yes. We knew each other for a while, but we didn't start dating until we were in college. I've always dated guys in my social circle who fit the same mold. They all came from money. They were going into majors that would set them up for prestigious careers. They were smart and charming and active in organizations on campus, be it fraternities, political groups, or something else."

"They wore collared shirts and boat shoes—even to sleep," Erik interrupts. He's hiding his smile behind his beer glass, which is still raised to his lips.

"Yes, Erik. They were all Chads. And I'm a Becky." I laugh because his description fits most guys I've dated—or even know. I reckon I fit the stereotype, too.

My youngest sister calls me Becky, a condescending term for a self-absorbed rich girl. She says the name comes from a '90s rap song.

"You wouldn't be a Becky," Erik corrects. "You'd be a Stacy. Stacy's are the perfect, beautiful, unattainable rich girls. Becky's are basic."

"Excuse me?"

"Shit, Maddie! I wasn't calling you a Stacy or a Becky. I was trying to explain the difference."

"I'm fully aware of how some people choose to see me, but I'm completely comfortable with myself, so their opinion doesn't matter."

Erik rubs a palm over his jaw. "Let me start that again. *You* don't fit into either of those lame stereotypes. *You* are a smart, strong, sexy, successful woman—*Southern* woman," he emphasizes.

Heat rushes from my cheeks straight up to my ears. Hearing Erik compliment me is like listening to my favorite song. It makes me smile, and I want to put it on repeat forever.

"Thank you," I say, "but if we're talking about Trent—he's a total Chad." I laugh. "He had similarities to the other guys, but he was more aggressive, I reckon. He came on strong, and that made me feel good—wanted. During our first week of dating, he told me he loved me. It was weird but also flattering. I don't know. It sounds so stupid to explain."

"Love bombing," Erik interjects.

"Excuse me?" I ask, confused by the phrase.

"It's a control tactic called called love-bombing. Abusers use excessive attention and affection to make you feel special. It builds trust and dependence on their opinion. When they flip the switch, you doubt yourself because you remember the person they were when you met. You think that person exists."

"I've never heard of that term. It makes a lot of sense., though," I say as I contemplate how Trent made me feel special when we first started dating. "Trent was very over the top at first. Out of all the guys I've dated, he was the one Mama and Daddy pushed me toward. He was handsome, from a successful family, and was on his way to Georgetown Law—at the time." I pause, realizing how shallow all of that sounds. Trent checked all the boxes of what I should've been looking for in a future husband. "It sounds so stupid."

"It doesn't sound stupid, Maddie. I've heard about the whole 'ring by spring' philosophy. I didn't think it still happened, but I've heard of it."

The term "ring by spring" catches me off guard. It's a phrase Emily used to mock me all the time. Now that Erik brought it up, I realize it describes exactly what traditional Southern parents want for their daughters—an engagement ring by graduation.

My education route was a bit different since I chose to go to the Savannah College of Art and Design. SCAD is the most prestigious art and fashion school in the South. It *was not* the place my parents wanted me to find a husband. They didn't want me to be with a creative. And it's unlikely to find a future hedge fund manager or attorney there.

Which is why they set me up with Trent, a good old boy who was majoring in pre-law at Duke. I really can't mock it. Back then, my goal was the same as theirs. I didn't change my mind until after Trent and I started dating.

My back stiffens, and I sit up straighter. "Maybe the idea seems archaic to some, but not me. I am college-educated, hard-working, and active in my community. I'm still a modern woman. But no matter how successful I am in my career, I will always put my family first. It's part of who I am and the way I was raised. I'm proud of both."

"I'm not insulting you, Maddie, believe me. I'm not from a traditional Southern family, so it's an old-fashioned concept to me."

"Old-fashioned isn't always bad."

"I didn't say it was." He slides a hand across the picnic table and places it on mine. "I'm not making fun of you. I respect you and your family. We can be different, think differently, and still be friends, right?"

My shoulders soften a bit as the tension leaves. "Of course."

Internally, I curse myself for getting so defensive. Trying to explain to people who don't understand is something I've battled for years. I'm not stupid. I'm not uneducated. I don't think everyone has to share my core beliefs, but it also doesn't mean I'll be mocked for them.

Family, above all, isn't a bad philosophy.

"When did you start realizing Trent wasn't as perfect as he seemed?" Erik asks, bringing me back on track.

"Thinking back on it now, I should have seen early signs, no matter how subtle. I thought he was being complimentary when he'd say he loved how I looked in a certain color or when my hair was styled a particular way." I lift my eyes to Erik. "Because we attended different schools, I went on with my life and did my own thing, not thinking too much about Trent's preferences. But when I was going to see him, I'd do things that made him happy. That's what you do in relationships, right? You think about the other person and do the little things you know they like. He loved when I wore my navy pencil skirt and had my hair tied back in a chic, loose chignon. It was easy enough for me."

Erik nods as if he understands.

"I didn't realize until about a year into our long-distance relationship that when he appreciated something about my appearance, it wasn't a compliment as much as a command."

"His comments weren't about being sweet; they were about control," he says.

"Exactly!" I say. Knowing Erik understands makes me think it wasn't all in my head, which Trent wanted me to believe. "I see so much now that I didn't see when I was in the relationship. Does that make sense?"

"Of course," Erik says. "That happens to everyone. It seems minor, but what Trent was doing was major. That's the thing about people who are good at manipulating. They make you feel like you're the one who needs to change. They make you think you're the one who has issues when they're projecting their issues onto you."

"Wow. Sounds like you get it."

"I've been in a few relationships." Erik winks. "I've gotta use the restroom. Be right back."

I know he's had girlfriends. I'm not naive. I also know we're only here together because he's helping me get away from Trent, and I'm helping him stay in the country. Nevertheless, hearing him talk about other relationships sends a ridiculous jealous twinge to my heart. And I'm not a jealous person. At least, I didn't think I was.

All this crap with Trent has me out of sorts. I know deciding to leave is the right choice, but I'm already at one of the lowest points in my life. I can't handle hearing about the other girls my long-time crush has been with.

After Erik excuses himself, crazy thoughts race around in my head. What if Trent has been watching us from the parking lot? What if he saw Erik go inside and uses the opportunity to confront me now that I'm alone?

Goosebumps break out across my arms. I roll my shoulders back and clasp my hands in my lap. Then I scan the patio, trying to look nonchalant as I check out the people occupying the other picnic tables.

At the table next to ours, the conversation two Americans are having with a guy from New Zealand is entertaining and enlightening.

"Have you ever had a BLT? A bacon, lettuce, and tomato sandwich?" the lady asks.

I almost laugh because it seems like such a silly question. Then I realize that, though I've traveled quite a bit, I've never been to New Zealand. Different countries and regions have their own cuisines. What seems normal to us may be completely unheard of to someone from another country.

I lean their way slightly to hear the answer.

He responds with, "Um, yeah. Bacon sandwiches are quite common where I'm from."

I straighten up in my seat. Mama always told me I should learn something new every day. I'm certain this wasn't what she meant, but knowledge is knowledge.

And it took my mind off Trent for a minute. That alone was reason enough to appreciate it.

I thought the knot in my stomach would subside when Erik returned to the table, but it's still there. As he throws a leg over the bench, he flashes me a smile. That's when I realized the knot isn't fear, like when walking to the brewery. It's excitement.

Being with Erik brings back all the innocent emotions I felt as a girl with a massive crush on a boy.

And now we're on a date.

It's fake. But for some reason, my mind refuses to allow that minor detail to stop my body from having all the feels. The butterflies that started in my stomach have moved south. Lust zings through my limbs and settles with a pulse between my legs. Just being around him turns me on.

"What's up?" he asks.

"Nothing. Why?" My answer comes out in a rush.

Am I blushing? I brush my fingers across my cheek to see if it's warm.

"You have this cute little smile on your face. Just wondering what put it there." He lifts his beer and takes a swig.

I watch every move, taking in details I've never had a chance to. The way his long fingers grip the pint glass. The way his tongue touches the rounded lip of the glass as he drinks. The way his Adam's apple bobs when he swallows.

How can he be so mean? He is sitting there, minding his own business, looking so incredibly sexy as he does everyday things like drinking his beer.

"There was a conversation about bacon. I love bacon."

I love bacon? I'm sitting across from the sexiest man alive and all I can say is I love bacon?

I take a pull of my beer, trying to wash down the embarrassment.

"Noted. Should I make you some tomorrow morning?"

I swallow fast, surprised by his bold question. Thankfully, the liquid didn't go down the wrong pipe, making me a coughing mess in front of him and everyone else. "Excuse me?"

"If I'm crashing at your place tonight, the least I can do is make breakfast."

I close my eyes and shake my head. My heart slams under my ribcage. "What are you talking about?" My voice is a gravelly mix of lust and thinly veiled outrage.

"I'm not letting you go home alone. I have this weird vibe that Trent might be there," Erik says without a hint of flirtation. He's all business. "You could come to my place if you want. I'm just up the road."

"Oh. Yeah, I-I didn't think about that." I nod. The butterflies exit through stage door left and fly out into the night. "It's not a good idea for me to be alone tonight. But, I mean, I can go to Liz's." I reach into my pocketbook and dig around for my phone.

Erik's arm snakes out, and he places his hand on my forearm. "We need to make this relationship look real. You said it yourself."

"You can hold your horses there, Bucko. I'm not the kind of girl who goes home with a man on the first date. No matter how long we've known each other. I'll stay with Liz or go to my parents' house."

The white lights, draping the branches of the potted tree next to our table, flicker, making his hazel eyes sparkle. But men only sparkle in paranormal vampire fiction, not real life.

His shoulders drop, and he removes his hand from my arm, leaving the skin cold where warmth once pulsed. "Okay. As long as you're not going home alone. That's all I care about."

I swallow back my pride. It's fake. It's all fake.

Why do I keep getting my hopes up? Why would I ever think Erik wants more than our agreement to help each other? He's had years to make a move or ask me out.

I'm such an idiot.

It shouldn't be this easy for me to fall back into the childish drama of a boy-crazed teenager. Time to put these ridiculous feelings aside and focus on why we're both doing this.

Erik's entire focus is keeping me safe, and I appreciate that.

In turn, I'll continue the charade so he can stay here in the U.S.—right where he belongs.

ERIK WASN'T KIDDING when he said he was going to protect me. He followed me to my parents' house and up their long driveway, then waited until I closed the door before driving away. I know because I watched him through the window, just like I used to do when I was younger.

Once inside, I lean against the door, unable to contain my smile or the tingle of excitement. The seemingly insignificant things—like waiting until I was safe in the house—make me giddy as a schoolgirl.

The few times Trent dropped me off after a date or event, he never waited. He put the pedal to the metal on his G Wagon as soon as I shut the passenger door. It annoyed me at the time, but then I got used to it.

Funny how the small things make such a big difference.

"Madeline, what are you doing here so late?" Mama asks.

My mother is, was, and always will be my role model. She's smart as a whip, drop-dead gorgeous, and always carries herself with class. Even now, in a cozy, black Cosabella pajama set, her frosted blonde hair twisted into small spiral buns and pinned against her head. I used to love watching her put them up and take them out. Perfect pin curls every time. It took me ages to learn, but I finally did.

"Is it okay if I stay here tonight?" I ask, peeling myself off the door. The question is a formality; I know I can stay with my parents anytime.

"Of course, sugar." Mama beckons me over. She reaches out once I'm close enough, skimming her hand over the back of my head. "Feels like the bump is gone already."

I nod. "It's still a little tender, though." Just like my nerves—tender, frayed. The physical effects of Trent's abuse may have faded, but the mental effects are still raw.

"Is something going on Uptown?" Mama asks.

"No, why?" I follow her to the kitchen.

Steam rises from a teacup sitting on the counter. The calming smell of cinnamon wafts through the air when she lifts the tea bag string and dips it a few times.

"Why aren't you staying at your condo tonight?" She rings the remaining water out of the bag by pressing it against a small spoon, then places both on the saucer. She extends the dainty, porcelain cup toward me. "Would you like this one? I can make another."

"No, thank you." I shake my head. "Honestly, Mama? I was afraid to go home."

"Why would you be afraid to go home? What's wrong?"

"It was an interesting night." Thankfully, the evening with Erik calmed me down.

"Does this have anything to do with your breakup with Trent?"

I should have known that Mama would already know. It hasn't even been four hours since it happened. Trent probably called his mama straightaway. I wonder if it was before or after he stormed into Amelia's?

"Yes. After we spoke, he followed me to a coffee shop, busted through like a wrecking ball, and started calling me a whore in front of God and everyone."

"Well, I'm not calling the kettle black, Madeline, but what is anyone supposed to think when you were at that coffee shop meeting another man just minutes after breaking up with your long-term boyfriend?" she snaps.

"That's not fair, Mama. I met up with a friend because I was nervous and upset. It wasn't a date with another man."

It wasn't. Maybe the part where we went to Home on the Range was, but that wasn't planned.

"Maybe so, but that's not what it sounds like to anyone else."

"Instead of talking about what it sounded like through the grapevine, can we address the fact that Trent followed me there and his psychotic outburst? Is there any wonder why I'm afraid to go home right now? He has a key to my condo. He could be there, waiting to do who knows what when I walk in the door."

"What's gotten into you, Madeline?"

"Excuse me?" I ask, confused.

Mama rarely scolds me. It's probably because we see eye-to-eye on most issues. Liz and Emily may have called me "Mayor Maddie" growing up, but Mama called me "Mini Magnolia," an offshoot of the nickname my grandfather on Daddy's side used to call her—Steel Magnolia—meaning she possessed both femininity and a strong will. I know how cliché it is for a Southern woman to be called a steel magnolia, but I like it. It describes us perfectly.

"Less than a week ago, you and Trent were happier than two pigs in the sun. Suddenly, you're accusing him of horrible things. You've even gone so far as to end your relationship. All of this came out of the blue, and I don't understand."

My heart sinks because she's right. The incident at the pool was frightening and eye-opening. I haven't discussed that with anyone and kept tight-lipped about Trent's treatment before that.

Liz said she could tell something was off between him and me, but she's my sister, my closest friend. She's always disliked Trent, so she watched with a critical eye.

Erik calling me out about the immensity of what Trent did triggered a string of alarming memories—things I can't push aside anymore.

Because of my silence on the issue, I can't expect anyone to understand.

"I told you things hadn't been going well between us for a while, Mama," I say quietly, treading lightly into the truth. "I just didn't say anything. It's not wise to air our dirty laundry for others to see, right?"

I know the code of conduct. The details of what goes on are kept within that relationship. What happens behind closed doors is no one else's business.

"Yes, that's right."

"I'm sorry I didn't say anything sooner, but I tried to make it work. I tried my hardest and lasted as long as possible."

"As long as you could?" Mama sets her teacup on the saucer. "You haven't even lived in the same town for a year!"

I don't have the energy to defend my decision or argue with her. Especially when I know there's no winning an argument with Mama. Either she's right, or she makes life hell.

"I know it's disappointing, Mama. I know I've let you down. But I'm still young; I'll find another man to marry."

At twenty-five, I probably seem like an old maid to her, who married Daddy a few days before her twentieth birthday. Things were different when they were younger. Her mother passed away shortly after she met him. I think that loss made her want to start her own family quickly—to have structure back in her life and become a mother herself. But she never talks about her past, so I can't say for sure.

Mama scoffs. "I'm not worried about your age or whether you'll find another boyfriend, Madeline. I'm concerned about the stores— and how much relies on our relationship with the Andersons. How many new sites are opening up between this year and next? Alfred is designing all of them, correct? Maybe we should have met before you abruptly ended things with his son."

A meeting about my love life. Not one of the things I realized I'd be signing up for when I chose to work in the family business.

"Sorry, I didn't reserve the conference room and call you all in before I made a decision about my personal life, Mama." I roll my eyes.

"Don't you dare get snippy with me, young lady." Mama points at me. "You, out of all my daughters, know how important relationships are. We're part of a tight-knit circle, and word gets around. Whether you like it or not, your business and personal decisions affect other people around you. I'm not saying you had to stay with Trent; I'm just asking you to give your Daddy and me a heads-up before you do something drastic."

"I did give you a heads-up," I protest. "I told you I wanted to break up with him."

"I meant before you did it. You blindsided all of us."

"I'm sorry I didn't run it by you and Daddy first, Mama. It's been weighing on me pretty heavily. And, despite what you may think, it wasn't an easy decision."

How sad is it that I had to think long and hard about severing ties with a man who has been physically, mentally, and verbally abusive to me for years? I've been silent for years so as not to rock the boat. Part of me thought it might be easier to go on with life as I had been until I remembered how concerned and frightened Erik had looked after he dragged me from the pool.

Finally, having the full support of a witness to Trent's abuse gave me the strength to break free.

"Whether it was a difficult decision or not, it's still something your father and I should have been aware of. We have to do damage control, Madeline. We have to look out for our business interests."

We'll go in circles for the rest of the night if I try to get Mama to understand my side—my feelings. For her, it's all about business and our reputation. "I know. I'm sorry, Mama."

"Why don't you go upstairs and take a shower?"

I nod. Before heading upstairs, I pause and say, "When I marry someone, I want to be as happy with him as you are with Daddy. That's always been my goal. I knew that wouldn't be the case with Trent Anderson."

"Good night, Madeline," Mama dismisses me.

It's not just me blowing smoke. I've always wanted a relationship like the one my parents have. Sure, they argue like any married couple —especially one in business together—but when it comes down to it, they love each other and do right by each other.

But as much as I love and admire Mama, she has one trait I never want to emulate—how cold she can be.

Chapter Eight

ERIK

I t's not like me to be nervous about taking a girl out, but the reality of picking Maddie up for a date has me feeling like an inexperienced teenager again.

I wipe my sweaty palms on my jeans before I open the door to enter the lobby of her Uptown Charlotte condo building. It's a huge, bright space with white-and-grey swirled marble floors and a calming waterfall streaming down a mahogany accent wall.

The concierge greets me with a smile and a nod from behind a massive desk. He's on the phone, so I shoot him a quick wave, then pull out my phone and text Maddie to let her know I'm here.

She said she'd be right down, so instead of sitting, I stand behind a gray-and-metal couch that looks straight out of a Restoration Hardware catalog, watching sports scores scroll across a huge flat-screen TV.

Though I've driven or walked by multiple times, I've never been in this building. Its clean, modern vibe is trendy and interesting but doesn't fit Maddie. She's warm and traditional, not stark and contemporary. Then again, she didn't design the building. Her personal space probably captures her vibe.

A few minutes later, I'm startled by someone grabbing my hand. I turn quickly and catch Maddie placing her lips on mine. The kiss is a complete surprise but not an unpleasant one. She pulls back immediately.

"Sorry!" She laughs. "I was going for your cheek, but you turned."

"I'm not mad about it."

Maddie smells like nostalgia. The sweet scent of lavender fills my mind with memories of sitting beside her, with our backs against that giant black walnut in her parents' yard, surrounded by English lavender plants.

The recollection makes me bold. I place my hands behind her ears, gently bring her face to mine, and drop my head to meet her lips again. This time, it's deliberate, and she responds by sliding her arms around my waist. Her reaction gives me permission to intensify the kiss. When I slip my tongue out to part her lips, she opens on contact. Our tongues touch, tangling for a few seconds.

I thought tasting her would calm my nerves, but it had the opposite effect. All I can think about is taking her back upstairs and showing her how much I want her.

It's not a new feeling.

And it's not fake.

But reality is not in the plan.

Her eyes were closed during the kiss, but when I pulled my lips from hers, they popped open with our faces just inches apart.

"That was nice," she whispers, looking at me through lush lashes.

I guide her toward the door with my hand on her bare skin, courtesy of the long-sleeved sweater she's wearing that's cropped at the midriff. It shows off a sliver of her tight stomach and hangs off one shoulder, giving me a double shot of warm, bronzed skin. Her dark, skin-tight jeans hug every curve of her hips and ass, and sexy, heeled sandals make her legs look a million miles long. This is what she wears bowling. She's going to kill me.

"You look delicious. I couldn't help it."

"Delicious?" Maddie asks, glancing at me over her shoulder while I hold the door for her.

"Absolutely devourable."

I can't lie. I need to bring it down a notch because I'll be walking around with a boner all night if I don't.

Which is uncomfortable for me and everyone around me.

At the corner of Fifth and Church, we turn right. We're meeting her sister, Liz, and her boyfriend for "Glow Bowling" at Strikers—a bowling alley a few blocks away.

I don't hang out in Charlotte's city center often, but I like Strikers. Especially for special nights like Glow Bowling—where blacklights make the balls glow neon. Is there anything more romantic than glowing balls and the creepy, ultra-white smiles from teeth that glow under a black light?

All kidding aside, I was stoked when Maddie chose bowling with her sister and her boyfriend for our first official date. It means she's taking the significance of our fake relationship seriously. If we want to be believable, we have to be loud and proud about it—in photos, at family gatherings, and in the whole she-bang. Hanging out with her sister in public is a great way to start.

"Liz and Austin are on lane seven."

I've never seen Liz's boyfriend, so I immediately scan the numbers on the lanes, searching for seven. Once I find them, my gaze travels to the people standing near the ball return.

"Uh, Maddie?" I ask, squinting to get a better look at the man in Liz Commons' embrace. "Is that Austin Williams from Drowned World?"

"Yeah. It's Liz's boyfriend."

"Liz is dating Austin Williams?"

"Yup."

"Why didn't you say anything?"

We stop at the counter to get our shoes, getting in line behind a family of four. The little boy turns around and shoots me with a finger gun. There's only one thing to do when that happens. I close my eyes and stagger back, bringing my hands to my heart as if he got me.

Maddie laughs at the interaction. "I told you we were going bowling with Liz and Austin."

"But you didn't tell me it was Austin *Williams*," I continue as if I didn't just get fake-shot. I'm getting good at pretending these days.

Maddie's gaze moves from our armed friend to me. A different kind of smile creeps across her face. "Are you fan-boying right now?"

"No," I scoff.

I'm not. But it's pretty damn surreal that I'm about to go bowling with the singer of one of the most popular bands in the country. Everyone's heard Drowned World songs on the radio.

Hell, I recently heard one in a car commercial. I can't remember what manufacturer, but stuff like that is big-time.

We grab our shoes from the attendant at the counter and pick out our balls before heading over to where Liz and Austin are already waiting for us.

"Hey!" Liz greets us with a huge smile. Maddie hugs her sister and Austin before turning to me.

"Liz, you know Erik," she says.

"Hey, Liz." I give her a quick hug. "Good to see you."

"You too, Erik." Liz smiles warmly. She's always been a nice person. I don't know why I expected her to look down on me or act surprised to see Maddie and me together. But her easy smile puts me at ease, and I don't feel uncomfortable.

"This is Austin," Liz says.

"Hey, man! Good to meet you." Austin holds out his hand, and I shake it firmly.

"You too."

"Y'all ready to get your butts kicked?" Maddie calls. She's setting the hot-pink ball she chose on the rack next to the red-and-black ones already there.

"I guess the pleasantries are over," I say, which makes Liz and Austin laugh.

I walk over to put my ball down, too. Maddie grabs my hand, kisses my cheek, then pulls a pair of socks out of her purse.

"Poor Erik. I don't think you know what you got yourself into." Liz shakes her head. "My sister is a force of nature."

It's interesting getting to know someone again. Though Maddie and I could be considered friends when we were teenagers, she's very different than she was then. Or at least different than the person she showed me back then. She's always been beautiful, confident, and energetic. But I'm seeing a competitive streak I never knew was there.

"Teams, or every man for himself?" Liz asks.

"Teams. It's more fun having a partner in life than being alone," Maddie says.

"Cool. You're up first, Mads." Liz presses a button on the digital scoreboard that starts our first game. On the screen mounted above us, a cursor blinks in the box for the first frame, waiting for Maddie to go. Down the lane, gray bars pop out of the gutters.

"You use bumpers?" I ask in amused disbelief.

"Just for the first game," she explains as if it's completely normal for someone over ten years old to use the bars that prevent gutter balls. "Gotta get my bowling groove back."

"To be fair," Liz says, "I used them for the first game, too."

Austin shrugs. "At least the Commons sisters aren't afraid of getting teased."

Maddie, who had started walking toward the alley, turns around. "Who's gonna tease us?"

Austin puts his hands up and backs away, taking a seat on the bench next to Liz. They immediately clasp hands. Liz leans her shoulder into him and smiles. Austin kisses the top of her head before they both turn their gazes to Maddie.

Those are the little things I want to do with Maddie. It's natural to want to touch the girl I'm dating. Not in a creepy way. When I like someone, I show it with physical connections.

Holding hands, touching her arm, or leading her by placing my hand on her back. Even though this is a fake relationship, I have the overwhelming urge to touch Maddie. We have a connection—a friendship if nothing else—so it seems natural. But I'm playing it cool. I'll let her take the lead on how touchy-feely she wants to get in front of people. I'll take it as slow as she needs, especially after her experiences with Trent.

Even with bumpers, Maddie's game starts pretty rough—only getting four of the ten pins down in her first two tries. I was hoping you wouldn't ask me how that's even possible without the ability to get a gutter ball.

It's probably because her ball moves slower than molasses in January.

Then again, after the first three frames, none of us have shown any indication that representatives from the Pro Bowlers Tour will be knocking on our doors.

Maddie's luck changes in the fourth frame. She walks up to the line with rigid determination, wheels her arm back, and flings the ball down the lane.

Her sweater rises.

All ten pins go down.

"Yes!" She jumps into the air.

Excitement propels me forward. I gather her in my arms, lift her off the ground, and spin her around once before placing her back on her feet. My fingers slide down her smooth, warm skin. "Great throw!"

Her cheeks are flushed when she looks up at me, and she's wearing the biggest grin. "I knew I'd get my groove."

"Nice job, Mads!" Liz slaps her hand in a high five as we return to our chairs.

"First strike of the night," Austin says. "Come on, Liz! Get your ass up there and get us a big X on the board."

"On it!" Liz jumps up, grabs her red ball, and launches it down the lane with gusto. It's a great throw, but only the eight middle pins go down, leaving her with a killer split. On her second throw, the ball slides straight down the middle without hitting anything.

"Ouch. Sorry, babe." Austin gives her a quick hug.

"No worries. We still have six frames left, right?"

"I like the positive attitude, Lizzie," Maddie says. "Now, go get 'em, Erik!"

I'm not much of a bowler, but if my girl wants a strike, I'm gonna try to get her a strike. As I lift my ball, I take a deep breath, silently praying to the dating gods to give me this moment to impress Maddie. Then I swing it back and send it down.

BOOM! Strike!

"That's how it's done!" Maddie yells.

Liz goes to the counter behind us and fills four plastic cups from a pitcher of beer. "Drinks are back here. We got the first round."

"You may be getting the second round, too," Maddie quips.

"Oh, it's like that?" Austin asks with a smile before getting up for his turn. The pressure brings out the best in all of us because Austin also bowls a strike. He celebrates by crossing his arms in an X and bouncing it off of his crotch.

"Classy," Maddie says as they pass in the aisle.

We all burst out laughing, except Maddie, whose eyebrows are knit in determination again as she grabs her ball.

To our surprise, she bowls another strike. After a sad start, she's got two strikes in a row, and though her ball still moves slowly, they're not bad throws. Maybe she did need to get her groove.

The rest of us finish the frame—no one except Maddie gets a strike this time.

After throwing what looks to be another freaking perfect ball, she stands at the end of the lane, watching with her hands like a steeple against her lips. It seems like she's praying to the bowling gods for one more strike. Like all her previous turns, the ball rolls as if in super slow motion. I think the rest of us are praying she puts a bit more power behind her swing so the ball gains more speed as the night goes on— but that's just me being petty. It obviously works for her.

And just like her last two turns, all ten pins go down.

She jumps up and claps her hands. "Gobble, gobble, bitches!" she says, a play on the "turkey" she just bowled, which is what three strikes in a row is called. She dances back toward us, then snaps her fingers and shakes her head in front of Liz and Austin.

"Are you allowed to brag when you're using bumpers?" Austin asks. He and Liz share a smile.

"Liz is using bumpers too!" Maddie cries.

I hold up my hand for a high five. "Nice work, partner," I say as she slaps it.

"I was in a league when I was a kid."

"Oh my gosh! You were seven, and your season average was twenty-five," Liz says.

"Guess I still got it," Maddie teases.

We enjoy four more pitchers over two more games and tons of fun and banter. Hanging out with Liz and Austin is a blast. Before we arrived, I thought it might be awkward hanging around the Commons sisters. I've only known Liz as Harris's oldest daughter—the one studying to be a doctor.

It didn't help when I saw Austin Williams when we got here. I wasn't intimidated, per se, but I expected him to be a douchey celebrity-type dude who was high on himself. Thankfully, that wasn't the case at all. Austin and both of the girls are so down-to-earth. They have a different demeanor when they aren't around their parents.

"That was a blast," I tell Maddie, grabbing her hand for the walk back to her condo. She squeezes it.

"It was! Gosh, I haven't had that much fun in forever. Can't even remember the last time I went bowling."

"You were terrific."

We chat about the evening as we walk. Once we reach her building, I hold the door open. Her ass brushes my hand as she scoots past me, which sends a rush of blood straight to my dick. I start counting slowly, hoping the erection straining against my zipper simmers down by the time I get to ten.

Maddie catches me entirely off guard when she reaches out and grabs my hand, yanking my body to hers. Our faces are inches apart, the tips of our noses almost touching. Her eyes are open, but her lids drop lower and lower with each erratic breath. I lean closer and slide my lips over hers so softly they barely touch. She makes the move, leaning in ever so slightly and pressing her lips on mine. When she opens her mouth, I slide my tongue in, then tilt my head to delve deeper into her mouth. She tastes like bubble gum and smells like sunshine.

She pulls back and whispers, "Come upstairs with me."

"We're playing with fire, Madeline."

"I like the heat," she says, clasping her hands behind my neck and holding me close.

"Most people say that until they get burned. Besides, there's no one to impress up there," I say.

It's a shitty thing to say because she's doing this as a huge, disastrous favor to me. But none of this is real, no matter how much I want it to be, and I have to be the one with a clear head.

I'm not trying to sound like a stereotypical ass, but it's a fact that women get more emotionally involved when things get intimate.

"You're right." She releases me immediately and yanks the hem of her sweater down as if trying to cover herself. "I don't know what I was thinking. Wrapped up in the moment."

The fabric pops back up, a reminder to both of us of how exposed she is. I don't want her to think I'm rejecting her, so I brush my palm over her face and slide my fingers into her hair. "I was right there with you, Maddie. An intimate situation is bound to get us riled up, whether it's real or not."

Maddie swallows hard. Her voice shakes slightly when she speaks. "Yeah. I'm riled up, all right."

It's not a secret, but hearing her say she's excited floods more blood to my cock, and I may have to wait a few minutes before I try to walk back to my truck. I jacked off before our date, but old boy is ready to go again.

"Madeline Commons! I am *not* letting you get in my pants on our second date, no matter how long we've known each other," I say in an exaggerated Southern accent. It matches what she said at Home on the Range Brewing. "You can march your sweet ass upstairs and take a cold shower."

Maddie bursts out laughing, which brings happiness to my heart. She's been dealing with a lot of dark issues with Trent. "Is that how I sound?" she asks.

"I'm teasing you."

Maddie's fingers dance down my chest until they reach my waistband. She looks up at me with a sensuous, mischievous gaze and hooks them into my jeans. "Maybe I'm the one teasing you."

"We can't start this." My head falls back, and I roll my eyes to the ceiling. My dick strains to make contact. Despite every single protesting voice in my head, I pull her hand out from inside my pants. "Get upstairs!" I command.

"Methinks thou dost protest too much, good sir." Maddie winks. But she spins around and starts toward the glass door leading to the elevator.

"I'll call you later," I call out.

"Promise?" She turns around, walking backward as she waits for my answer.

"Promise."

I wait, watching as she enters her code on the keypad that unlocks the doors to the elevator. Once she's out of sight, I slam my palms against the door to exit the building, gulping at the chilly evening air.

Having a fake relationship with someone you have no connection with is one thing. It's an entirely different situation when it's someone you've fantasized about for years.

It's not like I locked myself in my room, committed to a life of celibacy, pining for her. But Maddie has always been my dream girl.

Now that we have this arrangement, I'm facing a challenge I wasn't expecting. I could take it to the next level, and she'd be willing to participate.

If I allow myself to make our arrangement more than it is, she'll be devastated in six months.

I'm leaving the country—whether the U.S. government forces me to or not. I'm choosing to go because that's what I have to do to become a U.S. citizen someday.

There's nothing Maddie can do to change that. Marriage won't save me.

Being with her will be like balancing on a tightrope. If you lean too far one way, you won't be believable, and if you lean too far the other way, you'll be putting too many feelings at stake.

I'm supposed to be helping her recover from a man who crushed her heart, not be the next one to do it.

Chapter Nine

MADDIE

"Her pants were so tight. I could see her religion," Mary Hill Mitchell finishes a story about the fashion faux pas of an acquaintance we know at a recent party.

"Good lord!" Lucy Nelson shakes her head.

"Well, that's just trash," I say to keep up the conversation.

I felt butterflies attack my stomach the entire way to the restaurant, but being here with my friends is much more relaxing than I anticipated.

Normally, I'm all in for the recent gossip. I usually have a few stories to add myself, but with everything going on with work, Erik, and Trent, I'm a mess of nerves. The last thing on my mind is how tight someone's pants were.

But I haven't seen my friends since Trent and I broke up, so I'm grateful to be around them again.

Mary Hill, Lucy, and I met in our debutante class. There were fifteen girls, but four of us became close friends. For the past year or so, we've made it a point to have lunch together every month. We see each other outside of this, but monthly lunch is a tradition we wanted to keep alive when our lives got busy and pulled us in various directions.

I thought I'd have to fend off questions about the breakup, but so far so good. Neither woman has brought it up. Then again, the fourth member, the one person I expected to see, isn't here—yet.

My water glass is empty, so I look up to grab our waiter's attention. That's when I see Suzanne Anderson barreling through the restaurant like a wrecking ball in a baby blue, paisley, A-line dress. I take a deep breath and brace myself for the backlash Erik talked about.

Though we were in the same debutante class, Suzanne and I have been friends even longer. We've been joined at the hip since we met in high school. We chose all the same activities and sports and even went on multiple Spring Break trips together.

At one time, I called her my best friend, but she hasn't spoken to me since Trent and I broke up. So, I reckon the correct description now is Trent's sister.

"Hey, y'all! Sorry, I'm late," Suzanne says, placing her pocketbook on the back of her chair before sitting down. "I was helping at Junior League today and lost track of time."

"No problem, sugar." Mary Hill waves her hand. "I was telling the girls about the Brooks' party last Friday night."

"Did you tell them about Tricia's pants?" Suzanne asks immediately. The waiter stops to pour her a glass of water and refill mine from a silver pitcher. "Madeline." She nods at me curtly.

"Hey, Suzanne." I hoped she wouldn't show. I almost canceled because I knew she'd be here, but I didn't want anyone to think I was a coward. I made my decision and stand by it, even if I can't be entirely truthful about the reasons.

Thankfully, the conversation steers back to Brooks's party last Friday, which was obviously the place to be. I didn't even know about it. Which seems odd, but maybe I missed the invitation. I've been swamped at work and haven't been keeping up with personal email as often as I should have recently.

Our meals arrived quickly since we all ordered salads. I've just eaten a bite of the delicious Spinach, Cranberry, and Pecan salad I ordered when Suzanne turns to me.

"You must be doing well, hey, Madeline? I heard you're already seeing someone else. I reckon my brother was right about you."

It's imperative to finish chewing before answering, but the thick silence makes me uncomfortable. "And just what does that mean?" I finally squeak out.

"Well, it's no secret, is it? You've been out and about with him." Her beady, brown eyes pierce mine. They're an exact reflection of Trent's, which makes my stomach turn. "I never believed my brother when he said you were cheating on him. I thought I knew you better than that. But then he told me that you were already seeing someone."

"Madeline! Are you holding out on us?" Mary Hill asks. By the jovial tone of her voice, I'm sure she's trying to break the tension, but it's not helping. Not me, at least.

"For the record, I never cheated on Trent." I set my fork down and wipe my hands on the napkin in my lap. "But yes, I *am* seeing someone. It just sort of happened."

"I can't believe you held back this entire time." Lucy slaps the table lightly. "Tell us about him already."

"It's not something I want to talk about right now. It's all still new, nothing serious," I lie.

It is new, but it's gotten serious fairly fast—fueled by the fact that Erik and I had a previously established friendship. Since bowling with Liz and Austin, we've met up for multiple dates—axe throwing, a scavenger hunt to find all the murals in Plaza Midwood, the dog bar with Ramos—his black lab—and a few nights of movies and dinner delivery sprinkled in. No matter what we do, I enjoy my time with him. It's relaxing and exciting at the same time.

"Trent said he saw you with another man the same night you broke up with him. Is it the same guy, Madeline?" Suzanne asks. She's really going at it.

I clear my throat. None of this looks good for me, but I can't tell the girls about the agreement Erik and I have.

I promised Mama I'd never say anything about what Trent did at the pool. Though undiscussed, it's inferred that I won't tell anyone about the other times he's hurt me, either.

"It is. But it wasn't a date. I've known him for years. We were catching up at a coffee shop."

"Who is it?" Lucy asks.

These women have been my friends for years. We hang out in the same circles and have the same friends and acquaintances. They're assuming they'll know the guy.

"His name is Erik."

"What family is he from?" Mary Hill asks.

I shake my head. "No one you guys would know."

I don't want to hold back regarding my relationship with Erik, but he's *the landscaper*. The help.

I'm proud of Erik. He's a hardworking, savvy business owner. His occupation doesn't matter to me, but it certainly will to them.

I hate that I care about what they think. I hate that I'm omitting things about Erik to avoid their criticism. But I know I have to make the relationship look real, and telling my family and friends is as real as it gets.

"Did you meet him at SCAD?" Lucy asks. I should have known they wouldn't let it go quickly. I usually gush about everything—and everyone.

My stomach tightens. I know I've done this same thing to them, but it doesn't feel good to be on the receiving end of the interrogation, especially with Suzanne shooting daggers at me from the other side of the table.

"No. He's from Charlotte. But I don't think it's appropriate to talk about right now. Suzanne is obviously uncomfortable and angry about a breakup that has nothing to do with her," I say pointedly.

I can't help but be a little snippy. I understand she wants to protect her brother, but I didn't do anything wrong. Suzanne and I were friends before I started dating Trent. I didn't think our friendship hinged on me staying with him.

"I'm not angry that you broke up. I'm angry that you started dating someone so quickly after the breakup."

I swallow back the fear that tries to stop me from speaking the truth. Maybe I can't discuss exactly what happened, but I'm not going to keep my mouth shut. And I'm certainly not going to let her question my morals in front of our friends.

"Why does it matter? Things haven't been good between us since he moved to Charlotte. You know that. You've seen it."

Suzanne immediately casts her gaze on the table. Her eyebrows aren't knit together in anger anymore. She almost seems sorry.

Because she knows.

Suzanne has seen multiple instances of Trent's verbal and emotional abuse. She was at dinner the night Trent pushed me into the window of my apartment. She watched me walk into a high-end restaurant to dine with his family with a beautiful scarf wrapped around my head to hide the gash her brother had caused. She sat mute when he pointed out, in his condescending way, that the scarf was a piece from one of Commons' new collections. His exact words were, "Isn't it cute that she wears 'fashion for the common man'?" He purposely used my family store's slogan to mock me as I was hiding the injury he caused.

Not being able to confide in Suzanne was one of the hardest parts of being in a relationship with her brother. No matter how much she claims she'll be on my side, she won't—as today shows. She's been my best friend for years, but she's been Trent's sister for longer.

She'll always defend him. Family over everything. Blood over water. She's already done it on multiple occasions. But that's because Trent is just as angry and evil to her. It's like he has issues with all women, not just girlfriends. Gaslighting is a go-to for him.

"People break up. It came out of the blue, but it happens," Lucy says. "And it's still raw for everyone. It's understandable. Let's—"

"You thought it was out of the blue?" I ask.

Lucy doesn't hesitate in her answer. "Absolutely. Now that Trent has his law degree and is back in Charlotte, everyone thought you two would be engaged before the holidays."

Didn't anyone notice how Trent treated me? I thought I didn't see the full scope of his abuse because I was in the relationship. But my best friends are sitting here telling me they thought the breakup was out of the blue.

My entire sense of self is slowly sliding away. Am I really this fake? Did I put on such a good show for everyone, or are they choosing to see what they want to see?

After Trent and I had been dating for a few months, his compliments on my education and decision to go into the family business became backhanded. I didn't realize the switch until he began speaking down to me in public.

Unfortunately, growing up around the number of self-centered, pompous, high-powered men that I have, I've heard many of them talk down to women. But when I became the one being talked down to—by my boyfriend—I wasn't amused. Yet, I let it happen. I brushed off his comments with a sweet smile because Mama taught me to keep the peace, especially in front of our friends and colleagues.

Which is exactly what I decide to do now with my friends. Instead of making a bigger deal of the situation, it's time to sweep it under the rug like a good girl.

Realizing I've been slightly slumped over, I adjust my posture and square my shoulders. I'm not too proud to be the bigger person here.

"I'm sorry, Suzanne. I know this isn't the ideal situation. But I'm being honest when I say I didn't cheat on Trent. I'd like it if we could get past this. I know that may not happen today, but hopefully some-day. I value your friendship. I always have."

Am I lying? A little, but not completely. I did value Suzanne's friendship. We'll never have the same closeness because she'll always be Trent's sister, and I never want to be near or hear about him—again. Which is nothing but a dream, given how connected our families are.

Suzanne shakes her head. "You don't have to apologize, Madeline. I do. It wasn't my place to come in here with an attitude. What happened between you and Trent is your business. I'm sorry."

We're cut from the same cloth. We attended the same etiquette classes. The same type of women raised us. We know how to behave in public. We know when to let things go.

We also know that our friendship will never be the same.

While three of us focus on our food, Mary Hill launches into the details of the upcoming vacation she and her husband are taking to St. Bart's. It's the subject change we need to take the intensity down a notch.

By the end of lunch, I think I'd gotten through with only a few minor scratches until Suzanne's claws come out again as we're walking out.

"It was lovely to see you ladies. I do enjoy our monthly lunches," she says. Seems sweet enough.

"Same here," Lucy agrees, sliding on oversized, cat-eye sunglasses.

"Madeline, it's so funny. A friend of mine saw you out the other day. She said you were with a familiar face. Our lawn man—*Erik.*" There's a deliberate emphasis on the name.

"Wait," Lucy says, her smile faltering. "Didn't you say you were dating a guy named Erik? Are you dating the help?"

"He's not 'the help,'" I respond, using air quotes. "He owns the business. He has multiple—"

Lucy covers her mouth with her hands. Then, without listening to any of the words coming out of my mouth, she continues, "But isn't he all dirty and smelly?" She scrunches her nose. "Do his nails ever get clean?"

"Why don't you ask your granddaddy that, Lucy?" I snap. "Didn't he get all dirty and smelly after working on your family's tobacco farms? Don't tell me you forgot your roots now, girl."

Lucy glares at me. "I know my roots well, Madeline. You don't have to get defensive. It's not becoming."

"What did your parents say?" Mary Hill asks.

"I haven't told my parents yet. As I said before, we're just hanging out. It's nothing serious."

Suzanne stifles a laugh. "I'm sure they'll be thrilled to hear the news. You traded a lawyer for a lawn boy. Sounds like you're on the right track, Madeline."

I take a deep breath and hold my head high. "I traded a horrible human for a gorgeous man with a heart of gold. I've never been more excited about the track I'm on, thank you very much."

Clutching the strap of my pocketbook, I stalk away from my friends.

Mama will have my hide for saying Trent is a horrible human, but I refuse to let Suzanne get away with a vicious remark. And it's not like I explained why he's an awful human. Let them fester over it.

There's an indent in my hand from clutching my keys so tightly while walking to my car. I switch hands and shake it out. The security guard in front of the parking garage nods as I pass. Giving him a small smile, I pass quickly and head to the elevator.

My phone buzzes as soon as I reach the level where I left my car. A glance at the screen tells me it's Mary Hill. I don't know if I can take any more from my "friends" right now, but I answer because not doing so would be rude. It would also make it seem like I'm ashamed, which I am not.

"Hey, Mary Hill!" I answer in a sickly-sweet voice.

"Madeline, I'm so sorry about how lunch ended," she begins.

"Don't worry about it." I brush off the apology. Using my shoulder to hold the phone against my ear, I unlock the car door and swing it open. Once inside, I hook my phone to Bluetooth to talk and drive.

"I wasn't surprised about you and Trent."

"You weren't?" I ask. Her admission surprises me so much that I pause from backing up and shift the car into park.

"No. Everyone thought you two were a match made in heaven, but I never saw it working out long-term. You're far too different. You're bright, social, and bubbly. He's a boring, controlling curmudgeon."

I laugh. Only Mary Hill uses great words like curmudgeon. She and Liz are probably the most intelligent people I know. Her vocabulary is one of her most endearing qualities, though I admit having to look up some of her words.

"Well, he is," she confirms. "I don't know what happened with that man. He's so different than the rest of his family. His daddy is a social butterfly."

"And far too handsy," I add, relaxing in my seat. Mary Hill seems to understand my motivation, which removes some of the edginess I felt.

"Yeah, he's the creepy old man people always talk about," she agrees. "I just wanted to let you know that I understand. I don't know exactly what happened with you guys, but I think I have a good concept of when things are for show and when they aren't. I always thought your relationship with Trent was engineered by family rather than attraction. I'm sorry if I'm out of line saying that," she adds quickly.

"No! No, you're absolutely right. I didn't want to go out with him, but you know how persistent my mama is."

I stare at the BMW logo on my steering wheel. When I turned in my last car, I wanted an Audi, but Trent wouldn't let me. He said I needed a BMW or Mercedes Benz to fit in at business meetings and social events. A car is a status symbol and another way to prove my wealth constantly. Audi is a luxury brand; it just wasn't the right brand.

Mary Hill laughs, but there's a twinge of pity. Everyone knows how overbearing Mama is. It's no secret. If an issue or cause needs a leader, she's the first to volunteer. She's also the first to speak her mind when others stay silent. Or maybe they remain silent because she's so boisterous.

"Can I be honest with you, Mary Hill?" The question is just a formality. She's one of the few friends I know who can keep a secret.

"Please do, Madeline."

"I wish I had never gotten involved with Trent," I tell her, staring out the window at a massive concrete column in the parking garage. It reminds me of the exposed concrete in my condo. I have a similar column in my kitchen. "When our parents pushed us together, it seemed like a match made in heaven—two powerhouse families in Charlotte merging. But I didn't want to merge with Trent Anderson."

The only reason I chose Trent to be my escort for my debutante functions is because the rules state: no boyfriends. An escort should be a well-mannered family friend or "pal." Someone dependable, able to attend social events, and good to be seen within society. Debutante is stressful enough without adding messy boyfriend drama.

Then, our parents got involved. They started pressing for the match after seeing how well-received we were and how good we looked together. I held them off until junior year of college, telling Mama it would be impossible to date because we attended universities two states away—we'd never see each other.

The irony? I finally gave in for that exact reason. He was bearable in small doses, but I still had a separate life at school. Technically, we were dating, but we rarely saw each other, and I liked it just fine. I had my own life, free of fear of what kind of bullshit he'd pull next. But not free of all fear, he'd always find something to yell at me about, making me feel like I was doing something wrong.

Since he's been in Charlotte, I've had to walk on eggshells. I knew he would fly off the handle—I just never knew when.

"I know, Madeline," Mary Hill says. "I'm so sorry you're getting negativity about the breakup. I hate that people think they have a right to have an opinion about your personal life. It shouldn't be that way. Sometimes, people aren't meant to be together, no matter what the union can do for the family businesses. It's sad that people in our circle still think in terms of arranged marriages rather than love and companionship."

I swallow back emotion. She gets it. She truly gets it. I didn't think I'd have anyone to talk to about that.

"I know my role in my family. I chose it." I dab at one of my tear ducts with my ring finger. I can't have tears ruining my makeup. There's no way I could return to work with red-rimmed eyes or smudged eyeliner.

It looked good for Trent and me to attend social events together when we were both home in Charlotte. After graduating from law school, he moved back to work for his family's company, and we were forced into spending more time together than I could stomach. Almost immediately, I longed for the days he was at Georgetown.

"You chose to get the education and experience you needed to take over Commons Department Stores. You remember that, Madeline. You didn't choose to turn your personal life—and happiness—over to a man from the family who can do the most for the business. You are not a prostitute."

"Dang, Mary Hill!"

"Too much?" she asks.

"No. It's exactly what I've been thinking. Thank you for saying it."

"I know it probably sounds lame coming from me since I married the man my parents wanted me to, but—"

"Stop right there," I interrupt her. "Our situations are completely different. You love Jackson with all your heart. There is no denying that."

I can almost hear her smile on the other end of the line. "I do."

Mary Hill met her husband during first-year orientation at the University of North Carolina, and they've been inseparable ever since.

Because he's originally from Durham, he wasn't in the Charlotte social circle. Their relationship grew from genuine friendship into love, which is apparent to anyone who sees them.

"I'm sorry I didn't say anything in front of Lucy and Suzanne. I just agreed with you when you said it wasn't something to discuss right then. I knew Suzanne would make it about her. She always does."

I bite back a laugh. That's Suzanne. Taking every situation and bringing it back around to her. Even something that's not her business.

Out of the corner of my eye, I see the time. I've got to get back to the office soon. I have a phone call with one of our buyers in twenty minutes. "It's okay. I appreciate your call. It means a lot to me."

"I know you need to get back to work, but I have one more thing."

"No rush. I can talk while I'm driving," I say as I back out of my parking spot and start down the ramp toward the garage's exit.

"Erik, the landscaper is really, really hot. You get that, girl."

"Oh my gosh!" I laugh.

"He is! I am so excited for you! Did I ever tell you I had a huge crush on him as a teenager?"

"You did?" I'm not surprised. Erik has always been attractive. I don't think anyone was surprised he's grown up to be as hot and muscular as he is.

"Heck yes!" she exclaims. "But I'm pretty sure every girl at any property he worked on did, even if they won't admit it. It seemed like you guys had something going on back then. You gonna fess up now that you're dating?"

I appreciate how Mary Hill prods in a playful, silly way. That's how friends are supposed to be. It's not accusatory, like they're digging for something to use against you.

When I get to the bottom floor of the parking deck, I stop at the gate to insert my ticket and pay. "We were friends, I guess. Nothing ever happened. We just talked a lot."

"I knew there was something. You always had a sparkle in your eye when anyone mentioned seeing him."

"You know how boy crazy I was back then." I brush off her comment and toss my wallet onto the seat next to me.

"You were, but there was something more with Erik. You skipped your first day of college to attend Rusty Raines's funeral."

Erik's grandfather, Rusty, worked at our property before I was born. Of course, I'd attend his funeral. "Anyone would do that. His grandfather was like family."

"No, Madeline, not anyone would do that. Very few of his clients went."

Looking back, I guess I don't remember who had attended. I'd directed all of my attention to Erik, sitting in the front row of the church alone. No one saw it coming when Rusty, who always seemed to be in reasonably good shape and even better spirits, died suddenly from a massive heart attack.

They'd put Ginny, Erik's grandmother, in a nursing home just a few weeks before. It must have wrecked them, but neither Rusty nor Erik were trained nurses or caregivers. They did their best for as long as possible before it was too much. Her dementia had gotten so bad she couldn't even attend the service.

"It seemed wrong to miss it when Rusty was part of the family."

"I bet Erik appreciated you being there."

My car inches forward, and I lean over the steering wheel, craning my neck to see if any cars are coming before making a left onto Fifth Street.

"We've never discussed it," I say.

It's the truth. We barely spoke after the funeral. I went to college and moved out of my parents' house, and we never met up behind our black walnut again. It hurt at first, but the searing pain of losing a friendship slowly faded into a dull ache. We both went on with our lives.

"Maybe now is a good time," Mary Hill suggests earnestly. Then, in a more jovial tone, she says, "Well, I'm off. I just got to the tailors to pick up a suit Jackson had altered, and you know Mr. Smythe will talk my ear off once I get in there."

"Thanks again, Mary Hill. I really appreciate your call."

I press a button to hang up the Bluetooth, and "Open Your Heart" by Austin's band, Drowned World, blasts through the speakers.

Open your heart. Open my heart. Open Erik's heart.

After all these years, how do I bring up that painful day with Erik? The few times we saw each other, our conversations consisted of surface small talk: a wave and a hello, maybe a "How's school?" or "How's it going?" I never asked Erik how he was handling the loss, how his grandmother was doing, or if everything was going well with the business.

Deep down, I felt concerned, but I was selfish. I wasn't thinking about Erik and his loss anymore. I had school, internships in London and New York, and random social events on my mind. All of that was more important to me at the time—more important than a friend whose life had been devastated.

Everyone deserves a second chance.

Every new life experience is an opportunity to learn and grow. Instead of focusing on the past, I'm committed to the future. I can change from the person I was to the person I want to be. Anything is possible.

Chapter Ten

ERIK

Does anyone answer their door when they aren't expecting someone?

Ever since delivery companies started leaving things on the porch rather than knocking because they needed a signature, I can't remember the last time I answered my front door.

The sound probably wouldn't even register, except it makes my black lab, Ramos, go crazy. I usually just let him bark until the knocker leaves. Sometimes, I peek out the window, but I rarely ever answer.

Today is no different. Ramos stands directly in front of the door, yapping away, but I breeze right by on my way to the kitchen.

It's late, and I'm exhausted. All I can think about is stripping off my clothes, standing in the shower, and letting the stream of hot water pelt me for as long as possible. We'd spent all day laying pavers for a patio renovation at the home of one of my long-time clients. The work was backbreaking, but it turned out beautiful.

I'm so damn proud of what a great job my crew did, I took the guys out to dinner afterward. It was a quick trip to a burger place because we were all dirty and sweaty, but it was something to show my appreciation.

The knocking and barking continue.

"Ramos!" I yell, hoping to get him to back away.

I hope whoever is on the other side of the door will take the hint and leave. But after five more minutes, they're still there, and I feel like an idiot for letting it go on that long.

Nudging Ramos out of the way with my knee, I unlock the door and open it just enough to peek out. Using one leg to keep my dog back, I greet the man standing on my porch.

"Mr. Raines?" he asks.

"Can I help you?" I ask, appraising him. He doesn't seem intimidating: clean-shaven face. Perfect haircut. Wrinkle-free, navy-blue suit and crisp, white shirt with a bright pink tie. He doesn't look threatening, but can you tell by looking at someone?

"Yes," the man answers as he digs into the leather laptop bag hanging off his shoulder. He produces a legal-size white envelope. "I've been trying to reach you through letters and phone calls."

My heart pounds rapidly, and I swallow hard. The only thing I can think about is that this man is from Immigration and Customs Enforcement, coming to tell me this is it—I need to leave the country.

"Well, if I haven't answered your attempts to contact me, I'm probably not interested in whatever you're selling," I say, trying to keep my voice calm. The reality is that I don't know what he's here for since I haven't looked at the information he's given me yet, and I can't let the fear and uncertainty swirling around in my stomach get the best of me.

"I'm not selling anything, sir. My name is Thomas Lowell, and I'm here to follow up on multiple attempts to contact you. I need to make sure you understand what the future brings."

Shit.

My stomach drops, and the overwhelming urge to slam the door and climb out of my bedroom window takes over, but I know I can't escape. It's time to face the consequences of decisions others made for me as a child. I knew it was coming. I've been preparing myself; I didn't think it would happen right now. I thought I had more time.

"As you know—or should know—from previous correspondence, the land this building stands on was rezoned last year after the owner sold the property to a development company." He hands me the folder. "The demolition process on this building is scheduled to begin in less than three months."

"Excuse me?" I take the folder. My heart, which has been racing out of fear of thinking I was about to be presented with deportation papers, now pounds out of confusion. I have no clue what Thomas Lowell is talking about.

I remember seeing a notice about rezoning, but I skimmed it and tossed it into the trash. The city does what it wants, I don't have a say, so I didn't pay attention. I never realized it said this building was being torn down.

Thomas leans in and points to the folder. "If you look, you'll see copies of the letters we've sent regarding these changes and what was happening with this property. You've had over six months to find a new place to live."

"Fuck me," I say under my breath. The folder is marked with a Lowell Law logo. I pull the papers out and skim the top letter, trying to get a quick understanding, since I don't have time to read the information right now.

My area has changed immensely over the last ten to fifteen years. Buildings around me have been demolished, and others have been renovated and turned into housing or breweries. The complex isn't very big—about fifteen units—but it is tucked behind a large empty plot of land. People used the space for parking before a huge warning sign went up stating that vehicles parking without a permit would be booted and towed. When I see a moving truck, I never know if someone's coming or going.

I should pay more attention—and read my mail.

"None of this should come as a surprise, Mr. Raines," he says sharply. I cut my eyes to him, and he takes a slight step back. "But I understand that could be the case if you haven't been reading the correspondence."

"I didn't realize the rezoning affected me. I thought the letters were a formality."

Thomas Lowell nods. "I understand. That's why I'm following up with you and the remaining residents in person. You'll need to secure other housing soon."

"You said I have three months?"

"Technically, yes, but that's the day demolition starts, so you'll need to be out before that. There will be a lot of noise and action around here before then. This isn't something that can be stopped."

I nod absently. "I get it. Thank you."

"If you have any questions, please call. I put my card inside."

"Sure thing," I say as I shut the door, leaving Thomas Lowell on my doorstep.

Ramos follows me to the kitchen. I slide onto a bar stool while he heads for his water bowl. A quick skim over the papers confirms what Thomas Lowell said.

Rezoning notice, blah, blah, blah. The next is a letter from the building's former owner stating that they've sold to a development company and that all residents must move out by a specific date—two months from now.

Two months.

Fuck.

My apartment is relatively small and wide open. While sitting at the bar, I can see the entire space. The kitchen is in front of me, and the living room is directly behind me. The bedroom and bathroom doors are off the living room. I don't have much stuff, so sorting shit and packing up won't be a big deal. That's the good news.

Ramos sets his head on my thigh as if he knows I'm stressed. I rub his neck and ears. What am I going to do with him? Can I bring my dog to the Czech Republic? He's never been on a plane, and I don't know if a twelve-hour flight is the best way to introduce him to air travel.

No. I've got to find him a home here.

The thought crushes me. I rescued him from a shelter right after my grandfather's death. He's been the one thing I've been able to count on for comfort. We saved each other.

Where the fuck am I going to live after I leave here? I can afford one of those weekly hotels, but those places are shady as fuck. I don't have money to waste leasing someplace for a few months.

There's no doubt in my mind that Hugo, my crew leader, and his wife, Anna, would let me stay at their home. But they have their daughter, her boyfriend, and their three grandkids under that roof, and I'd never think about imposing—not when I have the means to stay somewhere else.

Sighing, I close my eyes and tap the letter against the counter. Up until this point, I've avoided thinking about the logistics of leaving. Not my most brilliant idea, but I kept holding onto a shred of hope that something would change. The walls are closing in, and there's nothing I can do to stop it. Everything I need to do to prepare feels like an anvil on my chest.

Maddie believes our arrangement can save me from having to leave the country when my work permit expires, but I know the truth.

Marrying her—or any U.S. citizen—won't help me stay in the country. According to my immigration lawyer, for me to continue my life in America—and eventually apply for citizenship—I must leave.

Currently, there's no way around it because my mother outstayed her Visa. I'm not here on a government-approved green card or work permit. I was eligible for Deferred Action because I was a childhood arrival. "Deferred" means my deportation was put off, not forgiven.

Every day, I get another clue to do the right thing: go to the Czech Republic for as long as I need to and try to get back to America legally. With the upcoming demolition forcing me out of my apartment, it feels like something—a higher being or universal energy, or whatever you want to call it—is pushing me to leave.

Who's going to take care of my grandma? Who's going to take care of Ramos? Who's going to protect Maddie?

These are reasons I have a problem believing in a higher being. I've lived my life as a good person. I've never gotten into major trouble. I do right by others. I've tried attending church and nightly prayers, but that wasn't my thing. And now I'm faced with losing my family, my business, and the girl I've loved for years.

What did I do to deserve this?

There's no time for an existential crisis. I need to roll with the punches and figure this shit out—like I've done my entire life.

I need solutions.

Ramos lifts his head when I shift to reach into my pocket and grab my phone. After entering the passcode quickly, I pull up a web browser. Taking a deep breath, I tap "capital of Czech Republic" into the search bar and hit return.

Prague.

Ready or not, here I come.

Chapter Eleven

MADDIE

"What brings you here today, my dear?" Daddy asks, lowering his newspaper as I lean over to kiss his cheek.

"I have a date, and I asked him to pick me up here." I try to keep my tone nonchalant as if it's normal for a woman my age to be picked up at her parents' house.

"A date?" He slides his glasses down his nose and looks at me over the top of the frames. "With whom?"

"Well, it's funny, Daddy," I begin, smiling broadly and avoiding his inquiring eyes. "It's not a real date. It's kind of this fake-relationship thing I'm doing to help out a friend."

Though I rehearsed a completely calm and professional way to tell my parents about Erik and me in the car on my way here, it all came out in a nervous jumble.

Daddy sits up in his chair and tosses his glasses onto his desk. "What do you mean by fake relationship?"

"It's nothing really. I have this friend who's going to be deported when his work permit expires in a few months, so, ya know?" I shrug and laugh nervously.

I sound like a Valley girl from those horrible '80s movies my friends and I watched at sleepovers. This couldn't have started off any worse.

"Back up, Madeline." Daddy closes his eyes, leans forward onto both elbows, and rubs his temples. "Who is this friend?"

"Erik Raines," I say, meeting his eyes for the first time since I arrived. I may be nervous about telling Mama and Daddy about our crazy plan, but I'm not embarrassed by Erik.

Confusion crosses Daddy's face briefly, then understanding. "He told you about his status?"

"Yes," I say, then quickly add, "but in confidence."

Daddy closes his eyes and pinches the bridge of his nose between his thumb and middle finger. "Who suggested a fake relationship?"

"I did. It's against the law to marry someone to keep them in the country, right?" It's a rhetorical question, so I keep talking. "We thought, well, I thought—it was completely my idea—I thought if we started dating while we tried to figure out other ways to keep Erik in the country, the marriage wouldn't look so shady."

"Why is keeping Erik in the country so important?" Mama asks as she enters the den, carrying a heaping plate of food.

I jerk my head toward her, surprised at how unaffected she could be. Erik's been with us for more than ten years. "Mama, how could you even ask something like that?"

She sets the plate in front of Daddy, then pulls the cloth napkin from her shoulder and hands it to him. "He's our landscaper. Why on earth do you care so much if he stays in this country?"

Daddy interrupts before I can answer. "I can't believe *you*, of all people, thought this was a good idea."

"I know it's a bit out of character, Daddy, but Erik has worked here so long. He's practically part of the family. And it's a harmless solution until we figure out how to keep him here for good."

"It's not harmless. You could get in a lot of trouble over this, Madeline. What you two are doing is illegal."

"It's not illegal until we bring the authorities into it and say, 'Hey, look at us!' We aren't lying to anyone right now. We're setting the stage in case we have to someday."

Thankfully, my nerves have settled, and I can discuss the business arrangement Erik and I entered into. Discussing business with my father is easy since I do it daily. I feel like I'm at a conference, offering a solution to a problem.

The number one piece of advice I'd give anyone for working with Daddy: if you come to him with a problem, you better have a suggestion for a solution, too. Complaining with no ideas to rectify the situation annoys him to no end.

"I'll look into his status, so it doesn't come to that," Daddy says before popping a potato chip into his mouth.

"Would you like some water, dear?" Mama asks, removing two glasses from the cupboard above the wet bar.

He nods. "Please."

"No thanks," I answer, though I'm pretty sure that "dear" was meant for Daddy. "You will?" I ask, bringing the conversation back to the matter at hand. "You'll help him?"

"Yes. I care about Erik's welfare, as well. He's worked hard for everything he has. The last thing I want is to see him deported."

Mama hands Daddy a glass of water, then slides into the soft, green leather chair across the desk from him. "You've always had a soft spot for that boy, Harris."

"Of course, I have, Cookie. We've seen him grow up. We've seen him through loss. We've seen him become a successful man."

"Sounds like the way you'd talk about a son." She rolls her eyes as she sips her water.

Daddy dismisses the comment. "He's not a criminal, Cookie. He had no choice in his situation."

"Yes, he did. He could have gone back where he came from as soon as he found out he was here illegally."

Daddy and I both turn to Mama, appalled by another callous remark.

"What do you have against Erik?" I ask.

"I don't have anything against him personally. But he had the chance to make things right years ago."

"He did make things right. He *willingly* chose to apply for a program that keeps him here legally. He made things right with the resources the government has in place."

"When he turned eighteen, he could have made an adult decision and handled his situation. He could have gone back to where he came from."

Mama buys into the click-bait—the scare tactics certain media outlets throw around without facts. I know because I used to believe blindly, as well. Like her, I thought immigrants who were in the country illegally were murderers, rapists, drug dealers. I imagined dangerous people living in the shadows to keep themselves hidden.

At the very least, I thought they were here to steal jobs from able-bodied Americans. I wasn't marching outside the White House about it, but deep down, I had those ridiculous, bigoted thoughts.

Until Erik told me he was undocumented.

He doesn't fit the profile I believed to be true. After our initial discussion, I researched the other side of the argument, the side I'd never looked at before. Reading articles from alternate sources helped me differentiate the lies from the facts.

When I researched the statistics, I learned that most undocumented immigrants are here because they overstayed their visas. Is it a crime? Technically. But it's a non-violent crime.

They aren't all murderers and rapists. No more than U.S.-born citizens are.

And they do jobs that Americans won't take—backbreaking labor for low wages.

Dreamers—the term used for people in the Deferred Action for Childhood Arrivals program—went to elementary or high school here. They're getting college degrees. They have jobs. They pay taxes. They contribute to our economy and help fund our federal programs.

They were brought here illegally; they didn't choose to do something illegal.

"Yes, he *could have*," I say, "but why would he? This country is all he's ever known. He hasn't been in the Czech Republic since he was a year old."

"Watch your tone now, Madeline. You may be upset, but I'm still your mama," she scolds while staying cool as a cucumber. "I've noticed changes in you over the last few weeks, but I didn't realize what it was until now. I'm concerned Erik's influence isn't a positive one."

I cross my arms over my chest. "Erik doesn't have an influence on me. I am my own person. I make my own decisions."

"A few months ago, I would have agreed, but you never mentioned problems with Trent until Erik carried you inside here after you fell in the pool. It doesn't make sense."

"You told me to keep quiet about the pool incident, Mama," I say sweetly.

Her jaw tightens, and she grips her glass tightly. It's very unlike Mama to lose her cool. It happens, but not very often.

"If something happened with Trent, you should have come to your father and me."

Throwing my hands up, I ask, "Why would I expect you to believe my word against his when I saw how you reacted to an eyewitness account of his abuse?"

"The eyewitness is Erik, correct? Which brings me back to my original concern."

"Let's just stop right here," Daddy interrupts.

"Erik and I have a business arrangement that serves both of us. I'm pretending to be his girlfriend until we find a better solution to keep him in the country."

"How does dating the landscaper serve you?" she asks.

"He's holding me accountable for making better choices."

"What in the world does that mean, Madeline?" Mama rolls her eyes.

Thankfully, the doorbell interrupts our conversation. Knowing Erik is standing on the front porch, waiting to pick me up like he might have done when we were teenagers, has my pulse racing.

I wish I could have warned him about the tense environment he's stepping into.

"That's Erik," I say. "We're going to visit his grandmother."

"In the nursing home?" Mama asks.

I nod. "Can y'all please let us do this our way? You don't have to be happy about it or agree with it, but please accept my choice to help my friend. No matter what you say, I'm sticking to our plan until we find another way."

"You've always had a beautiful heart, Madeline. The conversation is over for now." Daddy's easy retreat from the subject surprises me. He rises from his desk and kisses my forehead as he scoots past me, heading toward the door.

Oh no!

Before I can protest, he swings the front door open. "Erik! Madeline said you'd be picking her up." Daddy moves aside, giving my fake boyfriend room to enter. "Please, come in."

"Thanks, Harris." Erik nods as he steps inside. "Good to see you this morning, Cookie."

"Hello, Erik. Calling on us today would have been quite a surprise if Madeline hadn't told us about your *arrangement*," Mama says.

Subtle, Mama. Very subtle.

"She did?" Erik's eyes widen as he looks back and forth between Mama and Daddy. He slides next to me, whispering through a tight smile, "You did?"

"If we ever have to prove our relationship, my family will be some of the first people interviewed, right? I thought letting Mama and Daddy know what was happening made sense. I'm sorry I didn't say anything to you first."

"Yeah. No, it's okay." Erik takes my hand reassuringly. "It makes total sense." He glances at Daddy. "I know it's not the ideal option, but after the newest legislation passed, I'm exhausting all my options."

"We understand," Daddy says. "You know I'm always willing to help you, Erik. I'll speak with your immigration lawyer next week and see what I can come up with."

"Thank you, Harris. I appreciate that."

My parents handle most situations by acting like nothing is wrong, with no time to think about how to react. Daddy is calculated and controlled. He doesn't fly off the handle without thinking, which would only cause more damage control in the long run.

Still, it's going far too smoothly. We should leave before Mama says something cold or threatens Erik's job. She loves using the small power she has over him.

"Ready to get going?" I ask, tugging Erik's arm.

"Absolutely." He places his hand on my back and guides me to the door.

"How is Ginny doing, Erik?" Mama asks, picking at the flowers in a tall, slender vase on the table in the foyer.

Erik turns around. "Honestly, the same as she's been for the last few years, ma'am. She's never going to get any better, but she's no worse, I suppose."

Mama plucks five flowers and hands them to Erik. "Please take these to her. Something to brighten her spirits."

I don't know who's more surprised at her offering, Erik or me. I've known Mama for twenty-five years, and the abrupt shift in attitude gives me whiplash.

He reaches out, accepting them gingerly. "Thank you. That's...it's very thoughtful."

"Ginny always was a good woman," Mama says before edging past us. "Excuse me." The words come out in a whisper as she hurries up the stairs.

"Give Ginny my best," Daddy says. "I'm going to go check on your mother."

He follows her up the stairs, taking them two at a time, which is as fast as I've ever seen Daddy move. What in the world has gotten into Mama?

"Never expected that," Erik says quietly.

"Me neither." I glance up the stairs where my parents have disappeared from sight. "We should go."

Erik nods. Once outside, he helps me into his truck and then hands me the flowers to hold. I'm still thinking about Mama's reaction when Erik climbs in.

"Did Mama and your grandmother have a relationship that I didn't know about?" I lay the flowers on my lap as I reach for the seatbelt.

"I was about to ask you the same question."

"How often do you visit Ginny?" I ask.

"Every day."

"Every day?" I repeat.

Erik glances at me. "Yes. I make sure I'm there to feed her lunch. I know the nurses will do it, but they have so many residents to assist. Plus, it gives me my time with her. I can never make it for breakfast or dinner with my work schedule. I take a two-hour lunch every day."

"You do? That's, wow, that's so *European*." At first, I smile, but when I lift my eyes to Erik's, I realize my mistake. "I'm so sorry. That was supposed to be a joke, totally unrelated to your situation."

My stomach tightens. How could I be so insensitive? When am I going to learn to think before I blurt something? Of all the qualities my parents have that I could have picked up, why couldn't tact have been one of them?

"Is a long lunch a European thing?" he asks. "I didn't even realize. And I certainly didn't take offense. Geez, Maddie. Do you think I sit here waiting to pounce on something you say?"

"That's what I'm used to," I say quietly.

If Trent were in Erik's situation, he would have accused me of making a dig at him and his situation. The years with Trent tested how well I could hold my tongue, walk on eggshells, and ensure I delivered my point with the correct tone and inflection so Trent wouldn't be angered or offended. I didn't care as much if we were around friends because they always brushed off a 'faux pas' with a "That's just Madeline." I'd never been offended by it; I always used it to my advantage. Let people think I'm a ditzy fashionista.

"I'm sorry you had to live like that."

I don't want to ruin another minute thinking about Trent. I've wasted far too much time on that. Instead, I return to the original subject.

"Me too, but I don't live like that anymore. Thanks to you." I glance at him, hoping I don't look too lovesick. Being with him makes everything better. My tension releases. My problems don't seem as heavy. "It's wonderful that you make time for your grandma. I never realized you did that."

"Well, a lot has changed since the last time we had a deep conversation about her."

"True." His words are a reminder of how selfish I'd been. And how easy it was to forget him.

"I'm sorry I never asked you how you were doing, Erik. I never—"

"What are you talking about?" Erik's eyebrows veer together, making him look honestly perplexed. "We rarely saw each other after you went to college, Maddie. You didn't live with your parents anymore. When would you have had time to ask?"

"I could have made time."

"It's not something I dwell on." He reaches over the console and pats my knee. "We both had busy lives."

I lace my fingers with his. Everything is so easy. Touching, talking, kissing. I'm not on edge with Erik. If I start to feel that twinge, his actions nix it immediately.

Once we pull into the lot at the nursing home, Erik kills the engine and turns to me. "It's not pretty, Maddie."

"What?"

"Her life in there. It's—" He slams his hand against the wheel. "It's depressing as fuck."

"I know." I touch his face, sliding my hand across his cheek. "It's going to be okay. I'm here with you. You don't have to do this alone anymore."

He grabs my hand and plants a kiss on my palm. "That means the world to me."

Once inside, Erik leads me down a hallway to a dank, sterile room with two twin-sized hospital beds separated by nightstands. A frail skeleton of a woman sits in a wheelchair in the middle of the room, facing a dresser. There's nothing on the dresser. No photos. No TV. No artwork on the walls. It's eerie and heartbreaking.

"Hi, Grandma!" Erik greets her as he strides into the room. He stops beside her chair and presses his lips to her forehead before kneeling beside her. She doesn't look at him, but he keeps talking anyway. "It's cold out there today. You need a blanket."

He grabs the lavender afghan from the bed and drapes it over her lap. Ginny turns her head, her light brown eyes empty as she looks through her grandson. My heart breaks for him, but Erik smiles, talking to her as if she understands everything. He brushes wiry, white hair from her face and tucks it behind her ears. "We need to get you to the beauty shop, Grandma."

The smell of hospital food and illness makes my stomach roll. Though it's an involuntary reflex, the fleeting moment makes me feel like a horrible person. Since I only had a few interactions with her at the holiday parties my family throws for people who work for our family, I don't remember Ginny. But she's the equivalent of Erik's mama, not some random lady I'm meeting during volunteer work. She's family, and I need to treat her how I would treat my grandmother if she were in a facility like this.

"I brought a friend today." Erik glances up at me with bright eyes and a smile. "This is Maddie. Do you remember her? She's one of the Commons girls."

"Hi, Ginny." I take a deep breath, sucking up all of my selfishness and stepping toward her slowly. I drop to my knees next to Erik before saying, "My goodness, you look pretty today. I love this sweater. It makes your eyes pop." I brush my fingers over the pilled, purple wool.

"Purple is her favorite color." He glances at me before patting her leg.

"Oh!" I say, suddenly remembering the flowers I've been clutching since we left my parent's house. "These are for you."

Ginny smiles as I set them on her lap. It gives me hope that she understands and appreciates them somewhere in the depths of her mind.

Erik stands up, offering me a hand to help me rise. "Let's get you some lunch."

As he wheels his grandma's chair through the hallway, my eyes are locked on the walls—stark white with a thin maroon band three-quarters of the way up. When we pass a doorway, I tell myself not to look inside, but I can't help it. In one room, a resident rocks back and forth, talking and gesturing to a TV that isn't turned on.

My heart hurts, not just for the patients in the facility but for those working here. It takes someone with unlimited patience and a huge heart to devote their life to this work.

Erik turns into the dining room and wheels Ginny to a space at a large, round table. Multiple elderly people sit scattered at various tables. Most are already eating, some independently, while others have a nurse's assistance.

A nurse's aide calls out, "Hey, Miss Ginny! You're popular today!"

"Hey, Robin," Erik greets her. "This is my girlfriend, Maddie."

This is the first time Erik has introduced me to someone as his girlfriend, and I want to relish it, but the circumstances have me reining it in.

"Hi, Maddie," Robin says.

"It's nice to meet you." I smile, swallowing back the ache in my heart.

It's Saturday afternoon. I would have thought weekends would be hopping with visitors. Out of everyone in the room, Erik and I are the only ones who look like we don't work or live here. I wonder if that's always the case or if lunch is just a slow time.

Erik drags two chairs over to our table. He puts one on each side of Ginny and gestures for me to sit. "Be right back. I'm going to grab her tray."

I nod. Ginny turns her head. At first, I think she's following Erik, concerned about where he's going, but she stops when she reaches me.

"Thanks for letting me have lunch with you, Ginny," I say, following Erik's lead and speaking to her as I would anyone.

I'm not sure what to say. I've never spent time around anyone non-verbal—except babies.

In a different situation, my friends would tease me that she is the perfect audience since I like to talk so much, but it makes my heart ache for Erik. This is the woman who raised him. He's watched her decline rapidly over the years. He's watched her lose her ability to communicate.

Both of Daddy's parents are in excellent health. They still take vacations and are active in the community. I can't imagine having to watch someone I love forget me.

Erik returns with a tray of what's supposed to be food, and I'm appalled. It looks like dollar-store cat food. I must not be hiding my disgust well because he explains, "She has to have everything pureed. She doesn't have her teeth anymore. She has dentures, but they've been lost so many times that we decided to keep them out."

"Oh, yeah. That makes sense," I say, trying to smile.

Erik feeds Ginny her entire meal, telling her about what's happening at work. Then, we shared what we did on a few dates we had.

"They let you throw axes while drinking beer. Isn't that crazy,

Grandma?" he asks. "I can't imagine what kind of liability insurance a business like that needs, but it sure was fun."

She doesn't respond verbally or even with facial expressions. But she opens her mouth every time he lifts the spoon, so that's something.

After lunch, we wheel Ginny back to her room. Erik tucks the blanket under her legs to keep her cozy. He kneels beside her and kisses her forehead.

"I'll see you tomorrow. I love you."

In that tender moment, I realize what a fantastic man Erik is. He's caring, compassionate, family-oriented, driven, and so loving. He is everything I've always wanted in a partner. My feelings for Erik aren't as simple as lust or a silly teenage girl's crush.

I'm falling in love with Erik Raines.

"It's nice to meet you, Ginny. I'll see you again soon, okay?" I say, giving her a small wave as we leave the room.

Erik grabs my hand, and we walk silently down the hallway and out to the parking lot. I'm relieved to have a moment to corral my thoughts. I'm absolutely crushed and have no clue what to say. How in the world does he do this, day after day?

Once we're inside the truck, Erik speaks. "I don't know what will happen to her when I'm gone. She's getting the care she needs here, but I can't stand the thought of her not having any visitors." He runs a hand through his hair. "I know that sounds so stupid. She doesn't recognize anyone anyway; it's just that gnawing feeling in my gut. Deep down, I believe she knows I'm here, even if she can't communicate it. Sounds stupid, right?"

"No, not at all." I slide my palm over his cheek and hold his head up. "We don't know. That's the terrible part of the disease, right? We have no clue what happens when a person loses the ability to communicate."

He nods.

"Don't worry, Erik. You're not going to leave her. You'll be right here, and so will I. I'll visit her with you, or come at a different time. We can take turns to take some of the stress off you. Whatever makes it easier on you. I'm here."

"Thank you, Maddie. I know it's not easy to be there. It's not easy to see my grandma or the other residents. But I appreciate that you want to help. It means the world to me."

"Of course, I'll help, sugar. A relationship isn't only about the easy parts. It's support through the tough times, as well."

Sure, it was uncomfortable because I was unfamiliar with it, but I've done enough volunteer work to know I can handle it.

Ginny is family—and family comes before everything.

Chapter Twelve

ERIK

Hugo Lopez may be my employee, but he's more like family. Which is why he's the first and only person I thought of to run the business while I'm in Prague.

Thanks to technology, I can run the operations and payroll side from anywhere. Our timesheets are all digital—apps on the guys' phones that either Hugo or I click a button to sign off from before a payroll company cuts checks.

Raines Landscaping is a pretty well-oiled machine, but it's a hands-on business, and I need a partner to take my place and oversee the day-to-day operations, schedules, and equipment. I trust Hugo with my life, so I know I can trust him with my business.

"What's with the fancy dinner date, *amigo?*" Hugo asks, sliding into the red leather chair next to mine at the Capital Grille bar.

I laugh. "Only the best for you, *hermano.*"

"Anna's going to be jealous. She loves this place."

"Order her a meal before we leave and bring it to her. That'll be a surefire way to get some head," I tease.

Hugo laughs. "I don't need to bribe my woman for that. You should know. Don't you have a girlfriend now?" He nudges me with his elbow.

I chuckle. There's no keeping secrets around my guys. I mean, they saw Maddie and me in the front yard at her parents' house after the pool incident. They won't say anything to my face, but behind my back, they're all yapping about me getting it on with one of the clients. The rumors between my guys don't bother me. I can take a little good-natured heat.

"I do."

Hugo cocks his head. "Really? You and Miss Commons are a thing?"

I lean back in my chair and raise my drink. "Sort of. That's why I asked you here tonight. I have something I want to discuss with you."

"You want me to be the minister at your wedding?" Hugo slaps the bar. "I knew it. I've been waiting years for this moment, E!"

The comment startles me and I choke on the sip I just swallowed. "Years?" I ask after a minor coughing fit.

"Jack and ginger, please," Hugo says to the bartender before answering me. "You and Madeline have had stars in your eyes since the first time you met. Maria and I saw that puppy love from a mile away."

"Put it on my tab, please," I tell the bartender before he retreats.

I'm not surprised they noticed. Hugo and Maria aren't only close to me, they're very close to the Commons family. I wouldn't go as far as to call them friends, but Maria is Cookie's right-hand woman—the one she calls in any situation, from decorating the house to helping her cook. It makes sense, as she's worked at their home for twenty years.

"It's not like that. But Maddie *is* the reason for what I'm about to tell you," I begin. Even though I knew he would understand, I've never told Hugo about my illegal status. Sure, I'm here legally for the time being, but keeping as quiet as possible, even about that, seemed like the best plan. "This is completely hush-hush, right?"

"Do I ever tell your secrets?"

"Well, the guys know a lot more than I recall telling them about."

"It's because they see it with their eyes, *hermano*, not because I open my mouth." Hugo leans back in his chair. "You're the one who puts your business on display."

"Fair enough." I shrug and lift my eyes to the seven-point buck head mounted on the wall behind the bar.

"So, what's up? And what does Madeline have to do with it?"

Time to lay it all on the line. "I am not a legal citizen of the United States."

"You're not what now?" he asks, leaning closer as if he didn't hear correctly.

"I'm a *Dreamer*, Hugo. I was brought here illegally when I was a kid," I say quietly but firmly.

"Oh dang!" He places his elbow on the bar and covers his mouth with his hand. After processing for a moment, he straightens up. "What does that have to do with Madeline Commons?"

"Well, she came up with this crazy plan to start dating. To establish a relationship, so if we had to get married to keep me here, it would look like a natural progression."

Hugo stares at me with wary eyes. "You know—"

"Marriage won't keep me here?" I finish his sentence and nod. "Yes, I know that now."

"Damn, man. I can't believe she offered to do that!" He drains his drink and points to the empty glass, cueing the bartender to make him another. "She could get into major trouble."

"I know, and I can't let that happen." I sigh, dropping my shoulders in defeat. "I love my life, Hugo. I love the business and you and the guys. Charlotte is my home—the only place I've ever known. But"—I summon the courage to tell him my plan—"my DACA work permit expires in February. And I can't renew it again."

"No. Don't tell me that shit, E!" As understanding of what I'm saying—and what it means—sinks in, his eyes grow larger, and his hand flies up to rub his forehead.

"I'm moving to Prague in a few months," I finish. Getting it off my chest envelops me in a mixture of defeat and relief.

"Prague? Where the fuck is Prague?" He glances around the bar as if looking for a camera crew to pop out and tell him he's being pranked.

"The Czech Republic. That's where I was born." The bartender drops off new drinks for both of us. I slam mine, which is probably not the best decision since I drove here.

"Fuck, E. Fuck! You can't. You—"

"I don't have a choice. If I ever want to continue my life here or become an American citizen, I have to go back. We both know the current administration isn't going to pardon me."

"They might. You're so white you're almost translucent. They only want brown people like me gone."

"Hey now! My skin tans." I feign offense at the brutal description. "Isn't the Czech Republic on the Mediterranean or something?"

"You're from a landlocked country in white Europe." He slaps my shoulder. "You should really know that, man."

He's not wrong.

The bartender places an order of oysters I'd put in before he arrived in front of us. Without a pause, Hugo grabs one and slurps it down.

"I eat when I'm stressed out." He rubs his rotund belly. "Why would you tell me this now, E? It's the holiday season. My stomach can't take this much stress around the holidays."

"Sorry, I'm ruining the holiday for *you*." I roll my eyes.

He elbows me playfully. "You know what I mean, man. I love you like a brother."

"I love you too," I tell him honestly. "That's why I wanted to talk to you tonight."

"Fuck, E. Are you shutting down the business?" he asks. "Am I going home with a steak and a pink slip tonight?"

"No. Quite the opposite." I smile. "I want you to take over while I'm gone."

Hugo turns to me with cheeks full of oysters. He swallows hard and says, "You what?"

"Not just take over. I want you to be my business partner."

"Erik." He shakes his head. "I don't have money for a buy-in like that. Maria and I do okay, but with the kids living with us, it puts more strain—"

"I'm not talking about a buy-in, Hugo. You were the first employee Rusty and I hired. You've been just as instrumental in making this business successful as I have. I trust you with my life, literally. If you're in, I want you to be part owner of Raines Landscaping."

Tears well up in his eyes. People may be intimidated by his large frame, but he's an emotional teddy bear of a man.

"You're not fucking with me, right?"

"I would not fuck with you about my business. Ronaldo versus Messi, yes, but not my business," I tease. We've had a long-running "argument" about which futbol player is better: Cristiano Ronaldo or Lionel Messi. Though, the answer is obviously Ronaldo...

"I'm in. Whatever I can do to help, brother!"

"We'll have some meetings over the next few weeks to hash out what it will all look like. Then I'll have lawyers draw up some paperwork. But for now"—I pick up an oyster and hold it out for him like a toast—"we feast!"

Hugo clinks his oyster with mine, and we throw them down the hatch simultaneously.

The first step in my plan of action is complete, which brings a huge sense of relief. Hugo and I celebrate the rest of the evening, drinking and eating massive steaks.

I'm torn between two opposing emotions. I'm excited about starting an adventure in Prague, but I'm also wrecked when I think about leaving my grandmother and my friends.

The Czech Republic's capital looks pretty fucking cool, judging by what popped up in multiple searches I've done since putting my plans into full gear. Every time I look for apartments, my heart pounds a little faster, mesmerized by the city's beautiful architecture, a mix of various styles spanning hundreds of years.

Though I never went to college, I've done enough research for my landscaping designs to recognize the Baroque and Gothic-style buildings throughout Old Towne Square, the historic heart of the city. It's like nothing I've ever seen before. It's daunting to pick up and move to a place I don't know, but if I had to have been born in a foreign country, the Czech Republic seems like a win.

Except for that whole "landlocked" thing. That's a bummer.

After dinner, I make sure Hugo gets in the Lyft I called for him since neither one of us can drive. I'm about to enter my own address, but then I realize Maddie's condo is literally around the corner.

Madeline Commons, the beautiful, selfless woman who would risk getting into major trouble to help me stay in the country. I can't let her do that. The fact she would do that for me made me realize I have to take responsibility for myself. Since shifting my mindset from looking for loopholes in laws to stay here to making plans to return to America, I'm actually excited about whatever the future holds.

Each day, I fall deeper and deeper in love with Maddie. If our feelings for each other are real, I want the chance to be with her for the rest of my life. And in order to do that, I have to leave.

But right now, I'm here and plan on making the most of our "fake" relationship. I close the Lyft app and type out a quick text.

Me: I'm around the corner, mind if I stop by to say hi?
Maddie: Sure, come on up!

I shove my phone in my front pocket and practically run to her place. The drinks and newly-made plans have me high on life and feeling frisky. Hope Maddie's ready for me.

She's waiting in the lobby, wearing nothing but a tank top and shorts. It's borderline indecent, but I'm not complaining. It covers more than a bikini, technically. Plus, this is her home, so why would she feel uncomfortable?

She smiles and runs to me. "What a wonderful surprise!" she says, wrapping her arms around me. I'm slightly taken aback by how demonstrative she is, but I roll with it. My hands roam, feeling the rounds of her ass cheeks as her shorts ride up.

"Let's get upstairs." I turn her around and propel her forward, covering her like a blanket as we walk to the elevators.

"I've had a little bit of wine tonight," she whispers loudly as she presses her code into a keypad.

I nuzzle her neck, inhaling the soft, sweet scents of lavender and vanilla. "I've had a little bit of bourbon."

Thankfully, we're the only ones waiting for the elevator. When we get on, she presses the button for her floor, and I push her back against the wall and slam my mouth on hers. She grabs onto my shoulders. I place one hand on her waist and use the other to grope her breast, then slide up and into her hair. My erection presses against her stomach.

I'm so fucking aroused; I have no clue how long I'm going to last.

Maddie and I have never made out like this before. And the intensity is sexy as fuck.

We don't untangle, walking as if in a three-legged race to her condo.

"We should stop," I say, lifting my mouth from hers for two seconds. The time allows her to unlock the door.

"That seems silly," she says, holding my face to hers by sliding her fingers into my hair and pulling our mouths together. When she clutches, I dig deeper into the kiss.

"Can I lay next to you and kiss you tonight?"

Her eyes are wide as she stares at me. "We'll be doing a lot more than that, sugar."

I shake my head while taking the slightest step back. "Could you feel how much I want you?"

She nods.

"That feeling is not going to go away. But tonight, I just want to hold you. Would that be okay?"

She closes her eyes and smiles, then wraps her arms around my neck, hugging me. I lift her off her feet and carry her to the bedroom.

If Maddie and I have sex, this whole charade is over. I'm not a good enough actor to pretend I can fuck her without feeling anything. Without wanting more than either of us would be able to give.

Once we cross that line, it's all or nothing.

I'd rather hold off on the all, so I can handle being across the Atlantic with nothing.

Chapter Thirteen

MADDIE

My pulse spikes when I see Erik pull his black F-150 up to the curb in front of my parents' massive front yard. I've been watching from the window, waiting for him to arrive like I've done hundreds of times. Familiar feelings flood my mind and wreak havoc on my body: the racing heart, sweaty palms, and last-minute mirror-check to ensure I look good.

But this time is different. This time, I'm in love.

And love is a tricky little bugger.

It has me forgetting things, stumbling over my own feet, and thinking about him at the craziest times—during important work meetings, in the shower, and while driving. There was absolutely no reason to come to my parents' house today except for the pounding in my chest and the tension in my core, which tells me I need to see him at every opportunity.

I can't pretend anymore.

I'm in love with Erik Raines.

Every time I think about him—about us—another piece of the façade crumbles away, replaced by reality. I have to know if he feels the same or if this is still just an arrangement to keep him here.

Not that I'd walk away if that's all it is for him because I'll do anything to help him. It'll crush me if he doesn't feel the same, but I refuse to hold back. If Erik has taught me anything—it's to be true to myself and my feelings. Lying doesn't do anyone any good.

After the guys in his crew gather their equipment and scatter to various areas of the yard, Erik jumps into the back of his trailer, climbs onto his green-and-silver riding lawn mower, and backs it into the street.

When he sees me crossing the yard, he stops and climbs off. After raking the back of his arm across his forehead, he slides his headphones off and yanks the bandana from his nose and mouth.

"Hey! What's up? You need something?" Sweat rolls from his temple down his jawline, distracting me from his lips for a moment.

"No." I shake my head, momentarily forgetting the reason I came out here. "Yes. I—"

"You want to kiss me, don't you?"

"Excuse me?" I ask, completely forgetting my original mission.

"You can't get the feel of my lips out of your head."

"That's not what I came out here for, but since you brought it up." I shrug nonchalantly, even though the thought of kissing him has my stomach doing somersaults. "We might as well keep up our image."

"I'd love to kiss you, Maddie." Erik leans closer. I tense in anticipation of having his lips on mine again. My breathing gets heavier. "But not here. Not like this," he says against my lips.

"But our lips are already touching."

"I know. Feels nice, doesn't it? I keep mine in good shape. Scrubs and balms and all that stuff."

My eyes drop to his mouth, which is exactly what he wants.

Damn.

He leans back, smirking. "Kissing should be passionate and in the moment. Something special, don't you think?"

"It would be special." I gather his T-shirt in my fists and pull him close again. "It would be amazing and sexy. Rough. Raw. Right here. Right now."

"Begging. I like it." Erik replaces the bandana over his mouth, cutting off any chance of a kiss. "Though I'd like you on your knees when you're doing that."

Double damn.

I clench my muscles, trying to suppress the want pulsing between my legs.

If he thinks he won, he's wrong. I came out here to declare my love; he's the one who got us all hot and bothered with sexual fantasies. If he can tease, I can too.

I reach up, placing my fingertips on my collarbone. Then, I look him directly in the eyes as I slide my hand down, undo a few buttons on the silk blouse I'd worn under my blazer, and trace the top of my lacy bra.

I'm not opposed to using my feminine wiles to get what I want. And he should be used to it by now. I've always taken every chance I had to prance around him, looking my cutest.

At first, he keeps his eyes locked with mine, but the moment his gaze slips downward for a second, I go in for the kill.

"I just really think," I say in a sexy, sultry whisper, "it'd feel so good to have your mouth on—" I pause, holding my bottom lip with my teeth.

He jerks the bandana down again and grabs my hips, pulling me against him. He's rock-hard and pressing in the most delicious spot. "You show me any more of your tits, and I'll have my mouth on them right here in the yard for everyone to see."

"Promise?" I ask, sliding a hand into my bra and under my breast to lift it. The primal urge to feel his mouth on me trumps any common sense. Being in the front yard where all the neighbors can see excites me. I don't want to pretend anymore.

"What do you think Daddy will say when word gets back that the lawn guy assaulted you?"

His comment snaps me out of lust and into reality. I step back out of the safety of his arms. "It wouldn't be assault. Geez, Erik!"

"Stop with the charade, Maddie. Let me get back to work." He grabs his bandana again, but I reach out and stop him from placing it over his mouth.

"What if I want it to be real?"

"Excuse me?"

"What if I want this to be a real relationship?"

"We have a business agreement, Maddie." Erik swallows hard. "Don't get it twisted."

"Can you honestly tell me you don't feel anything for me, Erik?" I ask, bracing myself for the truth.

He grunts.

"Am I not your type? Are you ashamed of me? Am I only good enough to fake date?"

It's a low blow because Erik is very confident in who he is and what he offers. Although the type of work we do may differ—blue-collar versus white-collar—it's no secret that he makes great money.

I'm the one who worries about what other people will think about my relationship with him. I'm projecting my insecurities onto him because of how my friends reacted.

"Maddie." Erik sighs, taking a step closer to me. He slides his hand into my hair, cradling my head behind my ear. I tilt my head, leaning into his touch. "Do you really want to take this from a silly scheme into real life?"

"Do *you* want to?"

Erik closes his eyes for a second, then blows a puff of air out of his nose like he's a magic dragon. I know I frustrate him. But I want him to tell me he wants to be with me. I want him to know that this crazy plan was always rooted in how I feel about him.

I've never felt more like the person I'm meant to be than when I'm with him. He doesn't make me want the life I lived before the incident with Trent. He makes me feel comfortable in a tank top and yoga pants. No one has ever made me feel like I could be myself. I can be happy and bubbly and strong and smart without being fake. I've felt our connection for years. He has to feel it too.

"If you really want me to suck your tits in public that badly, you could just ask nicely. I'll put my mouth on any body part you want me to whenever, wherever. We can add fucking to the agreement. You don't have to pretend you want it to be real."

I turn around and stalk away from him. I'm a secure, positive person, but I don't have unlimited capacity. My confidence wears thin at some point.

No. I stop in my tracks, then spin around quickly. I will not allow him to turn this around on me. I will not keep my feelings bottled up. I promised myself I would only accept the truth from now on. No more living a lie.

"I'm in love with you, Erik," I say. "I'm head over heels in love with you, and I can't hold it back anymore. If you don't feel the same, I need to know now."

"Are you serious?" Erik asks. He seems a bit dazed as if I punched him in the stomach. "You love me?"

"As if you couldn't tell," I say softly.

The skin around his eyes crinkles as he smiles. "I've wanted to hear you say that for years, Maddie."

"You have?"

"Come on! I'm a fucking fool around you. I have been since I was a kid. Hell, I've always worn my best dirty shirts when I knew I was coming here," he says with a wink as a beautiful smile slides across his face. He takes a step toward me.

I move to him, closing the gap. "Do you want to try being together for real? Tell me the truth."

His eyes meet mine and don't waver, but he doesn't answer. Every part of me wants to plead my case, but at the same time, I shouldn't have to. If he feels more for me, he needs to say it. And I'm keeping my mouth shut until he does.

I gotta tell you, being silent is one of my least favorite things in the world. I'm the person who fills those uncomfortable gaps with mindless chatter.

But I'm trying to move away from the old me. Or parts of the old me.

"Are *you* all in? Or do you just want to keep fucking me?" he asks.

I can't help the burst of laughter that escapes my lips. "Please. If this was about sex, I could've had you years ago."

"You think?"

"Uh, yeah."

"You wanna take this to the backyard?"

"Can I ride on your mower?"

"I'd rather you ride my dick, but okay," he teases. Then he grabs my hand and yanks me toward him. I lose my footing and fall onto him, bracing myself against his chest. Our eyes lock. "You really want this to be real?"

"Absolutely." My answer comes out in a hushed whisper, with no hesitation.

"I love you too, Maddie. I wasn't sure if you felt the same way."

"You weren't? I thought it was pretty obvious, with all the staring, texting, and puppy-dog eyes."

"I just never thought it would happen. I thought you'd bottle up your emotions and keep this professional."

"I'm working on telling people how I feel. Maybe we should have done that from the start instead of waiting for fucked-up situations to bring us together."

"Maybe." Erik nuzzles his face into my neck. "But I don't think either of us would have been ready for this any sooner than it happened."

"That's true." I reach over and pat the seat of this mower. "Giddy up."

"Do you really think I'm going to fuck you in the backyard at your parents' house?"

"Hush with all the questions, sugar! We've established the fact that I want to be with you. Mind, body, soul."

"Soul?"

"When I'm in, I'm all in."

"Me too." He presses his pelvis against me. "Tonight."

I swallow back the lust that has my heart racing and blood pumping. "What does that mean?"

"I'm not gonna fuck you in the backyard, Maddie." He shrugs. "Well, not today. We can definitely consummate this place someday."

"Okay."

"We cool?"

"Yes," I say, though the rejection stings a bit. I know he's trying to be a gentleman about this, but it feels like a slap in the face. I'm not going to tell him that, though. Especially since I know he's making the right choice.

"Hey!" he says, placing a hand on my waist. "I'll be at your place at seven. Don't wear underwear."

I take in his words, searching for the perfect comeback. "Wasn't planning on it." I kiss his cheek quickly and walk away on wobbly legs.

The confidence is a ruse because the lusty promise has my insides melting. The anticipation of what tonight will bring will gnaw at me for the rest of the day.

Chapter Fourteen

ERIK

"Hey! How was your day?" Maddie calls.

"Awesome! I'm being evicted." I follow the amazing smell of Italian spices, leading me into the kitchen.

I hadn't planned on telling Maddie because my original plan was to be in Prague before leaving my apartment.

Everything changed when we declared our love. I don't want to leave Maddie any earlier than I have to, but the demolition deadline is approaching, and I need to find a place to live for a few months.

"What?" She's at the stove, stirring a pot of spaghetti sauce, with an apron tied around her tiny waist. It's so 1950s, but in a super-sexy way that sends all the blood to my dick. She glances at me over her shoulder. "Why?"

"My building is being bulldozed to make room for a new development—an outdoor mall or something." I move closer, hoping she'll offer me a taste of the sauce and because I like being near her. I haven't been able to get her out of my head after her shenanigans this afternoon at her parents' house. "That looks good."

She beams. "Want a taste?"

I groan and nip at her neck. "Yes."

Maddie laughs. Then she holds one hand under the spoon while bringing it to my lips. I blow on it gently before tasting it.

"That is phenomenal!" I exclaim. "Where did you learn to cook like that?"

"A Southern woman with any worth knows how to cook."

I laugh at her stereotypical comment. But when I look up at her, she's got a hand on her hip and a wooden spoon raised. "Oh, you weren't kidding."

"My mama raised me right, Erik. I am a college-educated executive who knows how to set a table, dance a waltz, and fix a dinner for my family."

"Simmer down, sexy. I love all of those things about you. I'm getting used to the Southern belle pride."

Her perfect pink lips turn up in a sexy smile, but she doesn't respond with a trademark snappy comeback. "Why don't you move in here?"

The suggestion catches me off guard, and I take a step back. "I don't know. That seems—"

Maddie spins around, so we're nose to nose. "I love you. You love me. You need a place to live. What's the problem?"

"We know this is real, but your parents don't." I look into her eyes. "What do you think they'll say?"

"We don't have to tell them."

"I'm sick of lying, Maddie."

"Well then, we can tell them." She laughs. "I'll follow your lead. I'm proud to be with you. I don't care if they know it's real."

I smile, hoping she doesn't see through how empty it is. I know I'm being frustrating, but I haven't told her I'm moving, no matter what. I can't break her heart right now. I took the demolition of my building as a sign.

Time's up, Erik. Go back to where you came from.

It was the kick in the ass I needed to get my plan together. Then love happened, and I can't bear to tell Maddie.

"Dinner will be ready in just a few minutes. Why don't you go pick a movie?"

I kiss her once more before shuffling to the couch. The best thing about her condo is the open floor plan. You can see and talk to each other from all rooms—except the bedrooms and bathroom.

"What are we watching?" Maddie asks, craning her neck to see the screen before reaching into the cupboard to retrieve two dinner plates. She sets the dishes on the counter and turns back to the stove.

"*The Mighty Ducks*."

"Are you joking?"

"You need to know me, Maddie. *Really* know me. If an interviewer ever asks what my favorite movies are, you gotta know how much I love these cheesy-ass movies."

"I can't believe we're spending a Friday night binging on children's movies."

"I love hockey. I started playing hockey because I wanted to be a Duck. Not in Anaheim," I explain, pointing at the screen. "I wanted to be on *this* team."

"So, you wanted to be an actor?" Maddie ladles spaghetti sauce onto a mountain of noodles. The heaping plate must be for me because there's no way she could eat all of that.

"No, I wanted to be an extra." I laugh. "They seemed like cool kids. I wanted to be their friend."

Maddie looks up from plating our meals. "That is the sweetest thing I've ever heard."

"I'm pretty good at hockey. Maybe my real dad is a hockey player in the Czech Republic."

"You never know, sugar." When she leans down to set the plate in front of me, she drops a kiss onto my lips. "Did you play when you were younger?"

"Thank you," I say, watching her grab her plate off the counter and carry it to the coffee table. She sits on the floor next to me. "Yeah, I played for years when I was a kid. I had to stop when I started working."

"Awww." Maddie pats my arm, then takes a bite of garlic bread.

"I wasn't good enough to make a higher-level team, so it was no big deal. I still play pick-up games. I'm in an adult league on Tuesday nights."

"You are?"

I can only nod since I stuffed my mouth with spaghetti after speaking.

"I've never seen a hockey game before," she says softly, as if I'm going to laugh or be angry. It's not surprising. Hockey is not a Southern sports staple. "Can I come watch you play sometime?"

"I'd love that." I wipe the sauce off my lips before pressing them onto her cheek. I point to my plate with my fork. "This is phenomenal, by the way."

"Thank you."

After dinner, we curl up on the couch to watch the movie. I wrap my arm around her, pulling her close. She snuggles next to me. But I can't concentrate on the story of the rag-tag hockey team being this close to the woman I love.

I slide one hand up her thigh to her hip. Nothing but skin. "Are you wearing underwear?"

"You told me not to," she says. "Your wish is my command."

I pull her onto me and press my mouth against hers. My hands rove across her back, over her ass. Within seconds, we've discovered the fast and furious pace we abandoned the other night.

This time, we don't stop kissing and touching, pulling and yanking until we reach her bedroom. We waste zero time undressing each other quickly and climbing onto the bed.

"Condoms are in the drawer," Maddie pants.

I reach over and slide open the drawer to her nightstand. Though condoms were my original mission, two hot-pink vibrators catch my eye, and my mind takes a major detour. I pick one up and hold it in front of Maddie.

"What's this?"

"Nothing. It doesn't even work." She squirms under me, silently begging me to touch her again.

"What, like it's not charged?" I ask, holding a button I assume turns it on. It immediately starts buzzing and shaking in my hand.

"No, it's supposed to be a G-spot vibrator, and it doesn't work. Maybe I don't have a G-spot."

"Maybe I should check."

Her eyes flash. "Erik—"

I trail the vibrator down her stomach and over her pussy. "I won't if you don't want me to, but I think I can help you find it." I kiss the inside of each thigh, then blow on her clit.

As her arousal grows, her pelvis rises to meet my mouth, but I lift my head. She's already soaking wet, so there's no need to moisten the toy with lube. Dropping my head again, I kiss her just below the belly button as I insert the vibrator slowly. She lifts her hips as I slide it farther inside. Her hips buck off the bed, jolting her pussy against my face.

"Mmmmmm. I love how excited you are, Madeline. It's so fucking sexy."

I press a few buttons, testing various speeds and rhythms. She moans when I get to a slow roll that builds to a more intense buzz. *That's the one.*

While one hand jerks the vibrator hard and fast against her G-spot, I lower my mouth to her clit, licking, sucking, and nibbling. She's rolling her pussy against my face and moaning, so I know it feels good.

That's when the brilliant idea strikes. I remove my face from between her legs and grab the other vibrator—a wand-type thing with a huge, bulbous head that pivots easily.

"Erik! Don't stop!"

With the G-spot toy still vibrating inside her, I flick the wand on and place it directly over her clit.

"Oh my God!" She thrashes under me, knocking the toy out of my hand.

"So fucking hot." I blow slowly on her pussy, then brace her with one arm before pressing the vibrator to her clit again.

"Fuck! Oh my god! Oh my god," she pants. "It's too much."

"Should I stop?" I ask, even though I know what her answer will be.

"No." She shakes her head. Her eyes are closed; she's writhing in ecstasy. "Fuck, Erik! How? I can't—I can't."

"Yeah, you can." My cock throbs, but I'm not giving it any attention until this girl is seeing stars. The intensity of both vibrators must have her close to exploding. And I want to taste it all. I press a button on the clit wand twice, which increases the speed. Using one hand to hold it on her clit, I wiggle the other vibrator, pulling it out and pushing it back in, hard and fast. It only takes a few jolts before she's screaming and bucking.

That's my cue to drop the wand and pull the G-spot vibrator out. I cover her pussy with my mouth, lapping her juices. She immediately closes her legs around my head and grinds against my face.

I grab hold of my cock and pump it in my fist a few times. It's not going to take me long to lose all control, not with how fucking hot Madeline looked getting wrecked by the double-vibrator orgasm.

"I'm gonna come," I tell her. My heart pounds against my chest, cock engorged in my hand. "Where do you want it?"

"On my tits. Come all over my tits," she begs, cupping her breasts with both hands and twisting her nipples between her fingers.

"Fuck!" I barely have time to rise onto my knees before I cover her beautiful breasts.

When I'm able to see straight again, I grab my boxer briefs off the floor and wipe my cum off Maddie's tits. It's definitely not the sweetest way to clean her off, but I'm completely spent, so it'll do until I get her in the shower later. Her eyes are still shut, and her breathing slows with each rise and fall of her chest, so it doesn't seem like she cares all that much.

"You are so fucking sexy, babe," I say, lying down next to her and gathering her in my arms.

"That was really hot," she says. "I have never done anything like that before."

Maddie's not shy, but doing things you're not familiar with in the bedroom takes a lot of trust in a partner. "Thank you for being so open."

Her head pops up, blue eyes blazing with fire. "What? Like, my legs?"

"No!" I laugh and kiss the top of her head. "Open, as in trusting me enough to try new things."

"Well, you never have to worry about things like that, sugar." Maddie relaxes and nestles into me, snuggling a little closer, if that's even possible since our sweaty, naked bodies are already completely molded together. "I trust you completely."

In the silence, her breathing slows. Listening to her makes me closer to her—like we're one in our hearts and bodies. Once our breathing syncs, our chests rising and falling together, I know it's the right time to confess everything that's been building in my heart.

"I've never felt as connected to someone as I do to you, Maddie. I've never wanted to spend every single second with another person. I've never been so proud of someone else's success and accomplishments. I—" *Why the fuck am I rambling about bullshit stuff?* "What it comes down to is, I love you more with every breath I take. I feel like our souls have had this connection since we were kids, and it's just gotten stronger over the last few months. I can't imagine my life without you in it."

Maddie is silent, which might be the first time that's happened in twenty-five years. Maybe she's digesting the information. Maybe she's overcome with emotion. Maybe she's contemplating what to say.

After a few seconds, I can't take it anymore; I look down, hoping to catch her eye. The slow and steady rhythm of her breathing should have clued me in. She's sound asleep.

As we lay tangled in each other, my thoughts wander to earlier when Maddie asked me a million questions about hockey while we were watching the movie.

I love that she's interested in my hobbies and what makes me happy. I love that she's proud to be with me and that she wants to tell her parents about us.

All of those things give me hope—hope that when I tell her I'm leaving, she'll understand that I want to spend the rest of my life with her without the repercussions of a fake marriage.

I hope she understands I'm leaving for us.

Chapter Fifteen

MADDIE

When I checked my calendar first thing this morning, I saw "Trent Anderson" on the schedule for the conference room, which is why I've steered clear of that part of the office. Still, it surprises me when I look up to see him looming in my doorway, his bulky frame taking up the entire space.

Blocking my exit.

A shiver rushes through me like the air conditioner is on full blast. Fear-induced adrenaline pumps through me.

"I haven't seen the contracts for the new designers come through my email yet. Is there a reason for that?" His demeaning tone and the way he phrases things grate on my nerves. He's not my supervisor.

Since we use his services as our company's attorney, he's nothing more than the hired help. Thinking about him that way makes me laugh and gives me a much-needed burst of empowerment.

"I'll have them to you when I'm finished. I'm quite capable of doing my job without you reminding me."

"Well, demolition for the site of the mall starts in a few weeks, and you were supposed to have all the designer's contracts in by demolition. Isn't that correct?" His voice is hard and mocking.

"What are you talking about?" I ask. "We haven't decided on a location yet. How can demolition be starting?"

"Didn't Harris tell you? We pulled the trigger quickly on some land that came up for sale in NoDa. There's a decrepit apartment complex on some of it right now. Owner needed a fast out. The contract has been signed for months. Residents have been notified."

Technically, the location of the new mall doesn't have anything to do with my particular position, but anything regarding the timeline certainly does. If demolition starts in a few weeks, not months, that moves the construction schedule up significantly, which means this mall will be completed much sooner than I'd planned.

How could my father not tell me? Even if I wasn't in on the meeting, how could there not have been an email chain or something? Is Trent right? Did I miss it and drop the ball?

My plan was to have five new designers lined up for the grand opening. I've been working on a three-year plan, including meeting with the designers on the various lines, when each would come out, and how we would market them. I've got four of the designers lined up, but this information changes my timeline drastically. It's not the end of the world, but it means I need to contact all the designers and start putting together a very specific—and fast—plan.

"Seems like you've been off lately, Madeline. Not quite the professional face of the Commons brand we're used to."

"I always work at the top of my game and you're well aware of that," I tell him in a clipped voice. "If that's all the business you need to discuss with me, you can leave. I have a lot of work to do."

"I know how hard it is. I'll let you get to it." He tosses a folder onto my desk.

With an exasperated sigh, I push back from my desk and stand up. "Look, I understand you may still be hurt and upset with me, but we need to get past it. We're going to have to work together. We need to put our feelings aside for the greater good."

"Get over yourself, Madeline. Our relationship was nothing more than the obligatory courting before an arranged marriage. Our parents matched us for a specific reason. You're a doormat. A beautiful girl with a bubbly personality and low self-esteem. You'll smile and nod and do your cute little fashion work for now, but once you're married, you'll leave the business world to have babies and plan playdates with your girlfriends. Everyone knows it. It's how your father marketed you. That's the only reason anyone dated you. I'm glad you broke it off because now, I won't be stuck with a sad, weak woman as my wife. Honestly"—he looks down at his nails—"I feel sorry for the man who has to marry you."

My stomach tightens as if he just punched me. I bite my lip hard. The pain gives me something to focus on so I keep my composure.

"Get out of my office."

Trent laughs. "Best mind your manners, Madeline. We're going to have to work together, remember."

He chuckles, brushes off one arm of his suit coat, then pulls the door closed behind him.

The solitude gives me the minute I need to break down. I slump over my desk and rub my face with both hands. There's no time to cry. It's not even an option. I haven't cried at work once in my life, and I'm not about to start today.

I'm stronger than that.

My body shakes, but I manage to take five deep breaths, which is what I always do to calm myself. I won't let him get in my head. I won't let him get me down. I have too much to accomplish today.

It's almost ten o'clock. In an hour, we have a photo shoot and I have to be on top of my game. With a shake of the mouse, my blank computer screen comes to life. The light blinks on my phone, alerting me to a new voicemail. As I listen to the message, I scan my emails.

What on earth is going on today? Did I unknowingly put some kind of bad karma into the world that's making the universe spit on me?

The art director got a flat tire while driving in from Greensboro and can't make it. The models aren't here yet because the photographer told them the shoot was this afternoon instead of this morning. And my assistant, Katie, just burst into my office with a huge smile and an armful of orange flowers.

It's a gorgeous arrangement, but I asked for pink flowers for this shoot. And I need a heck of a lot more than one freaking bouquet.

I'm about to lose it.

In addition to the work I'm doing to prepare for the upcoming store at the outdoor mall, Commons just brought on a new local designer and we're doing a huge advertising campaign for the first line, which will come out in the spring of next year. Orange doesn't go with the outfits I have planned for the photo shoot. Orange is a fall color. Orange is—

"I asked for pink flowers. Pink. I reckon it's not that difficult to get pink flowers. Aren't pink flowers everywhere? Isn't pink, like, the main color of flowers?" I'm talking to myself, but Katie is still in the room, so I assume she deems it necessary to answer my rhetorical question.

"Maddie, they're—"

"They're wrong is what they are!" I snap. "Look, I know *you* didn't order me orange flowers when I specifically asked for pink, but can you please find out who did, because I'm going to fire—"

"Why do you hate orange?" Erik asks.

My head jerks up in surprise upon hearing his voice. But there he is, standing in the doorway, looking hot as blazes in a crisp, white button-down shirt and dark jeans. He's squinting as if confused but has the cutest half-smile on his face.

"What? No, I—" I scramble for words. Maybe it's hard to form words because I'm fighting to keep my tongue in my mouth. I have never seen him look so irresistible. "What are you doing here?"

"I wanted to say hi...and bring you flowers."

I glance at Katie, who's still holding the bouquet in her arms, though her smile is gone. The poor girl looks like a dam of tears is about to break.

Jumping from my seat, I grab the flowers from her arms and apologize. "I'm so sorry, Katie! I'm stressed out and frustrated this morning."

"It's okay, Maddie. I get it."

"Can you check the ETA for the models?"

"On it." She nods.

"And can you figure out where the pink flowers we ordered are? If they don't get here soon, I'm gonna have to have you run up to the farmers market."

"Absolutely."

As she shuffles out, I take a moment to compose myself—again. This time, I take deep breaths with my nose buried in the lovely orange flowers Erik brought. I can appreciate how gorgeous they are now that I know they aren't meant for the photo shoot.

He slips into my office and shuts the door behind him. "Rough day?"

Yes." I lift my face out of the flora and smile. "But it's better now."

"I didn't expect to catch you in full boss mode."

"Boss or bitch?" I ask, setting the vase on the upper corner of my desk.

"I gotta admit, it was pretty hot seeing you in charge. A little scary." He holds his fingers less than an inch apart. "But still hot."

I drop my face in my hands. "I'm so sorry. It's been a stressful day already."

"No, I'm sorry for dropping in unannounced. I should've texted first."

"If it wasn't this, it would be something else. I feel like things are spinning out of control recently."

"What's up?"

"We have this new line launching, which is fabulous, don't get me wrong. But we also have five new stores in various stages. The one in Richmond, Virginia, is set to open in two weeks. Then, there's a new one in Charlotte that we've secured the land to build on. It's moving fast now."

"Another store in Charlotte? I thought all the major malls had one."

"They do. This one will be the anchor store of—" I pause and glance at the door. I'm not worried about sharing with Erik; I trust him completely. I'm not going to tell him all the Commons Store secrets, but this one is one I can share. Lowering my voice, I continue, "We're going to be the anchor store of a beautiful, new outdoor mall."

"Really?" Erik lowers himself into the chair across from me and crosses his legs—ankle resting on the opposite knee. He looks so relaxed and comfortable in my office. But it's not like I can climb over my desk and straddle his lap. My eyes veer to his crotch.

"What are you thinking about, Maddie?"

"Hmmm?" I lift my gaze to his quickly. Heat rushes to my cheeks. Not because I'm embarrassed—on the contrary. If we didn't have a group of people on their way to the office for this photo shoot...

"Seriously. What are you thinking?" Erik asks again. "You keep looking at my dick, and you've got this devilish smile on your face."

"Seems like you already know what I'm thinking about."

He glances over his shoulder toward the door. "Wanna?"

"No!" I dismiss his question with a wave. "Although that would be a way to take my stress down a notch."

"I should have called," Erik says again. "Sorry."

"Please don't apologize. I appreciate you dropping in. I've never had anyone do that before."

Trent never dropped by my office when we were dating. Every part of his day was planned to the minute in his calendar. I hate to keep comparing Erik to Trent because they are completely different people, but Trent is the only boyfriend I've had since being in an executive role at Commons.

Sure, I had boyfriends in high school drop by when I was a cashier at the South Park Mall store, but that was different. My friends hung out at the mall all the time.

"Really?"

"My daily schedule is usually pretty packed." My eyes drop to his chest. "I thought yours was too. Why are you all dressed up? Aren't you working today?"

"I am. But I had an appointment with a lawyer this morning."

"Everything okay?"

"Yeah." He nods. "Just making sure I'm doing everything right to be able to become a U.S. citizen one day."

I get up, walk around the desk, and drop myself in his lap. Wrapping my arms around him, I say, "I'm glad you stopped by. It makes me happy when you do sweet things like that."

Erik kisses my forehead. "You're the first thing I think about when I wake up and the last thing I think about before I fall asleep. Doing sweet things for you is as easy as breathing."

Every word makes my heart beat faster. I'm not used to the kindness and compliments. "I'm very lucky to be yours." I rub my hand across his chest.

"You like this look?" he asks, glancing at his button-down.

"Absolutely. But I like you in muddy work boots and sweaty, smelly T-shirts too."

He laughs. "Good to know."

"I like you however I get you. Clean and debonair or dirty and rough." I nip his ear and wiggle my butt against him. His erection grows beneath me.

"You come across so proper," he growls. One hand slips underneath my skirt and glides across my thigh. "But I know you like it dirty."

I swallow back the lust. As much as I want to pursue this right now, I honestly don't have time. "I do. And I'm going to schedule you in for this on a day that I have free time."

Erik throws his head back and laughs. "Way to ruin the mood."

"What?"

"Let me schedule sex," he says in a high-pitched voice.

"I'm a busy—"

"Executive! I know," he teases. Instead of continuing his original sexual pursuit, he starts squeezing my thigh in multiple places. I curl into his chest. "A bossy, hot, Southern, smart, sexy, executive that I get to fuck every night."

"That's the spirit," I say with a laugh.

"I love every minute I get to spend with you, Madeline Commons," Erik whispers. "Always remember that."

After Erik leaves, I peer into the folder Trent brought to my office earlier. It contains a set of colored brochures with information about the site of the outdoor mall in Charlotte. I skim the bullet points and scan the map. The area pictured sets off an alarm in my head.

After closer inspection, I realize why the street names sound familiar.

The outdoor mall is being built on the site of Erik's apartment building.

He was displaced because of us.

Chapter Sixteen

ERIK

"Is this all you have?" Maddie asks, eyeing the boxes in the back of my truck.

"I've got a dog and two duffel bags in the front." I point over my shoulder with my thumb while shifting a few boxes that got jostled around in the bed of my truck on the drive to Maddie's. I'm bringing most of them over to Hugo's garage, which is where I store my trailer and equipment. Anything I'll need over the next few months is in the duffels.

"This is all you own?" she asks again. I think it's confusion, but her voice has a gloomy lilt. "Everything fits in your truck?"

I donated all of my furniture and a ton of random household things to the Habitat Restore, but I don't want to tell Maddie. "Well"—I scratch my head—"I took a lot of stuff to Hugo's already. No reason to bring it here since you have furniture and everything I need for the kitchen and bathroom."

She nods. "What about personal belongings? Books?"

"Anything like that is packed up, but honestly, I don't keep a lot of stuff. I live pretty simply."

Minimalism isn't a hard concept for me. Growing up with grand-parents who were teetering on the line of hoarder territory, made me realize the value of experiences over things. What's the point in having a house full of stuff you never touch?

My grandfather owned every Beatles album ever recorded, but his record player had been broken since the day I moved in. My grandmother had three closets overflowing with clothes but wore the same outfits over and over—saving her "good" blouses and slacks for special occasions that never came.

They had a houseful of unused stuff that they wouldn't part with. Every time I tried to gather items for a garage sale or Salvation Army donations, they fought me tooth and nail over every little thing. Finally, I stopped asking.

Their house was a bitch to clean out after Grandpa passed away. I hate piles of stuff lying around—whether it's mail, magazines, or dishes in the sink. I hate knickknacks and tchotchkes. Maybe I take it to the opposite extreme—but it's the end I'd rather be on.

She nods, but there's a look of awe on her face.

"My grandparents hoarded stuff, not garbage or anything gross, just things. Cleaning out their house after my grandpa died was a nightmare," I explain. "I felt bad getting rid of their possessions, but it had to be done because they kept *everything*."

Maybe that's why I don't have sentimental attachments to things. I remember every fishing trip with my grandpa and every pie I watched my grandma bake, but I didn't need to save the fishing pole or the pie tin.

"Oh, well, that makes a sense." She smiles.

"I saved a few of my grandfather's old flannels. I wear them, so it's not like they're just hanging around."

"Vintage hipster," Maddie quips.

"I also kept my grandparents' wedding album and some family photos. I'm not completely heartless." I give her a quick kiss as I pass. "I'll be the easiest roommate ever. All I need is a bed, electricity, and water."

"I want you to feel at home here. You don't have to be a ghost."

"That's a great comparison! I'm a ghost. Call me Casper."

"Do you need any help getting these boxes upstairs, Casper?"

"You can see me?" I whisper, faking astonishment.

"You aren't right in the head." Maddie yanks the passenger door open and Ramos bursts out, immediately jumping up to give her love.

"Ramos! Down!" I command, but both the dog and Maddie ignore me. Maybe I am a ghost.

"Hey, baby!" she greets him, scratching him behind his ears with both hands, as he bounces on his hind legs. His front paws claw her T-shirt straight over her tits, and suddenly I wish I'd greeted her that way.

Wonder if she'd give me a rubdown?

I heft two duffle bags onto each shoulder and follow Maddie and my pup into the elevator that will take us to her condo. Having to go up and down an elevator to take Ramos out is gonna suck, but I can't complain since Maddie was kind enough to let me live with her for a few weeks.

I've been to Maddie's place multiple times, but I've never had Ramos with me. When she opens the door, the bright, white sofa practically glows. I drop one of my duffle bags and grab Ramos's collar, holding him back from bursting into the condo and jumping on her immaculate furniture.

She turns around. "What are you doing?"

"His paws are all muddy and he's going to jump right on—"

"It's okay, Erik." She looks me in the eye when she speaks, which is how I know it's really okay. "It's his home now. And I have stain-guard stuff on all my furniture. Dirt will come out."

Even though I know she's being honest, I still hesitate while Ramos practically chokes himself trying to bust out of my grasp and get in.

"Come on in, Ramos!" Maddie lowers herself to one knee. The simple beckon brings out his super-lab strength. He jerks out of my grasp and runs to Maddie. She grabs his head and scratches him heartily. "Your daddy is so silly. I invited him to live here, and he's dirtier than you are most days."

"Touché," I say, picking up the duffel bag I'd dropped entering Maddie's condo, and shut the door behind me with my foot.

"I've had this furniture for years. It's very lived-in." Maddie lets go of Ramos. To my surprise, he doesn't head straight for the couch.

Instead, he puts his nose down, exploring the place by sniffing every crack and crevice in each room.

"Thanks for letting two dirty boys move in with you." I stop to kiss her before taking my bags to the guest room. As I pass the couch, I notice it does not look lived-in. Not even a little bit. It looks like it came off the delivery truck yesterday. "How often do you have it cleaned?"

"Well, I usually have the furniture professionally vacuumed and shampooed every three months."

That's not high-maintenance at all, I think as I set my bags in the guest room. I make a mental note to schedule someone to clean the furniture after Ramos and I leave.

"I've never heard of anyone doing that," I tell her when I return to the living area.

"I'm not a germaphobe, I swear," Maddie says. "I know it sounds that way, but I'm not. I like having everything cleaned. I could probably do it twice a year, like Mama does, but I like how it feels and smells."

"Well, it's gonna smell like dog and man soon."

"I know! I'm so excited!" Maddie grabs a remote from the coffee table and presses a few buttons until music comes on. Then, she flicks a switch on the wall, flooding the room in darkness, except for a few candles flickering throughout the room. "Time to celebrate."

"Sex?" I ask.

"Dancing." She tugs my hand, but I'm frozen in place. "Come on."

"I don't dance, Maddie," I say.

"It's easy, just put your hands on my waist and move your hips."

I place my hands on her waist and move my hips from side to side, slow and stiff. It's meant to exaggerate my lack of skills. My hands drop back to my side.

Maddie cocks her head and stares at me, blinking once, before saying. "It's just us, Erik. No one's watching. Just try, please."

"There may not be anyone else in here, but there's a ton of people out there." I nod toward the floor-to-ceiling windows that span an entire wall of her condo. The view is breathtaking, especially now, with darkness falling and the city sparkling with lights as far as the eye can see.

"No one can see us way up here." She places her hands on my hips and guides them in a slower, rolling motion. "Loosen up. Feel the music."

"I *hear* the music, I can't *feel* it," I say, laughing at her instructions. "I don't have any rhythm."

"Look at me and follow my lead." She places her hands on my cheeks and presses her body against mine. My automatic response is to grab her hips. Then she starts swaying and moving her hips slowly. I mimic her actions because I don't want her body to slip away for mine. I love the feeling of having her so close.

Maddie raises on her tiptoes, leans in, and whispers, "See? It's easy."

Her lips tickle my ear as she speaks, which sends a jolt of lust through me. I pull her closer. "Being with you is easy."

"Is it?" she asks, stopping our movements just as I started getting my groove.

Concentrating on the music and staying in rhythm with her helps keep my mind off how much I love her. I could get used to moments like this: swaying together in the safety and warmth of our home—errr —her home.

"Yeah," I tell her. "You're fun and willing to try anything. I'll do anything with you, even things I'd never see myself doing before."

"I feel the same way about you." She places her hands on my face and kisses me softly.

Now that I'm not distracted by trying to keep rhythm, my thoughts veer straight back to the fact that we're in front of a huge window. Suddenly the prospect that someone could look up and see us isn't embarrassing—it's fucking hot.

I spin her around and wrap my arms around her waist, so we're gazing out at the sprawling city together. Lowering my lips to her ear, I say, "What do you want to try that you haven't done before?"

She must feel my erection pressing against her because she grinds her ass into my crotch. "Surprise me."

Chapter Seventeen

MADDIE

Erik presses his chest against my back, leans close to my ear, and whispers, "Put your palms on the window."

My breath hitches, but I do as he commands, closing my eyes and shivering as my body reacts to his soft, sensual timbre. I try to squeeze my legs together, a natural reaction to the excitement tightening my stomach, but Erik places his thigh between mine and nudges them farther apart with his knee.

"You're gorgeous, Maddie." He slides a fingertip down my back, then kneels behind me and places his lips in the middle, right above my ass. Despite his calloused hands, his touch is soft, gentle, and tender.

A shiver shakes my entire body. My heart speeds up in anticipation of what he'll do next. He slides his hands over my hips and down the outside of my thighs. His lips are still on my back, his breath hot on my skin. Slowly, he reaches up and finds my clit. He alternates between rubbing and flicking, then he dips one finger inside me, and my knees almost buckle. I feel him smile against my back before he slips another digit into me.

I'm so wet, his fingers slide easily as he pumps them in and out. It's nothing new. When I'm around Erik, my arousal is almost instant. All he has to do is look at me, and I'm drenched.

"You're so beautiful," he whispers.

I'm rocking against his hand, wanting more, needing more. Just when I'm getting used to the rhythm, he pulls out. Before I can protest, his mouth is between my legs, his tongue taking the place of his fingers. The low moan that escapes doesn't even sound like me. He pushes his fingers into me again, forcing me slightly forward. His teeth graze my clit, but it's when he sucks softly that he sends me over the edge. I grind down, moving through the orgasm. He doesn't let up, sucking and nibbling. I didn't even realize an orgasm could last so long, but he keeps letting me ride his face, so I'm not complaining.

Once he's gotten everything from me, he licks my pussy before standing up. He slides his hands up and down my hips again, his soft touch mesmerizing me into a haze. I'm expecting something sweet and soft again, but he surprises me by grabbing my hips and pushing into me hard from behind.

The force propels me forward, and I brace myself, splaying my palms against the glass. Being fucked against a window is a completely new and exhilarating experience. In the back of my mind, I know no one can see us. All the lights are off in the condo, and there's no other building as far as we can see.

Still, the excitement of being seen is there. I never thought I would enjoy being naked in front of an open window, but I can't deny the way my body reacts.

I'm breaking all the rules with Erik. Taking fears and prejudices and tossing them aside like the black, lacy lingerie he pulled off me tonight.

"Yes! Erik! Oh my god!" I say, urging him to keep going. Every time he thrusts, it's a bit harder and a bit deeper, and I love it. But my head is dangerously close to hitting the window, and the memory of Trent pushing me into it, causes terror to rip through me.

As if Erik can read my mind or maybe sense my tension, he raises his arm and places a hand palm down against the window at my head level. I rest my forehead on the back of his hand in silent appreciation.

"I've got you, Madeline. Don't hold back," Erik growls in my ear. "You can let go with me."

He wraps the other arm around me, caging me in, then reaches around and places his fingers on my clit, rubbing as he continues thrusting. When my head falls back onto his shoulder, he kisses my neck, grazing my skin with his teeth. The sensations make me dizzy, lightheaded, and about to lose it again. I nod, clenching his cock with all my strength.

"You ready, sweetheart?"

I nod again and push my ass back, letting him know that he can keep pumping into me, filling me deeper and deeper until he gives me everything he's got. I want it all. I want his essence to flow through my blood. I'd give anything to be one-tenth of the strong, amazing person Erik is.

LIVING with Erik gets better with each passing day. He leaves me notes on the bathroom mirror daily, fixes things around the condo, and takes my car to get washed every week.

I don't need those things, but it's really sweet that he does them. He's always thinking of me. It's only been a month, so maybe we're still in the honeymoon stage, but from everything I know about him, it's just more ways that show how thoughtful he is.

After the crazy, stressful day I had, I don't want to have to think about anything. All I want to do is change into super-comfy clothes and binge something mundane on Netflix until he gets home. Then have a ton of sex.

Ramos greets me at the door, tail wagging and tongue hanging out of his mouth. Before I do anything else, I latch a leash onto his collar and take him outside to do his business. Settler's Cemetery, Charlotte's oldest, is across the street from my building. It's a well-kept, beautiful park-like space, which may seem weird, but I think it's wonderful. Walking amongst the final resting spot for people who were in the city from the beginning gives me a rush of pride for how far we've come.

The entire lobby smells like garlic wafting in from the upscale Thai restaurant next door. It's not a bad smell, but it gets overwhelming at certain parts of the night. Before heading back up to my condo, I stop to check my mail.

Once we're back inside, I remove Ramos' leash and hang it on the hook next to the door, then I kick off my shoes and round the counter to the kitchen. After grabbing a glass from the cabinet and placing it on the counter, I open the fridge, praying a bottle of wine is chilling. If not, I need to hit the market down the road. Today was the kind of day where I need to chill out with wine and hibachi takeout. Thankfully, a Pinot Grigio bottle awaits me on the top shelf. There's a yellow Post-it note taped to the bottle.

Hope you had a great day, beautiful! Pour yourself a drink and relax! Can't wait to get home to see you.

My lips turn up in a smile, and butterflies zoom inside my belly as I think about how sweet it is that Erik thought of me. I grab the bottle and move to the drawer where I keep the opener.

Trent never left me notes—sweet or otherwise.

I shuffle to the couch with a glass of wine in one hand and my cell phone already opened up to a food-delivery app in the other. As soon as I sit down, Ramos joins me, curling up next to me and resting his head on my thigh. Erik gets annoyed when the dog jumps on my furniture, but I don't mind.

I've never had a pet. Mama is allergic to cats and never wanted the responsibility and hassle of having a dog. I totally understand. Between all the long hours Daddy worked, the countless activities Mama had us girls in, and vacations, having a dog didn't fit into our lifestyle.

I set my wine glass on the coffee table and run my hand across Ramos's soft fur. Erik's concerns are out of respect for my home. He thinks muddy dog paws will ruin my furniture. But, hell, Erik comes home muddy and grimy from work every day, and I let *him* on the furniture. I want him here—in my home and my life. Having Ramos with us makes me feel like we're a family.

I stop petting the dog to send a quick thank you text to Erik.

> Thanks for the wine. Can't wait to see you tonight.

Because he's still working, I don't expect him to text back right away, but seeing the tiny dots on my screen that tell me he's typing makes my heart flutter.

> I've been thinking about you all day. Can we snuggle on the couch with a movie tonight?

> Sure, after you ravish me.

> Well, that's a given. I can't focus on a movie with my dick pressed against your back. ;)

> Hurry home.

> I'll be there as soon as I can, love.

Letting Erik move in was a no-brainer. Our relationship is legitimate, and we need to document the steps to prove it. I'm still hoping that the laws will change while he's here, but I know it's unlikely.

How can a hard-working man with an impeccable reputation and no criminal record be deported? I highly doubt the Department of Homeland Security is out there cracking down on illegal immigrants like him. Wouldn't they focus on the real criminals? He's not a bad person just because doesn't have correct paperwork.

I like having him here. It's funny because the thought of moving in with Trent never once crossed my mind—which is ridiculous since marriage was supposed to be the long-term plan.

Offering to share my condo with Erik popped into my head immediately and without hesitation.

Everything is easy and fun with him, whether we're strolling around the city hand in hand with Ramos in tow or snuggling on the couch after a long day of work. Life with him is exactly what I dreamed of when I thought about a happy, loving relationship.

Being with him makes me realize how unhappy I was in my last relationship. Trent was rigid and busy. He made me schedule time with his paralegal, who runs his calendar at the law firm. We never had cute, fun dates, like mural-hunting in Plaza Midwood or bowling with Austin and Liz.

Trent would never set foot in a nursing home, let alone be there for one of his grandma's meals every single day. Trent and I were all for show. We attended formal events, threw dinner parties, and met colleagues and friends at the trendiest establishments.

Over the last few months with Erik, I've realized how much I missed being in a loving, trusting relationship. Having the complete freedom to go out with friends or my sisters and not have to explain or justify my choices is priceless.

Then there's the passion. I barely wanted to kiss Trent, but I can't keep my hands off Erik. I want him all the time—on the furniture, the bed, the kitchen, the shower. I can't resist him.

I'm lost in my thoughts when Erik's face lights up my screen. I slide my thumb over it to answer.

"Hey!" I greet him, unable to keep the silly grin off my face. This is what relationships are supposed to be like. Smiling when you're thinking about the person. Getting excited about every call or text, even if you saw them earlier.

"Hey, Mads! My truck won't start. I'm gonna call a Lyft to get me and Hugo home. Just wanted to let you know I'd be a little late tonight."

"Don't call Lyft. I can pick you up."

"Are you sure? You don't have to do that."

"I know I don't have to, but I want to," I tell him, getting off the couch and placing my wine glass in the fridge. "Hold tight. I'll be there soon."

"You're the best, babe. See you soon."

After all the little fix-it jobs Erik has taken care of at my condo, the least I can do is help him. I like having the relationship we have. Always being there for each other. Being able to count on someone. Not having to walk on eggshells when asking for a favor. Not being worried about anything.

When I get to the address Erik gave me, they're in the road, standing next to his trailer. But his truck is nowhere to be seen.

"Where's your truck?" I ask through an open window as I pull up next to them.

"Tow truck just hauled her off." Erik leans in and pecks my lips quickly. "Thanks so much for doing this."

"I'm here for you, always."

Erik hops in the backseat, which is probably a good thing. Hugo is a very large man—he's over six feet and probably close to three hundred pounds. I don't know if he could squeeze into the tiny back-seat of my sports car.

"Thanks, Miss Commons," Hugo says as he stands next to the open passenger door. He hesitates before getting in.

"Come on in, Hugo."

He bites his bottom lip as his eyes scan the seat. "I'm all dirty, Miss."

I pat the seat. "You sit right down. You know darn well I've never been afraid of a little dirt."

He smiles and squeezes into the car. Once I input his address into my navigation system, we're off.

We've been driving for less than five minutes when I notice a police car pull out behind me. My shoulders tense, and I immediately drop my gaze to the dash to check my speed. Relieved I'm going a few miles per hour under the limit, I relax and continue.

"How's Anna?" I ask Hugo. Anna, his wife, works for my parents. Housecleaning mostly, but she does a ton of odd jobs for them. She's been with our family for over twenty years, so we trust her with everything.

"Good. She's on a fitness kick. Keeps asking me to do all these dance classes with her." He glances at his belly and squeezes a roll. "I'm not in shape for dancing."

"Oh, come on! I know you've got a little salsa in you. I've seen you work that weed wacker," Erik teases.

"It's not the same," Hugo says with a laugh. "The weed wacker doesn't yell at me."

"Have you tried, at least?" I ask. Out of the corner of my eye, I see Erik lean forward in the middle of the backseat. He's lifting his phone as if he's trying to get a signal or something.

Before Hugo has a chance to answer, I'm distracted when the lights on the police car behind me start flashing. I check all my mirrors and even glance at my blind spots. I'm the only car on the road.

"What in the world? I wasn't doing anything wrong, was I?" I ask out loud. I'm not expecting an answer, but Erik speaks.

"Not a thing," he confirms, lowering his phone to his lap.

As the officer approaches, I keep my hands on the wheel, waiting for him to tap on the window before pressing the button to roll it down.

Before speaking, he peers into the car. His dark eyes stay on Hugo for a second too long, as if he's assessing him. That and the slight downward turn of his pale, thin lips annoys me. Hugo and Erik are both still in their work clothes—dingy, white T-shirts and faded jeans tinged with grass and mud stains.

"Everything okay, Miss?" he asks.

What the hell does that mean? Why wouldn't everything be okay?

Instead of asking, I answer with a strong, "Yes, sir."

"Do you know why I pulled you over?"

"No."

"You were speeding."

"I don't reckon I was, sir. I was going the speed limit. Maybe even a little under."

"When you came down that hill on Idlewild."

"Bullshit," Erik mumbles under his breath.

The cop peers into the car, eyebrows furrowed in anger. "Excuse me, boy? Do you have something to say to me?"

My hands clench the steering wheel.

"License and registration," the cop barks at me.

I lean down to grab my purse at Hugo's feet, dig my license out of my wallet, and hand it to the officer. Then I lean over him and reach out toward my glove compartment to grab my registration.

"What are you doing?" the cop asks. I glance back, catching the slight movement of his hand to the holster at his hip.

My heart speeds up. "You asked for my registration. I'm getting my registration."

After retrieving it, I hand it to the cop. He grabs it and stalks back to his patrol car.

"I swear I wasn't speeding," I say once he's gone.

"You weren't," Erik assures me.

"Are you serious or just being sweet?"

"Dead serious. I started videotaping your dashboard as soon as I saw that cop start following you."

"You did?" It seems odd, but at least it explains what he was doing on his phone.

He nods solemnly. Then he lifts his phone and shows me the screen. Together, we watch the video of me going the speed limit. At one point, I might have exceeded it by one mile per hour over, but never more.

"It doesn't make any sense. If I wasn't speeding, why would he pull me over?"

"Because you're driving with brown," Erik mutters.

Color me confused. "What does that mean?"

"A white girl driving with a Mexican," Hugo explains.

"That's not why!" I start to dismiss the explanation, then I pause. "Is it?"

"You don't know anything about our reality, Maddie."

I'm not sure what he means by "our reality" since his skin is as white as mine. He wouldn't be mistaken for a man of color, even with a summer tan.

"Tell me then. I want to know. I'm not just a ditzy blonde who only cares about herself." Erik laughs, and my heart sinks. "Is that what you think of me?" I ask in a whisper.

"No. Maddie, I—"

It hurts to know that he still sees me as a callous girl who cares only about herself and her own interests—a ditz with no comprehension of what goes on in our society.

Maybe I haven't had much experience or many friends of color, but it doesn't mean I have to live the rest of my life that way. I can try to make changes. If I got pulled over for driving with Hugo because of the color of his skin, then I need to do something about it—tell someone at the very least.

Daddy knows the police chief. Maybe he can help put a stop to behavior like that. It's not that I actively participate; I just don't think about it. I feel terrible admitting that I don't pay attention to other people's issues until they're brought to my attention.

I'm ashamed of myself.

The officer's heavy footsteps pounding the pavement shake me out of my thoughts.

He reaches into the car and hands me my license and registration. "I only wrote you for five over," he says, looking at Hugo as he hands me the ticket.

"What do you mean, you wrote me for five over? I wasn't speeding!" I say, dropping my license and registration into the cup holder.

"Miss—" he begins, but I cut him off.

"You know you work for me, right? It's not the other way around. *I* pay *your* salary." Adrenaline pumps through me, fueled by rage at the hateful reason that made this officer stop and the lies he tells to justify it.

It's apparent that the cop wasn't expecting any resistance from me. Maybe he thought I'd be driven by fear. But he doesn't know me. Once I know something is wrong, I won't stop until it's right.

I won't lie and say I do this all the time. Quite the contrary. I've never given a police officer anything but respect before, but this time is different. This is my chance to stand up for what's right in the small way I'm able.

"*Dios mío,*" Hugo whispers and turns his head to look out the passenger-side window.

I'm not sure what it means, but I'm positive it's not good. This should probably be a clue for me to shut my mouth, but I've never been good at stopping once I've started something.

"If you have a problem with the ticket, you can take it to court," he says, writing something on his pad before handing it to me.

"Take it to court? Waste more taxpayers' money than we're wasting right now to fight a bull-hockey ticket? That's ridiculous! I have a—" Erik puts a hand on my shoulder, which derails my thoughts. He shakes his head slightly when I glance back at him, but I'm not letting this go. "This isn't going to make it to court. My father will have a field day with this. Harris Commons—you know him, right?"

The cop, who seemed frustrated, but still slightly amused, now stares at me with hard, unwavering eyes.

"Please stop, Maddie," Erik urges quietly from behind me.

"I can see you do. Enjoy the rest of your shift, Officer. You might want to put the windows down, enjoy the wind in your"—I glance at his smooth bald head—"hair. Because you'll be behind a desk by next week."

Without waiting for a response, I crumple the ticket and let it drop into my lap, all while keeping eye contact with the officer. Then I roll up the window, dismissing him completely.

It may have seemed collected, but my heart was pounding like a racehorse at the Derby. I finally let out a breath, and my shoulders relax.

"What the fuck was that, Maddie?" Erik asks.

"What?" I glance at him in my rearview mirror as I pull back onto the road. He shakes his head as if disappointed. "Are you mad at me? For defending myself from an asshole who thinks he can use his power to intimidate people?"

"I'm not mad. But I will admit I was fucking freaked out."

"Same," Hugo agrees.

"Why?" I ask, looking at Hugo quickly.

He shifts uncomfortably in his seat and sighs as if he doesn't want to answer but feels obligated to. "If I talked to a cop like that, I'd be face first on the concrete." He rubs his forehead with his fingers. "I almost thought I would be anyway, with the way it was going."

"Really?" I ask.

I'm appalled at myself for making Hugo uncomfortable. I thought my standing up to the cop was a way to help.

Hugo turns to me. "It's different for me, Ms. Commons, for reasons you'll never have to worry about."

"I'm so sorry," I say quietly. "I didn't mean to put you in that situation. I didn't realize—" I stop because, though I'm sincere, my apology means nothing. My ignorance could have made the situation horrible for him.

Neither man says anything else, so I keep driving in silence. Hugo only speaks to point out his house.

Shame seeps through me, filling every crack. Erik was correct. I don't know Hugo's reality. I was too wrapped up, thinking I could use my influence—privilege—to get some sort of justice that I didn't even think about the consequences for either of them. It never even crossed my mind that the cop could have taken the fuss I was making out on Hugo.

After I drop Hugo off, Erik moves into the front seat. He doesn't speak, and it kills me. I hate when people are mad at me. I especially hate it when it's because I did something that unintentionally hurt someone. I never intended to put Hugo or Erik in a bad situation.

Being afraid of the police is nothing I've ever had to think about. The only other time I've been stopped was when I was speeding while coming home from the beach a few years ago. I apologized profusely, said I'd never do it again, pretended to cry, and the officer let me go without a ticket.

Chapter Eighteen

ERIK

"I'm really sorry, Erik," Maddie whispers as tears fill her eyes.

I grab her hand. "Don't ever apologize for standing up for what's right."

"I didn't even think about the consequences for Hugo—or you. I just ran my mouth like a privileged white girl. That's exactly why we'll never work in the long run, isn't it?"

"Hey! Hey! What are you talking about?" I've never heard her talk like that, and the drastic swing away from her normally cheerful disposition concerns me.

"I can't even see simple things from a different perspective. I didn't even stop to think about Hugo."

"Pull over, Maddie."

"What?" she asks, tugging her hand from mine to place both on the steering wheel. Her knuckles turn white while her arms shake.

"Pull over. We need to talk."

Without another word, she checks her surroundings, searching for a place to pull over. She chooses the parking lot of a chain pharmacy that's closed for the night, whips the car between two white lines, and then shifts into park.

Without hesitation, I lean closer and take her face in my hands.

"You absolutely did think about Hugo and I. You knew what that officer was doing was wrong, and you stood up for yourself—for us. That's fucking amazing. I haven't met many people who would stand up for another person like that."

"But it could have turned out horribly for you both, Erik. I've got a lot to learn."

"Who doesn't?" I laugh softly. "Look, I'm not gonna lie, I was a bit shocked by how you handled the situation, but I know you can be"—I pause, looking for a word that won't offend her or make her feel worse —"impulsive," I finish. "But the point is that you chose to act on an injustice. And that means the world to me, Maddie."

"I reckon I should keep my mouth shut from now on." She shakes her head and casts her gaze to her lap as if dismissing herself.

"No! Please don't." I tilt her head so we're eye to eye. "You've experienced something you never had before. Now you recognize it. I wish more people did. That's how things change."

"I can't do anything right. When I try to help, I'm doing it wrong. If I don't help, I'm not doing my part to make a change. I'm the white devil."

"Jesus, Maddie. I'm so sorry if I made you feel that way. Every time you stand up for someone that's being marginalized, you're helping. I'm sorry if I made it sound like you weren't."

"I want to do what I can to make things right. I can't change an entire systemic problem this minute, but I can start somewhere. Isn't that the point? People who have influence starting somewhere? It's hard to help when I'm trying and getting slammed down." She closes her eyes and shakes her head. "I'm not looking for pity. I know this isn't about me, believe me. Hugo and his family face these kinds of reactions and hardships every day—I'm not diminishing that. I'm asking from my heart, what do you want me to do?"

"Keep being you, Maddie. Keep standing up for people. Look at what you did for me. You put your neck on the line, knowing you could get in huge trouble by helping me stay in the country."

"Once I get something in my head—"

"I know!" I interrupt her. "Remember that time when you made me take home that box of kittens you found at school?"

"Well, I knew Mama would just drop them off at a shelter and they'd be euthanized. I had to give them a chance."

"Yeah, and you got Grandpa on your side. You guys teamed up on me."

"Rusty had such a beautiful heart," she says softly. "I loved being around him."

"Me too." I brush my thumb across her cheek. "He would have liked this, ya know? Us together."

"Really?"

"Yeah. He loved you. He loved your bubbly, vibrant personality. Liz was always really quiet and, shit, we barely ever saw Emily. But you, you're a force, Maddie. It's not possible for people to be uncomfortable around you. You make everyone feel wanted, included, loved."

"That's not always a good thing. Being a people-pleaser."

"Is that what you think of yourself?"

"I don't know. I guess I've always felt I had to be the hostess. Bring people together. Make everyone happy—my parents, my friends, boyfriends."

"Sounds like an exhausting life. Living for what everyone else thinks."

"It is, but at the same time—I enjoy it. I don't even know how to explain."

"You want it all because you can handle it all. I want to be part of your life. I want to help you be the best human you can be."

"You already do that, Erik." She pauses. "What did you mean when you said I don't understand your reality? You used the term as though you understand what it's like to be Hugo."

"Ever since I found out I was undocumented, I've done my best not to get into any trouble. I didn't make waves and didn't stand up for things I should have because I needed to protect my secret. I thought having any kind of black marks on my record—even a speeding ticket—would make me a criminal." I turn my head and gaze out the window as memories rush through my head. Situations where I could have been a better friend, a better advocate for change. I'm ashamed that I let the fear of my situation get in the way of standing up for my friends. "When I said that, I didn't mean I knew anything about the sort of racism Hugo had been through. I just meant I understand not being able to say and do everything I want to make things right."

When Maddie takes my hand, I shift my gaze. "Now that everything is out in the open. You can be a catalyst for change."

"*We*," I say, squeezing her hand. "We can be catalysts for change together."

I hope Maddie sees how many changes she's made since gathering the courage to leave Trent. She sees the world with different eyes.

It gives me hope that she'll be able to forgive me when I leave.

Chapter Nineteen

MADDIE

"I got a call from a friend at the police department," Daddy says as soon as I walk in my parents' front door to the annual holiday party we throw for people who work for our family.

It's one of my favorite traditions, probably because I'm the one who suggested it back when I was in high school.

No "hello." No hug. Straight to business, as always.

News travels fast through the grapevine. I thought I'd hear from him the day after it happened, but it's more his style to wait until he sees someone in person. He loves confrontation. He loves intimidation. He knew I'd never miss this gathering.

"Well, hello to you too, Daddy." I lean over and kiss his cheek.

"You got a ticket?" he asks.

"I did, yes. The officer said it was for speeding, but I wasn't speeding," I explain while hanging my gorgeous new jacket in the hall closet. Before closing the door, I give it one last look. Stella Carney, one of the designers I chose to create a line for the Commons Stores next year, sent it to me for Christmas.

"What do you mean you weren't speeding? If you weren't, why would he say that, Madeline?"

I shrug, then straighten the bow on my black silk top. "I don't know, but I wasn't speeding. I have a video showing that I was going the limit. I'm going to use it in court."

"You will do no such thing."

Wait. Is he angry with me?

"It's totally bogus, Daddy! I only got stopped because I was driving Hugo home."

"Excuse me?" His eyebrows knit together in confusion. "Who's Hugo?"

I pause. He knows damn well who Hugo is. Instead of taking the conversation off track, I answer, "Our landscaper."

"Why were you driving him home?"

"Erik's truck broke down, so I picked them up and drove them home."

There's no need to tell Daddy I drove Erik to *my* home. Or that we hung out in bed the entire next day. I haven't even told Mama and Daddy that Erik and I are actually dating now. They know about our agreement, but I haven't come clean about our real feelings. But they certainly wouldn't understand him moving in even if I did.

"That racist cop gave me a ticket for driving with Hugo."

"You can stop that right now, Madeline."

"No, Daddy. It's a farce. It's also—"

"Stop! Now."

I close my mouth and glare at my father, completely taken aback by his attitude. Why isn't he concerned? I thought he would be on Hugo's side. He's always been kind to him.

"You shouldn't be driving him home, Madeline. I don't want you in that area."

"What could I do, Daddy? They were stuck."

"Hugo has friends he can call."

"Making him wait on friends when I was right there to drive him home doesn't sound like the kind of thing a good Christian girl would do."

Daddy glares at me. I know I've taken it too far by bringing religion into it, but I don't care. Mama and Daddy raised us on "good Christian values." I guess I can only use my Christian values when it's people they regard as worthy of it.

"There are multiple options to get home these days. Cab, Lyft, Uber."

"Limo?" I offer sarcastically.

"I'm not sure why you came here with an attitude, especially when you're the one who made a poor choice. You have no right to use *my* name to threaten an officer's job because you got a ticket and had a hissy fit."

I roll my eyes, even though I know it's the most childish way I could react. I imagine the glint of suppressed laughter in Erik's eyes if he were here to see me react this way.

"It wasn't about the ticket itself. It was about racial profiling," I snap

"If you can't conduct yourself like a lady, you can leave."

Giving him a fake sweet smile, I lower my voice and calm myself. "Can we get back to the issue, Daddy?"

"I've covered the issue."

"No, the issue is that I was pulled over by a racist jerk because I was driving with a Mexican man."

"You have zero proof of that, Madeline."

"I have a video!"

"Does the video prove racism?"

"No, it proves I wasn't speeding."

"You have nothing." He lifts a glass decanter off the bar and pours himself two fingers of bourbon.

"Daddy, you're not getting the point," I plead. "It was racial profiling."

He lifts his glass to his lips before saying, "I've heard enough."

"You don't think it's wrong?"

"I'm telling you to let it go. Our guests will be arriving soon." His voice is stern, wavering on anger. This is the point where I've always backed down. Challenging him isn't worth his wrath. Mama is the only person I know who can hold a grudge longer than Daddy.

"You're powerful in the community, Daddy. You could do something about it."

He chuckles. "You think I have far more influence than I really have."

A mix of emotions swirls in my stomach. I've always had him on a pedestal. Far more than Liz or Emily ever did.

I'm the epitome of a daddy's girl. The one who begged him to take me to every father-daughter dance at the country club—despite there being three of us girls to choose from. The one who always wanted him to play the part of Prince Charming, saving me from ferocious dragons and evil sisters. The one who always trusted his decisions, even when my sisters balked. The one who went into the family business to take after him—and take it over from him.

Suddenly, he doesn't seem so heroic. I know he has influence. He makes things happen in this city. People respect him. People fear him.

Why wouldn't he back Hugo, a man who has worked with our family for years? We trust him and Maria with absolutely every part of our home. We've hosted them for intimate family gatherings throughout the years. They're like family.

The window over the kitchen sink looks out over our beautifully manicured backyard—the intricate plan of bushes, flowers, and trees on every side of a glittering in-ground swimming pool—the one Erik jumped in to save my life.

Erik created the entire plan. He drew it up, modified it to my mother's liking, and put every piece in place with the help of his crew. That was years ago. It looked beautiful when he first did it, but it's gorgeous now. Everything he imagined has matured and pops when in full bloom. He's a true artist.

And the kindest person I've ever known. True kindness. Not for show or personal gain. He's got the sweetest soul.

"I see you differently than you see yourself, Daddy. I've seen you use your influence for things you want to accomplish. Why not use that influence to make a change?"

"I use my so-called influence to make changes every single day, Madeline."

"Yes, for your business interests and friends. But what do you do for the people who need your influence and voice? The ones who face discrimination and oppression every day?"

"While I feel for Hugo, it's not my battle, Madeline. You're asking me to try to dismantle a system you think is broken all of a sudden over a speeding ticket. That's ridiculous and, frankly, quite bratty."

"This isn't about a speeding ticket!" I stomp my stiletto against the hardwood floor, sliding right into his brat-depiction of me.

"You have no proof that it's racial profiling, Madeline. I don't care what kind of video you have. To accuse an officer who puts his life on the line for citizens daily is disrespectful. I have a good relationship with the police chief, officers, judges, and attorneys all over this city. I see people who do the best job they can rather than as a problem that needs to be fixed. As I said, it's not my battle, and it's not something I'll waste my time on."

"It *is* your battle. It's all of our battle," I interject pointedly.

Daddy's indifference is part of what keeps the system the way it is. People with the means to create change sit back and do nothing because it doesn't directly affect them.

There's a point in every child's life where we see our parents as human beings rather than superheroes. This is that moment for me.

Hearing my father say he isn't willing to do anything—even admit there is an issue—is eye-opening. I'm not saying I've agreed with and understood all of his decisions over the years, in our family or business, but I've trusted him. I trusted that he made decisions for the right reasons. I trusted the people he chose to do business with.

"I'm not saying I don't care—" he starts, but I don't let him finish.

"Have you always been this cold?" I ask. "Have I been so blinded by the pedestal I have you on that I didn't see what a heartless man you are?"

"What's gotten into you, Madeline? Since when did you become a crusader for justice?"

Since I almost died at the hands of someone he set me up with. Someone he trusts.

That's what I want to say, but I hold my tongue. If I speak, I might break down.

"Are you finished with your fit?" Daddy takes another sip of his drink. "Because I don't want to hear another word about it."

"All these years, I thought I believed in you. I thought you cared about all these people you claim to help."

"I will not have my daughter question my integrity. You can talk that way to your sisters or your friends, but you will not talk that way to me. Is that understood, Madeline?"

"Yes, *sir.*" Mocking respect is all I have to give right now.

While it was disrespectful to lash out at Daddy, I won't lie and say I'm sorry I did it. Maybe I've never been a crusader for justice before, but it doesn't mean I can't change.

All it takes is for people to start standing up for what's right.

Like Erik did for me.

After I realized I could trust him, it allowed me to open up about my relationship with Trent. If he hadn't fished me out of that pool, I'm sure I would have followed the path set for me and stayed with Trent.

Well, that's assuming I'd be alive if he hadn't fished me out.

What's gotten into me?

Erik.

"If you don't have anything else to say, you can help your mother in the kitchen."

Oh, I have something to say, alright. I'm ready to let him know everything.

"Trent Anderson pushed me into the pool and left me for dead. He pushed me into a window at my apartment. He pushed me down staircases. He left so many bruises on my body, I learned to be clever in how I covered them—outside *and* in here." I tap my temple. "Trent manipulated me physically and emotionally for years. He still tries to. And you let it all happen. You set us up. You continue to make me interact with him because of business and your friendships and contracts with the Old Boys' network."

"If any of that happened, why didn't you say anything, Madeline? After the pool incident, you insisted it was an accident. That you slipped and fell. Do you see how hard it is to believe that now, you're telling the 'truth,'" Daddy asks, using air quotes when he says the word truth.

"Erik saw what happened," I whisper, choking back emotion. "Erik saw what Trent did. And it was Erik who jumped into the pool and dragged me out. Erik saved my life."

Daddy's hard gaze softens slightly. He might actually be listening now.

"Erik believed me. Erik listened to me and believed me. Erik helped me heal."

"Just how close have you and Erik gotten in this fake relationship, Madeline?" Daddy's voice booms.

So, that's what made him listen. He wasn't softened, listening to the horrible things Trent did to me or Erik's heroic actions. He's listening because I confided in Erik.

Time to drop the biggest bomb of all—just for spite.

I wasn't planning on telling my parents that Erik moved in. But after this conversation, I have no choice. I want them to know how much I love him and that Erik is a better man than Trent will ever be.

"He moved in with me last month," I declare.

Daddy's glass slips out of his hand and crashes onto the edge of the marble sink.

An audio engineer on a movie set couldn't have planned the timing more perfectly.

Mama rushes into the room. "What happened?"

"Hi, Mama."

I know I've just shocked my father beyond measure. Out of anyone in our family, I'm the last person Daddy would ever think would go against the grain and fall in love with someone outside of our social circle. I'm the one who loved living in the world my parents created. I'm the one who—

"Good evening, Madeline." Her eyes bounce between me and Daddy as if watching a tennis match. "What's going on, Harris?"

Daddy doesn't answer. He storms out, leaving broken glass and an irreparable mess behind.

Quickly, I squat down as much as I can in my pink, sequined pencil skirt and begin picking up the largest pieces.

"Leave that, sugar. I don't want you to cut yourself," Mama says.

A part of me does want to cut myself—and that's not something that's ever run through my thoughts before. I can't scream right now, though I want to so badly, and the pain might be the distraction I need.

I've steered clear of painful emotions for someone who runs her mouth as much as I do. I've always tucked them away to deal with later, to keep up the facade of a strong woman with a perfect life. I'd paste on a smile and nod my head.

Homage to the perfect life I supposedly had with Trent—the man who almost killed me. The man my parents still want me to be with.

But I can't keep it up anymore because I'm finally awake. Not just to the world around me but to things happening in my bubble. The bubble I loved living in for twenty-five years.

My father would rather I be with a man like the one who almost killed me than the one who saved my life—because of class, money, and the business ties we have with a family.

And that's absolutely disgusting.

"What happened, Madeline?"

"I have to go, Mama," I say, dropping the large chunks of glass into the trash and bolting out of the room.

"Madeline! The guests are arriving!" Mama calls.

On my way out the front door, I smack into Emily, my tatted-up younger sister.

What the hell is Emily doing here?

"Whoa! Hey, Maddie!" she says, grabbing my arm.

I don't respond. I can't process my situation, let alone try to figure out what brought Emily into the lion's den of a Commons holiday party after sporadic attendance over the last few years.

Instead, I wiggle out of her grasp, push past her, and rush to my car. Once inside, I let the tears flow freely. Amidst the blur of tears, I find my phone and call Erik.

He answers immediately. "Hey, babe! Miss me already?"

Tears stream down my cheeks and over my lips before dropping onto my silk blouse. My back bounces against the leather seat with each heaving sob.

"Maddie, what's wrong? Where are you? I'm coming to get you."

I clutch the phone with both hands. "No!" Tears stream down my cheeks, dotting the silk with wet splotches.

"Babe, please tell me what's wrong?"

"I'm at..." I begin through heaving sobs. "I'm at my parents. I just told Daddy that—"

"Told him what?" Erik asks slowly.

"That you moved in."

There's silence on the other end.

Everything floods me at once, and at that particular moment, I realize I may have just fucked everything up. Not only with my parents but also with Erik.

We haven't discussed when or how we'd tell my parents that real emotions replaced our fake relationship. Mouthing off to Daddy isn't something I normally do, but the fact that I brought Erik into it shows how selfish I am. I thought Erik taught me about caring for others and standing up for people.

And yet, in my anger, I used someone I love against my father because I knew it would hurt him. I knew it would make him furious.

I'm no better than he is.

My ignorant hissy fit might cause Erik a huge loss in income. If my father fires him, the trickle-down effect would be set into motion immediately. When Daddy pulls out, he'll instruct his cronies to follow suit. Someone doesn't get fired without the trickle-down effect. Erik could lose multiple jobs over the way I acted.

How would he survive if he gets deported? How would he pay for his grandmother's care?

The selfishness of opening my big mouth without thinking about the repercussions again weighs heavy on me.

"Jesus, Erik, I'm so sorry. I didn't even think about the consequences, I just—"

"It's okay, Maddie. It's okay. I wish I would have been there, but we'll face it together. I love you."

Those words.

I love you.

How could he still love me after fucking up this badly?

Erik's voice pulls me out of my trance. "I'm already on my way. Do not move."

"No!" I wipe the tears away with my fingers. "No! Daddy is angry, and everyone is about to show up, and—"

"I've been invited to this party every year for over ten years, Maddie. I'm on my way. We'll talk to him together."

A pair of headlights shine in my rearview mirror. The party is underway. "This isn't the time to talk. Guests are starting to arrive. We can't talk about this in front of everyone."

"So, we're going to sweep it under the rug, put on our fake smiles, and pretend to enjoy the party while tension seeps into every crack of that house? I thought you were over that life?"

I appreciate Erik's optimism, but I know my father—my family. This won't go well. They won't allow this to go well. I'm certain of that.

Still, he's right. I'm over the charade. It's time to face all the secrets and lies.

The mess I caused inside before a holiday party to thank our employees and contract workers.

The truth about Trent.

The consequences of suggesting a fake relationship while knowing mutual attraction fueled the decision.

How did I ever think this could be simple? How did I ever think I could hold back my emotions with someone I have so many feelings for? I didn't realize it was possible to fall in love in mere months because I had never been in love in twenty-five years.

But that was a lie—I have been in love. I've been in love with Erik since I was a teenager.

Words are words. Anyone can say them.

Hell, Trent told me he loved me, all the while using me as a punching bag and grinding my self-confidence into the ground day after day. Throwing passive-aggressive insults. Twisting my words and actions into something they weren't.

I know, more than anyone, that actions matter above all else.

Erik's desire to confront my father when he arrives tells me everything I need to know about love and action.

"Maddie, are you still there?"

I nod, forgetting for a second that I'm still on the phone. "Yes," I squeak out.

"It'll be hella awkward, but we're going to face it together, just like everything else in life. We can do it, Madeline. I've got your back from now until the end of time."

"Thank you."

"I'll be there soon, babe. I love you."

"I love you."

Just as I'm hanging up with Erik, a knock on my window startles me, causing me to drop my phone.

Emily pounds again, her heavily made-up face twisted with concern. Don't get me wrong, she looks gorgeous. My sister is a master of makeup—she just wears a ton of it. She could step onto a Broadway stage and be seen from the farthest seat.

"Maddie, what's going on?" she asks through the glass. With frigid fingers, I press the engine button and roll down the window.

"Just telling the truth and ruining people's lives," I admit.

Her tan, knee-length coat is gorgeous. It looks like vintage suede, but she doesn't use animal products as a vegan, so it must be synthetic.

"The truth has a way of doing that. That's why people avoid it." She pulls her jacket closed and rounds the car, yanking the passenger door handle before jumping in next to me. The overpowering smell of marijuana envelops the small space.

"You smell like Cheech and Kong," I say, coughing and batting the air as though that will dissipate the nauseating stench.

Emily laughs. "Chong."

"What?"

"Cheech and Chong. Not Kong."

I glare at her. "Whatever. I'll have to drive with my windows down for a week to air it out."

"Don't be pissy with me; I came out to help."

"I don't need your help," I say, rolling up my window despite the odor. It may trap the smell, but since I can't stop shivering, I don't have a choice.

"Mayor Maddie is sitting alone in a freezing-cold car before a party is about to start. I'd say you need someone right now. Like it or not, here I am." She gives me an exaggerated grin and holds up wiggling jazz hands. I can't help but smile. "What's the truth that's ruining everyone's lives?"

"I'm in love with Erik Raines."

"The hot landscaper?" Emily exclaims.

I nod.

"Does he love you back?" she asks tentatively.

I nod.

She slaps her thigh. "You lucky bitch!"

I *am* lucky—lucky that Erik loves me. Lucky that he wants to stand up for me, and face my parents with me. There's nothing wrong with falling in love. I don't owe them an explanation for my personal choices.

"I'm surprised you let it happen. He's a little beneath you, isn't he?"

The old Maddie would bark back with a biting comment. My sister and I thrive on a relationship ripe with sarcasm and one-upmanship. Emily and I were never very close. We had nothing in common growing up except our love for art. It's still the only thing we have in common—we just took two different routes: fashion for me and tattooing for her.

Over the last few months, I've learned to see past my self-imposed blinders, my prejudices against people who choose a path I might not understand—like hers. I'm slowly learning to appreciate her as she is, not as who I expected or wanted her to be.

Maybe her attitude isn't about defiance. Maybe she's standing up for herself and her choices. Just because we don't agree on our ideal lifestyles doesn't mean hers is wrong.

"I don't need to be chastised right now, Em. I need support"—I drop my eyes to my lap—"and maybe a hug."

Without hesitation, Emily wraps her arms around me. "I'm sorry, Mads." She squeezes me tight. After a few seconds of soaking up strength through her embrace, I give her a quick rundown of what happened over the last few months. I'm almost finished when my phone beeps with a text.

Thought you were inside, so I knocked on the door and got pulled into your dad's den. It's go time.

"Shit!" I shove my phone into my pocketbook. "I've gotta get in there right now."

Emily scrambles out of the car, hot on my heels on the way to the door. "What's going on?"

"Erik is confronting Mama and Daddy about us."

Let the fireworks begin.

Chapter Twenty

ERIK

When I arrived at the Commons' house, I expected Maddie to answer the door. I figured she'd been waiting impatiently since we got off the phone. Usually, one of the Commons girls greets guests with a mega-watt smile and the standard holiday welcome: *"Merry Christmas! Come on in. What can I get you to drink?"*

When the door swings open, Harris stands in the foyer. Wordlessly, he ushers me into his den.

He follows me into the huge, octagonal room, which is lined with mahogany bookshelves. An ornate crystal chandelier hangs from the twelve-foot ceiling, and gas lanterns flicker between the bookshelves.

Harris shuts the door behind us, then wastes no time getting straight to the meat of the matter.

"You moved in with Madeline? I thought this was a fake arrangement?" he roars.

The level of his voice tells me I'm most likely the first guest to arrive. As Maddie says, it's not the Commons' way to air their dirty laundry out for all to see or hear.

"Look—" I begin when I'm interrupted by the doorbell.

Harris takes a deep breath, then lets it out slowly. He holds one finger up as if to say he'll be right back.

While he's gone, I send Maddie a quick text. I have no problem handling Harris myself, but I'd appreciate a united front.

When Harris enters again, Maddie is on his heels. As soon as she slides in the door, she hurries to my side.

"Someone better tell me what the hell is going on," he demands, shutting the door behind him.

"My apartment complex is being demolished," I begin. "Maddie was kind enough to let me stay with her for a few months."

"You didn't have any other friends to stay with?" Harris snaps.

He and I have always had a great relationship, so I've rarely seen him irate. Nor did I ever want to be the person who stoked the anger. With multiple veins straining his neck, it looks like he's about to show me the side I never wanted to see.

"I did, but—"

Maddie interrupts me before I finish, "But since the Commons family is the reason he had to leave his home, I figured the least I could do is offer mine."

"What?" Harris and I ask at the same time. I pivot my body toward Maddie.

"Erik's apartment complex currently stands on the site of a future outdoor mall—the mall that Commons Department store will anchor. It's our fault he's been displaced."

Holy shit. I didn't realize the mall Maddie mentioned in her office a few weeks back was the project going up on the land. It doesn't matter; it's not like they did it on purpose, but still.

"Did you offer the other residents a place to live as well, Madeline?" Harris asks sarcastically.

"No, Daddy. I might have, but I'm not in love with any of them," she retorts, grabbing my hand and lacing her fingers through mine. "Just Erik."

Bomb dropped.

"Jesus Christ," he whispers, rubbing the bridge of his nose with his thumb and index finger. When he focuses again, his hard gaze sears through me.

Harris's gaze doesn't scare me with Maddie's hand in mine. This is exactly what I wanted after her father steered me into his office. A united front sharing the truth. No more secrets or lies.

Despite knowing that my actions will only provoke Harris further, I lean over and kiss her quickly. She smiles shyly, and her face flushes pink.

It's beautiful. It gives me life. Knowing she's felt the same way I've felt about her emphasizes how pure our love is. It reinforces how much I want this to work out, even if it started as a crazy plan to keep me in the country.

"Look, I understand that you might think this is love. A fake relationship can feel real—"

"It's real, Daddy."

"Did Erik make it clear to you that dating, living together—even getting married—will not keep a *dreamer* such as Erik in the country? Deferred action doesn't work that way."

Shit.

I haven't told Maddie that part yet. I was working my way there, but the right time to hurt her never came up.

"I—we—" Maddie falters slightly. "It may not be enough to keep him in the country. But we're in love, and we want to be together. Living together and getting married can't hurt in the long run."

Despite being blindsided by the news, Maddie explained our motivation with conviction. Her unique, energetic spirit and quick-thinking ability are some of her greatest strengths. No matter how outlandish her idea sounds, you find yourself fighting for her—with her.

I curse myself for not telling her sooner. She shouldn't have had to cover for me on the fly.

"I hear you both throwing around the word 'love.' Why would someone who loves you allow you to put yourself in a position where you could go to jail for helping him? Doesn't that seem selfish to you, Madeline?"

She's the light of Harris's life. I've seen that for years. She truly is a daddy's girl. Always by his side. His right-hand "man" in business. He doesn't want to be angry with her. That's her advantage over him.

Maddie is the perfect daughter. The one Cookie and Harris pride themselves on getting right.

It makes complete sense he'd be appalled that she fell in love with me.

"With all due respect, sir," I speak before Maddie answers. "I never wanted Madeline to get in trouble. I had a different motivation when I agreed to the arrangement."

"Do tell."

"I wanted her to have a reason to break up with Trent Anderson. He almost killed her once. I won't let that happen again."

"Trent didn't—" Harris starts.

It's crazy how he's trying to rewrite a memory of an incident I saw with my own eyes. Harris wasn't there; I was.

This is how history books get written, by people who weren't there and have an agenda for how the story gets told.

It's gaslighting when you use it with people who love and trust you. If you tell them how something happened a certain way over and over again, their memory of it changes. They start to believe the lie, even if they know the truth.

Memories are easy to manipulate.

"Daddy, stop!" Maddie interrupts this time. Which surprises Harris, but not me.

I know how strong she is. I know she won't be pushed around anymore. From this point forward, she can love and respect her parents but also create her own narrative.

"Erik saved my life. I wanted to repay him. He wanted to help me. That's how it all started."

"And then we fell in love," I add confidently.

"We were already in love. If we weren't, neither one of us would have agreed to the plan," Maddie confirms, She takes my hand and squeezes it. Then she continues, "It was inevitable. It was set in motion the second Erik set foot on our property."

Most people will remember a moment like this as happy, maybe even triumphant, but I can feel the tension draping the room like a thick London fog.

Suddenly, the door bursts open and Cookie slides in. "What in the world is going on in here? The guests are arriving and I'm still plating the appetizers. I need some help out there."

"Erik and Madeline are in love, Cookie. They're living together," Harris says.

It may seem as though he finally understands, but with every second that passes, I practically hear the gears turning in his head. I feel his cold glare. I see his jaw tighten.

He seems cool and collected, but there's no way he's letting his daughter—the heir to his business empire—stay with me. I've known from the beginning, but I stuck with it because I wanted to experience Maddie's love. Even for a short time before real life took away our fairy tale.

She deserves to know what real love is before she gets swept back into a world where marriages are business transactions and where families match their kids to enhance their power and influence.

"What?" she exclaims, then checks her tone and continues, whispering loudly, "I can't believe you two." She shifts her narrowed gaze from Maddie to me. "I tolerated the 'fake relationship' when you asked me to because you insisted you were helping a friend. But nothing about this is cute. Or funny," she says in a biting tone. "What you're doing is unacceptable. How are you so calm about this, Harris?"

"They're in love, Cookie," Harris says. "You remember what it felt like at the beginning, don't you?"

I bite back a sarcastic laugh because I can't imagine Harris and Cookie married for love. He's too rich and she's too conniving.

A smile spreads across Maddie's face and she squeezes my hand.

She still trusts her father. She still sees good in him.

She thinks love won. She thinks *we* won.

But I know better.

I know this is the beginning of the end.

Chapter Twenty-One

MADDIE

It takes me an hour, but I finally finish getting the condo set up exactly as I want it. Rose petals create a path from the door to the living room and continue straight onto our bed. Battery-operated tealights illuminate the petal path, while real candles burn on every surface of the apartment.

Our relationship is out in the open—and my parents appear to have accepted it. Mama will take a bit more convincing, but having Daddy on our side is a huge win.

None of this would have happened if Erik hadn't fished me out of a swimming pool. If there was ever a reason to have an over-the-top romantic celebration, I'd say that's a good one.

I've just finished sliding a nude gloss on my lips that makes them appear sexy and pouty when I hear Erik unlocking the door. My heart pounds with excitement and anticipation, thinking about how he'll receive my surprise.

"What's all this?" he asks.

"If it weren't for you, I'd be an angel up in heaven," I say as I walk from the bedroom to the living room. "To celebrate, I decided to be your angel here on earth."

"Awww, babe, that's—" He stops dead in his tracks when he glances up. His eyes bulge and his jaw drops. It's the exact reaction I wanted when I chose my outfit—a headband halo made of silver garland and white lace everything else, from my matching bra-and-panty combo to the top of my thigh-high stockings.

"Holy fuck, Madeline." His hockey bag slides off his shoulder and hits the floor with a *thud*. He crosses the room in three strides and grabs my hips. "Holy fuck," he repeats, his breath increasing as he takes in every inch of me.

He smells fresh and clean, straight from the shower. Inhaling lifts my chest, which catches Erik's eye. He lowers his head and kisses my neck, then trails his mouth to my breasts. His hand cups the underside and one boob spills out. He covers my nipple with his mouth and sucks gently. Then he grazes his teeth over it and I arch into him.

He pulls back, biting his bottom lip as he devours me with his eyes. "You're absolutely gorgeous," he whispers reverently. His hands slide up and down my thighs. One finger dips under my thong and he groans. "I need to taste you now."

Erik drops to his knees, pushes the fabric away, and begins to lick between my legs. I swallow hard and squeeze my eyes shut, praying I can stay standing when he goes harder. He wraps one arm around my legs, holding me firm, as the other hand pushes down his pants and boxer briefs. My fingers curl into his hair while my pelvis grinds against his face.

It doesn't take long for me to fall over the edge. Erik releases the grip on my legs and I wobble. He grabs my hips to hold me steady and rises to his feet. After kicking his clothes off, he backs me up until we fall onto the bed together. He reaches for the handle to the nightstand drawer, but I stop him, flipping him onto his back and climbing on top. He watches, breathing heavily, as I lean down, kissing a trail from his muscular chest to his flat stomach.

When I reach the promised land, I cup his balls gently and fondle them between my fingers. He moans, lifting his hips slightly. Then I take his long, hard cock in my hand and start sliding up and down, squeezing and pumping faster and faster. His breath increases, getting heavier the faster I go. I wrap my mouth around his cock and slide down as far as I can until the tip hits the back of my throat. After pulling off completely, I spit on his dick to get it nice and wet and do it again. Soon, my mouth matches the rhythm of my hand, which makes Erik shout, "Fuck! I'm gonna come."

I remove my mouth, despite his groan of protest, and grab a condom out of the nightstand. I've never rolled one on so quickly, but I want him to come inside me, so I have to be fast. Once the condom is in place, I slide onto his dick and ride him hard. I fall forward, rubbing against his pelvic bone, which brings me to another orgasm within seconds.

"Fuck!" we roar at the same time, as we climax together. When it's over, I collapse onto Erik's chest. He hugs me to him, allowing me to calm my racing heart in the comfort of his arms.

After taking a minute to clean up, we crawl back into bed and snuggle into each other. I throw one leg over his and rest my head on his chest. We lie there, basking in the comfortable quiet. The beat of his heart lulls me into a sleepy haze.

"Maddie, we need to talk about something," Erik says softly, breaking the silence.

"What is it?"

Butterflies flit around my stomach in anticipation, wondering what he wants to talk about. I'm hoping he'll propose. His work permit expires soon, and we have no clue how long he has left in the country after that. He could be deported once his time is up.

After the blow-up at my parent's house, I now know marrying me won't keep him here, but it certainly doesn't hurt his chances.

Especially since the sham that started as a way to get him to stay in the country turned into real, lasting love. Some people might say it was fast, but we have a history. A love story that started years ago, blossoming over the last several months. There's nothing fake—or illegal—about it.

"I love you, Madeline. Please know that." He squeezes me to his chest.

"I know you do," I say tentatively. My stomach swirls in anticipation of something unpleasant coming next. "And I love you."

"I'm moving to Prague at the end of the month."

Using his chest to brace my hands, I bolt upright. "What do you mean? Did you get notified? Are you being deported?"

Erik sits up, taking my hands in his. "No."

"Well, then what do you mean you're moving to Prague?" My voice cracks and my body shakes. He squeezes my hands.

"I have to leave the country if I ever want to come back. The laws aren't going to change anytime soon. They aren't going to give immigrants—even immigrants who were brought here as babies—a blanket pardon." Erik's eyes are glassy, but he doesn't take his gaze from mine. "You know that. We've talked about it."

I nod.

"I don't know how any of this works, but I figure, if I do this now, on my terms, maybe that will help me get back into the country sooner."

My jaw tightens. It makes sense, but I don't want to hear it. We've been so focused on keeping him here that we never discussed what would happen if he had to leave—or, in this case, if he *chose* to leave.

"What if you never get deported? Think about how many people are here illegally. Why would you choose to go when you aren't being kicked out?" I can't keep the hysterical shrill out of my voice.

"Because I want to do this right. I don't want to live in hiding or fear. I don't want to be afraid to check the mail or answer the door. I don't want to put the people I love in a bad position. But mostly—I don't want to lie anymore."

"Is this a lie? Are *we* a lie?"

"No." Erik wraps his arms around me and pulls me to his chest. "We are not a lie. *We* are the reason I'm doing this. The faster I can get back to this country, the faster I can be with you, forever, without any obstacles in our way."

The tears spill over my cheeks and onto his chest. "Isn't there any other way?" I plead, though I know the answer. We've exhausted every possible avenue. All roads lead to the same answer.

The truth is, he may never be allowed back into the country. If the process gets that far, it could be years before he's approved.

Erik lifts my chin so we're staring into each other's eyes. "You are the kindest, sweetest, most wonderful human being I've ever known.

Whether we had fallen in love or not, you chose to do something completely selfless. Illegal"—he chuckles—"but selfless, just to help me. You stood up for what you thought was right. You're strong and brave, and you have the most beautiful heart. I'm thankful each day that you are in my life."

"I must be a mirror—because that's what I see in you, Erik. You are the most honest man I've ever met. You have integrity and courage. You can't be bought or bribed. As much as it will hurt to say goodbye to you, I know you have to do this. I'm so proud of you," I say as the tears flow again. "I'm wrecked. But I'm proud of the man you are."

"Jesus." Erik blinks a few times. Is he crying? I've never seen him cry—not even at Rusty's funeral. "I don't want to break up, Maddie. I mean, I know that I can't ask you to put your life on hold, but—"

"We're not breaking up," I agree. "We're going to utilize every damn form of technology there is to stay in touch."

"Mmmmmm." Erik drops his mouth to my neck, kissing his way to my earlobe before taking it in his teeth and tugging gently. "Maybe some sexy video calls?"

"That sounds fun," I say, tilting my head so he has better access to the sweet spot.

"We've got one month to see me off with a bang."

"We can bang wherever you want, Sugar."

He lifts his head, showing me a silly grin and wide eyes. "On your desk at the office?"

"Absolutely."

"But first..." His mouth presses against mine and I fall back onto the bed. He climbs on top, gliding his palm across my cheek and through my hair while gazing into my eyes. "I love you, Madeline. I want to spend the rest of my life with you."

A tear slips out and slides down my temple and onto the pillow below me.

This may be the end of what we have right now, but it's not the end of us. If I could make a long-distance relationship work with a man I loathed, I can certainly make it work with the man I love.

Chapter Twenty-Two

ERIK

W hen Harris texted me, telling me he needed to meet with me as soon as possible, I let it go for a few days. It may seem like I'm playing a game of whose dick is bigger, but it's really because, after confessing to Maddie that I'm moving, Harris has nothing over me anymore. I don't have to jump when he says jump. But I need to tell him my plans, so I agree to meet.

"Please sit." Harris nods to an antique settee, upholstered in worn, green leather. While I get comfortable, he strides to the bar and pours brown liquor into two highball glasses. He hands me one and drops into the seat behind the oversized desk in his home office. It's probably meant to be subtly intimidating, but it doesn't affect me.

"After Madeline told us she'd entered into an arrangement with you to keep you in the country, I spoke with your immigration lawyer." He sets his glass on a coaster and grabs a pair of eyeglasses from a tray. "I've always been willing to help you with your status," he says, sliding the glasses onto his face.

"You have. And I've always appreciated that." I take a small sip of the drink—bourbon—before setting it on the desk.

He opens a drawer, removes a thin, document-sized envelope, and then leans across the desk to offer it to me.

"What's this?" I ask, meeting his eyes briefly as I take it, before sliding my fingers under the flap and removing the paperwork.

"It's a birth certificate. If you stop this ridiculous charade with Madeline, you are an official citizen of the United States."

More lies. More illegal activities. He's asking me to replace one illegal charade with another—by offering me a doctored birth certificate. It's the epitome of hypocrisy.

"It's not a charade, Harris." I shove the document back into the envelope. "I lo—"

"Don't say it, Erik," Harris commands. "I'm very fond of you. You know that. I've done the best I can for you. I won't cancel the Raines Landscaping contract here, but you'll send a crew from now on. I'll even set you up in an apartment of your own until we figure out what's going on with your status. I want you to stay away from Madeline."

Anger boils in my chest, my heart pounds to get out. Clenching my fists at my sides, I silently count to ten and take breaths—any calming technique I can think of, so as not to use him as a punching bag.

I can't forget how good Harris has been to me and my family. Twenty years ago, he hired my grandfather as a landscaper. Over time, he referred a huge group of his friends to him. Back then, it was just me and Grandpa working our tails off for those families. As business grew, we hired additional guys to help us make the jobs faster and more efficient, enabling us to take on more.

My grandfather didn't want to expand, but I knew we had to diversify—and I'm glad we did. If Harris fires me and his friends follow suit, the business will take a hit—but it'll be okay. I may be frustrated and angry, but I'll never hate him because he is the sole reason we were able to create the thriving business I have today.

"There are plenty of women out there, Erik. You're handsome and hardworking. You have a good heart. You'll make a fine husband. I'm sure of it."

"Then why am I not good enough for Maddie? You've said that you've always been fond of me. I'm a good person. I work my ass off. I have a thriving business. Even if I lost you and your friends as clients, I'll still be successful. I'm not trying to live off Maddie."

"It's not about that, Erik! This isn't about your social status or your financial success, or if I think you're trying to use her for her money. Which, for the record, I don't think at all." He takes off his glasses. "This is about Madeline and her future. Simply put: I cannot have my daughter get in trouble for conspiring to a fake marriage to keep you in the country. Do you understand what that could do to her—and to our business?"

"What we have isn't fake."

"I understand you believe that. But we both know that Madeline has a soft heart. She would do anything to help anyone—especially you since you two were quite friendly when you were children. But you need to leave her out of your ordeal. Her career—her life—is on the line. She's the future of the Commons stores. I can't have her involved in something illegal. Her reputation is already tarnished."

"Tarnished? How?"

"The aftermath of her breakup. I know she went through a rough time with Trent—"

I jump to my feet and look down at him. "A 'rough time?' He almost killed her, and you call it a 'rough time?'"

Harris stands, refusing to be overpowered, even in body language. "I've already discussed the incident with Trent. He insists it wasn't that at all."

"Oh my God!" I roll my eyes to the crystal chandelier above our heads. My body shakes so hard, it feels like the room is moving. "Sometimes you make it hard to appreciate you, Harris."

"Excuse me?"

"Listen to yourself? How could you believe that manipulative, abusive scumbag over her?"

He shakes his head and holds a hand up. "Enough of this."

"Harris, I will promise to walk away from Madeline if you promise not to push her toward Trent."

"You're not really in a place to compromise."

"You don't understand how much I love her. Someone has to protect her—especially if you won't."

Harris scowls as if I've slapped him in the face.

"I'm not worried about being deported. I'll go to the Czech

Republic and start a life there. What I *am* worried about is Trent hurting Maddie again."

"He didn't hurt—"

"Ask her!" I yell, interrupting any ignorant comment about to come out of his mouth. Harris could have my head on a platter, but I don't care. He needs to hear the truth. "Ask your daughter about everything he did to her, Harris! But ask her with an open mind, not as if you're trying to prove her wrong."

He's staring at me in disbelief as if I'd used my fists instead of words against him. But he's listening now and this is my chance to help him see the truth about Trent.

Maddie isn't a pawn in a family business. She's a human being—a wonderful human being who's being sent to the den of a hungry lion every time she's forced to interact with Trent.

"You're standing here, telling me you're worried about her future. You're worried about the trouble she could get into for marrying an illegal immigrant, and I get that. But you'll let a narcissistic sociopath abuse her—maybe even kill her?"

"Was it that bad?" Harris asks quietly as if entertaining the thought for the first time. His hands brace the top of his chair.

I lift my arms as if to shake him, but I know I can't, so I clench my fists in frustration. "Yes. He's violent and emotionally abusive. How have you never seen it?"

"He's never laid a hand on her in my presence."

"No shit," I snap. "What about how he talks to her?"

"It's no different than—" Harris pauses, stopping himself from saying anything else.

It's no different than how he talks to Cookie? It's no different than how his associates speak to women. I'm not saying I haven't benefited from a patriarchal system or values, but fuck—unchecked patriarchy is a sad, disrespectful way to live. Especially when you can't see outside of it.

I can't say that to him, and honestly, it wouldn't do any good. I'll never change his mind, but maybe I can get him to see it from another perspective.

"Madeline has idolized you her entire life," I say tentatively. "She never had any doubts about wanting to work in your family business—to work directly with you. This is your chance to be the hero, Harris. To be the man she's always seen through those beautiful blue eyes."

He taps the envelope against his thigh, contemplating what to say next. I honestly have no clue if I'm getting through to him.

Finally, he squares his jaw and looks me in the eye. "I don't know if she'll ever see me that way again."

"That's up to you. But if you don't start listening to her concerns, you'll lose the only daughter who's always been on your side."

"I have your word that you won't let her continue this charade?"

"If I have your word you will take her concerns about Trent seriously and keep him away from her."

"I'll make sure the Trent Anderson situation is handled immediately."

A "thank you" rushes out with the breath I've been holding. "I'll end our arrangement. You have my word. I don't want her involved in anything that could get her in trouble, either. It's gone too far."

Though my feelings for Maddie are very real, I can honestly say I don't want her to be involved in any of this. I certainly don't want to be linked to any shady, fake birth certificate that Harris Commons can make happen. I'm done living with lies.

I have to take responsibility for my own life. I can't blame anyone anymore. If Maddie and I are meant to be together, it will happen. Someday. We live in a world where communication overseas is easy. We may not be together as a couple, but we can keep in touch.

He holds the envelope out to me. I shake my head in refusal.

"Make sure that record gets wiped off the planet, Harris. I don't want my name tied to any of that fake-document shit. I'm doing this the legal way."

By the way his eyebrows inch up, he's surprised by my stern command.

There's no reason to be intimidated because he doesn't have anything to hold over my head anymore. Not the secret of my citizenship. Not my business. Not my relationship with his daughter.

Despite his surprise, he keeps a cool demeanor, shoving a hand in his pocket and shifting his stance casually before asking, "How so?"

"I'm moving to Prague at the end of the month." The relief of finally taking control of my life gives me confidence. "Everything is in place."

Harris breaks eye contact to toss the envelope on his desk. He leans over and grabs his bourbon. "Does Madeline know?"

"Yes," I say firmly.

Harris's eyes fly to mine in surprise.

"She understands I'm doing it because I love her. And I will do anything in my power to keep her safe and out of trouble—even if it means breaking her heart."

Chapter Twenty-Three

MADDIE

When Erik told me he was moving to Prague, it was the hardest thing I've ever had to process. Though it felt like my heart was being ripped out of my chest, I played it cool because there was no reason to get upset or make him more upset. I knew there was no changing his mind.

We understand the reality. If he wants to legally enter America after his work permit expires, he *must* leave the country.

We have no clue how long it will be until he's allowed back.

Because he chose to admit that he was brought here illegally as a child and took the appropriate steps to stay here, we're hoping his process to re-enter the country will be a little easier. The policies on the status of *Dreamers* could change a hundred times over the next few months or even years. Still, it's improbable that all of them would ever be given blanket U.S. citizenship, no matter how many Homeland Security policy changes happen. It doesn't do him any good to wait if the solution will always be the same.

I never thought he would choose to leave, and as much as it hurts, I understand why he has to.

I was prepared to handle his absence with a broken heart and my head high. Until I realized...

Erik can't stay in America, but nothing is stopping me from going to the Czech Republic with him.

We've been discussing how to keep him here all this time, but going with him never came up once. I'm pretty sure he never mentioned it because he thinks I have this grand life that I couldn't possibly leave behind, and maybe I felt that myself once—before us.

I'm a different person now than I was a few months ago, but one thing has remained the same: family is the most important thing in the world.

And Erik is my family now.

I knew he'd never agree to my suggestion unless I settled a few things beforehand—not just in my life, but also things that weigh heavily on him. If I can get everything I need to sorted out in the next few weeks, I'm free to move to wherever I damn well please.

If the man I love moves to Prague, I'm going with him.

I KNOCK on the doorframe of my father's office. Like a college professor, he has open-door hours at work. This policy is part of a company-wide plan to create a more open, friendly workplace.

We're a family business and want our employees to feel like family. *Open-door hours* give employees specific times to reach managers in person. Although executives can only reach Daddy this way, it's still helpful.

"Daddy, I need to talk to you about my future with Commons Department Stores."

"Excuse me?" He looks up from his computer screen.

"I'm moving to Prague at the end of the month," I say matter-of-factly, though I know the news will be a significant blow. "I may not be able to efficiently handle all of the duties of the Vice President of Apparel and Cosmetics remotely. I need to talk with you about a different position or hiring an Assistant VP to take care of things I need to be present for during that time. I assume hiring someone is cheaper than flying me back and forth. I'd like to know my other options with the company."

"Hold on a second, Madeline! What do you mean you're moving to Prague?"

"Erik has to move, and I'm going with him."

Daddy stares at me. He looks at the computer screen, then at me again. "Come in and sit down, please."

I step into his office. "I can't stay long, Daddy. As you can imagine, I have a to-do list a million miles long. I need to know if it's something we can work on or if I need to look for a position in Prague."

"Madeline, you've made your point. You love him. I can handle that." He removes his glasses, tossing them on the desk, and rises from his chair. "But giving up your career? Moving to a foreign country?"

"Erik stood up for me when no one else would. Erik stands up for everybody." I gaze out the window because I can't quite face my father when the pain is still so raw. "You wouldn't stand up for me when I told you about Trent. I'm your *daughter*." I turn back to him with tears in my eyes. "I can't keep putting on a strong face every day and be forced to work alongside Trent. Something has to—"

Daddy raises his hand, a well-known nonverbal command to silence me. It's ingrained. "I spoke to Jessie Piper and told him that Trent Anderson is not to be involved in any matters that involve Commons Department Stores or the Commons family. He is not to have access to records. He is not to communicate with our family in any legal matter. And if they don't adhere to those rules, we will pull all of our business from their firm."

"But—" I close my eyes and shake my head, trying to understand. "You—"

Within a few strides, he's at my side. He places his hands on my shoulder and looks me straight in the eye. "You are more important to me than Trent Anderson. You always have been, and you always will be. I'm sorry if my actions have ever made you doubt that."

"Thank you, Daddy."

"Now that we've handled that." He kisses my forehead and starts to walk toward his desk.

"Does that mean I'll be able to stay in my current position while in Prague?" I ask.

He spins around, eyes wide with surprise. "I thought I just established that you won't have to work with Trent again. You can stay here."

"While I truly appreciate that you finally stood up for me, Trent has little to do with my decision. I want to be with Erik. He's my family. I won't let him move to a foreign country alone."

He tilts his head before pleading, "Madeline—"

"Harris," I say firmly. "I'm going to Prague. I want to do it on good terms. I want you to be proud of me. But I'm going with or without your approval. Will I have a job or not?"

The silence is thick for a few seconds. Finally, he sighs heavily, his shoulders dropping when he says, "Yes. You will have a job. Let's put together some ideas about what it will look like and meet next week."

"Thank you." I turn to leave his office.

"Madeline!" Daddy calls. I turn around slowly, bracing for the wrath of speaking to my father so sternly.

"I'll always be proud of you."

I'VE BARELY MADE it to my car when a text pings. After a quick swipe of the screen, I see:

> Madeline, you get your butt to the house this minute!

Ah, shit. I should've known Daddy would call Mama as soon as I left his office. My stilettos clap against the asphalt as I hurry to the car.

"I'm here, Mama!" I call as I enter the house. "Do your worst."

"I'm in the kitchen!" she calls.

Taking a deep breath, I brace myself for the wrath. Mama is fantastic at making me feel guilty for my choices. Or making me feel like if I don't make the decision she wants me to make, it's flat-out wrong.

Thankfully, I've been sailing through Cookie's waters my entire life, so I know how to navigate the storm brewing. I am my mother's daughter, and like her, once I've made up my mind, nothing will change it.

Not even one of her guilt trips.

She's at the bar when I enter the kitchen, clicking away on a laptop. She stops to pat the chair next to her.

"Pull up a seat, Madeline."

Tentatively, I walk toward her, surprised at how calm everything seems. It's not how I expected this to go. Maybe Daddy didn't call her? They're thick as thieves, so that's out of the question.

I hang my pocketbook on the back of the chair and slide in next to her. Peering at the screen, I notice she's logged into the website she uses to coordinate meals for our friends who have had significant life events happen and need extra help or love. She'll enlist people to make a meal and bring it to the family so they can focus on the event, whether it's a family member who passed away or a new baby in the house.

"Who's that for?" I ask.

"Ginny."

My head snaps to Mama. "What?"

She switches back and forth between a browser with her email to the sign-up website, her eyes never veering from the screen. "I'm making a schedule for who's going to visit Ginny while you and Erik are away," she says. "There won't be one day where she has no visitors."

"Mama—" I start, but the words catch in my throat. I press my lips together, trying to compose myself as tears pool in my eyes.

"I've made it very clear that visiting during mealtime is ideal, but I do hope it's okay if there's a day or two that it's just a visit." She finally looks at me.

I don't even stop the tears as they slide down my cheeks. "Thank you, Mama," I say softly.

She wraps her arms around me and hugs me tight. Suddenly, her body begins to shake, and I realize Mama might be crying. I pull back to confirm, and we're both blubbering.

She reaches across the counter and grabs a dish towel. "I'm going to miss you, Madeline," she says, taking a moment to dab her eyes. "But I won't stop you from being with the person you love."

On the drive from my office to the house, I considered what I still needed to do to make moving to Prague work. Because I knew Ginny's lack of a visitor was one of Erik's major concerns about his having to leave, I wanted to make sure I took care of it before I told him I was going with him. I didn't know how to pull it together, but I never imagined Mama would.

I'd prepared for this moment with Mama, ready to fight. Yet, instead of coming at me angrily, she began organizing the very thing I needed help with. Suddenly, I'm reminded of her immense kindness. She might do or say things I perceive to be cold, but when it comes down to it, she does what she needs to do for her family. And she'll fight tooth and nail for us.

"Thank you, Mama. This means the world to me—to *us*." I pull her back in my arms because I don't have any other words to express my appreciation. "I love you so much."

I HAVE one last pressing issue to resolve before returning home tonight, and I know just who to call.

"What's up, Mayor?" Emily greets me upon answering her phone.

"I need a favor."

"You want a tattoo?" she teases.

"Fat chance."

"Someday, you're gonna get one. And I'm going to say—"

I interrupt her ridiculous rambling. "I'm moving to Prague with Erik. Can you foster our dog for a few years?"

"Fuck yes!" she answers.

And just like that, Erik and I are free to go.

Chapter Twenty-Four

ERIK

"I'm going with you to Prague," Maddie declares as soon as I set foot in the condo.

My girl has lost her mind. She can't possibly go with me. Her entire life is here—in Charlotte. And she loves it. I lean down to pet Ramos, who zoomed past her in his beeline to greet me. "Maddie. That's ridiculous. You can't—"

"I can," she says firmly. "I love you and don't want to live without you. Nothing means more to me than you." She moves closer, gently kneeing Ramos out of the way.

"I appreciate that, love." I kiss her lips quickly, inhaling the sweet scent of bubble gum. "But your career is here. Your family is here."

"You're right. But you mean more to me than my job. And I'm a U.S. citizen." She shrugs. "Technically, I can come back and visit my family anytime I want."

"Way to rub it in," I tease.

I know her by now. I know her body language and the tone of her voice. She's completely serious. Her mind is made up.

"Sweetheart, I love you too—so much that it hurts my heart. But you cannot move to the Czech Republic with me. You cannot leave your entire life behind. You may not see the consequences right now, but I do. You may not care about them, but I do."

"Erik."

"Stop, please. I won't let you turn your back on everything you know and love because of me. You'll lose your family and the career you worked hard for. You'll miss your friends," I say, inching past her to get to the living room. I've never let her see any weakness in my decision, and I'm not about to now. "I don't know what the Czech Republic will be like. I have a place to live, but I don't have any real plans. I have no clue what I'm doing. I can't bring you into that unknown."

"Erik." Maddie reaches out and grabs my arm. I turn to face her again. "I told you before that I will do anything to help you. A couple of years in another country isn't going to break me. It's an adventure. I *want* to go on this adventure with you. If you can't stay here, I'm going with you."

I won't let her make a decision that will ruin everything she worked for in her life. It's that easy. But since she's stuck on another crazy idea, I have to pull out the big guns.

"What about my grandma, Maddie? I feel good about leaving because I trust you'll take good care of her." It's a bit of a low blow since Ginny is not Maddie's responsibility in any way, but I had to hit below the belt to get her to realize it would be a mistake to leave her life here.

"There's a line out the door of people who want to help care for Ginny. Mama already started a signup sheet. Emily, Liz, Austin—even Austin's mama. They all assured us that there won't be one day where Ginny doesn't have someone there."

Surprised and slightly stunned by her thoughtfulness and the fact that so many people want to help, I stumble back until my calves hit the couch and fall onto it.

"And Emily said she'd take care of Ramos for the time we're gone," Maddie says, reading my mind before I can ask about him.

"You did all that for me?"

She sinks next to me and takes my hand. "I did it for us. I'm not letting you do this alone, Erik. My family is your family, and your family is mine. We're in this together. And we have people we can count on to help us."

"Are you sure, Maddie?" I whisper.

Fuck the tears that are stinging my eyes. I refuse to let them spill.

"I've never been more sure about anything in my life."

My knee shakes as I consider the possibility of Maddie coming with me. "What about your parents?" My concern is weak because Maddie is an adult, but their opposition would be a significant roadblock.

"My parents are fine with it."

"I don't believe that." I shake my head stubbornly. I refuse to let her ruin her ties with her family. That would break her.

"You don't have to believe me. As soon as you stop resisting, we can hop in that big old truck of yours, race to Mama and Daddy's, and you can ask them yourself. Heck, Daddy's the one who helped me get my visa paperwork started."

"This is ridiculous." I run both hands through my hair, squeezing the back of my head in frustration.

"We're like two mules fighting over a turnip right now, I swear." She huffs.

My head snaps up to get a translation of her Southern sayings. "Excuse me?"

"We've gotta come to an agreement, Sugar. We both want the same thing, don't we?" Maddie asks.

"Yes."

"You love me, don't you?"

"You know I do."

"I'm not buckling in for a twelve-hour flight with a stubborn ass. So, stop all this fussin' and kiss me already."

The woman sitting next to me is so much different from the woman I've known for years. She's not concerned about how others perceive her or about making other people happy. Her only concern is me.

I stare into her eyes, trying to determine if she's completely serious about this crazy plan. Is she making a good choice or being completely unreasonable?

Her stiletto taps against the hardwood floor, reminding me that even the split-second I've taken is too long because when a beautiful, Southern woman demands you kiss her—you kiss her.

I grab her waist and pull her onto my lap, then cover her mouth with mine. She melts into me, sliding her hands across my back before clasping them around my neck. Our tongues tangle for a few seconds, and when I pull away, the taste of bubble gum lingers. I open my mouth to speak, but Maddie interrupts before I can say a word.

"If you're about to argue again, you can just hush."

I can't help but smile. "I'm not going to argue. I'm going to say thank you." I nudge her nose with mine. "I cannot believe you're giving up your entire life for me."

"I'm not giving up my life, Erik. I'm starting it. I thought it was pretty clear that *you* are my life. *You* are my family. *You* are the person I want to spend the rest of my days with. We'll be on the front porch swing when we're old and gray, sipping iced tea together. I don't care what country that porch is in as long as I'm with you."

Tears spring to my eyes, a sign of how completely overwhelmed I am by how much thought she's put into this. And the fact that she's willing to drop everything to go with me. The only other people who loved me like this were my grandparents, who took me in and cared for me, even though I wasn't a blood relation.

"Oh, Erik." Maddie smiles and brings her hands to my face, gently sweeping the pads of her thumbs across my eyes.

I sniff a few times and clear my throat. Done.

"I'm not arguing, but—" I begin tentatively. "What about your career? You've worked hard to be where you are at Commons."

She shrugs. "I spoke to Daddy about working remotely—maybe not in my current position, but something. If we come to an agreement that works, that's great. If not, the visa I'm applying for will allow me to work. I'll email my resume to every business in Prague until I find something. I'm not worried, Erik. I'm confident I'm an asset to any company, not just my family's."

"I agree, one hundred percent."

"So, we're doing this?" Maddie asks, pulling back slightly. Her eyes are as bright as her smile.

I chuckle. "I guess we are."

Maddie clenches our fists together and pumps it into the air. "I'm so excited."

Though not relevant at this particular moment, I can't help but wonder how Maddie will fit all of her stuff into a few suitcases.

She extends her arm in front of her and slides it through the air as if our names are in lights on a marquis. "Maddie and Erik take Europe."

"Dramatic much?" I ask, tightening my grip and hugging her to me again.

Never in a million years did I think Madeline Commons would drop everything to move to another country—at all, let alone with me.

Asking her never crossed my mind. I'm not sure why. I didn't doubt her love for me, but asking her to move so far from everything she knew didn't seem like an easy request. I wouldn't have asked it of anyone.

But the fact that *she* made that decision, and all the work she put into answering my doubts, reinforces my belief that what we have is real.

"This is so surreal, Maddie."

She snuggles into my chest. "I know. It's going to be an amazing adventure. I'm excited to build a life together away from everyone and everything. We can start fresh."

"Sounds wonderful." I squeeze her tighter.

"Erik, can I ask you something crazy?" Her words are muffled because her face is buried in my chest. I lean back.

"You can ask me anything."

"Will you marry me?"

"Yes."

"Hear me out!" She rushes into her following sentence. "It makes sense that we're already married when we move to Prague. It means this is real. We're both all in. No one can question our commitment."

"Sweetheart." I tilt her chin upwards with my fingers. "I said yes."

"Oh. Well, all right then. It's settled."

It's settled. We've chosen our path. We've chosen each other after all the years—maybe because of all the years. And the truth set both of us free.

Life is a series of decisions.

We choose to lie or choose to tell the truth. Sometimes, the truth is the hardest thing we'll ever face, but I've found the most challenging decisions have the greatest reward.

EPILOGUE

Maddie

E rik and I sing along to "We Are the Champions" at the top of
our lungs as he pulls his truck into my parents' driveway.

He shifts into park and turns to me. "Last family brunch for a
while," he says, squeezing my knee. "You ready?"

Over the past few weeks, there have been many "lasts": my Last day
at the office and my last lunch with my girlfriends.

Moving is stressful, whether you're going across town, across the
country, or across an ocean. Between applying for the documents I'd
need to work in the Czech Republic, whittling my wardrobe down to
almost nothing, and pulling multiple overnighters to get everything
else done to prepare to leave the country, the exhaustion has hit me
hard. But I have zero complaints because the excitement of starting a
new life with Erik keeps me going.

"Yes," I answer honestly. "Though, I am gonna miss Mama's cooking. There are some recipes I can't recreate."

"Wanna know a secret?" Erik lowers his voice to a conspiratorial
tone, though it's just us in the truck. "I like your cooking better." He
winks and leans over to kiss me.

I peck his lips. "You're just saying that because I'm all you'll have for the next few years." I unbuckle my seatbelt and grab my pocketbook from the floor.

"I'm not!" Erik climbs out. He walks around the front of the truck and grabs my hand when he gets to me. "You have the Southern staples down pat, but you can also cook other cuisines. You make the best lasagna I've ever had in my life."

"You're the sweetest man." I lean over and kiss his cheek as we approach my parents' front door.

"Hello!" I call as I open the door. "The guests of honor have arrived! Drinks, please!"

"Cookie's gonna love that," Erik mumbles.

I wink at him. "She'll get over it."

Mama appears from the kitchen with two full punch glasses in her hand. "I almost thought it was your younger sister with a greeting like that."

As she hands us our drinks, she looks as immaculate as ever. Her hair is perfectly curled, with the sides pinned up. A black-and-white flowered A-line dress fits her figure, cinching her waist and hitting just below her knee.

I'm going to miss this—brunch with my family. Mama taking care of me. Learning from her.

My heart sinks momentarily, but I don't let it show. I made a decision for my future—the future I want with Erik. I'm not upset with my choice, but leaving my family will be difficult. I straighten my shoulders.

"Thanks, Mama." I lean in and kiss each of her cheeks. Erik does the same.

"You look beautiful, Mrs. Commons," he says.

She flashes him a smile. "Thank you, Erik."

The difference between how Mama treats Erik since she decided to be Ginny's new champion is night and day.

Maybe it's her way of apologizing to him for being rude during the last few months. Maybe it's because the caretaker in her loves having someone to look after. All of us girls are out of the house, and I'm leaving the country, so maybe it's her way of coping.

"Have you heard from Emily?" Mama asks. "I thought she'd be here to see you off."

I shrug. "She said she would be."

My little sister and I don't talk very often, but we bonded a bit when things went haywire with Daddy before the holiday party, and I wasn't about to leave the country for who-knows-how-long without inviting her to my going-away brunch.

Over the last week, my phone has been ringing constantly, with people wanting to wish Erik and me well on our new adventure. When it rings, I glance at it quickly, ready to dismiss the call. But Emily's name and picture are on the screen.

"Speak of the devil," I answer as I walk into the hallway. "Your ears must've been burning because—"

"Maddie, can you please put Liz on the phone?"

"If you wanted to speak with Liz, why did you call me?"

"Because her phone is going straight to voicemail," Emily explains with an irritated clip to her tone.

"Well, that's a nice how-do-you-do," I mumble, remembering why Emily and I barely speak anymore.

"Madeline! Can you *please* put Liz on the phone?" The irritation changes to desperation.

I roll my eyes. Of course. Insult me, then ask for help. It's such an Emily thing to do.

"Liz and Austin are in the other room, sitting close as cat's breath. I doubt they want to be interrupted. Anything I can help with, or do you want me to get her?"

There's silence on the other end. Then, in a meek voice, I hear, "Can you come get me?"

"From where?" I ask, holding back my annoyed sigh.

"You promise not to tell, Mama?"

I take a deep breath. "Emily, so help me—"

"Jail."

Thank you so much for reading LIVE TO TELL!

I hope you love Maddie and Erik.

Can't wait to find out what Emily got herself into? Dive right into CRAZY FOR YOU, a sexy enemies-to-lovers, age-gap romance that will tug at your heartstrings and steam up the pages.

Read CRAZY FOR YOU today!

"Amazing story!"

"The chemistry between the two is off the charts."

"There isn't anything that Sophia Henry can't write and write well."

-- ★★★★★ Reader Reviews

ARE you dying to discover how Maddie's' parents, Cookie and Harris, got together and created their empire? Check out DEVIL IN DISGUISE, the prequel to the Material Girls series.

WARNING: Be ready for a sexy Russian Mafia hitman, a dangerous love triangle, and a shocking twist!

Grab DEVIL IN DISGUISE now!

Turn the page for an excerpt from Devil in Disguise...

DO YOU HEAR WEDDING BELLS?

Sign up for Sophia's newsletter to read a Bonus Epilogue that gives you a front row seat to Maddie and Erik's big day!

Grab the Bonus Epilogue!

BE KIND. LOVE HARD.

At the beginning of my career, I vowed to give a portion of royalties from each of my books to charity. I choose charities that are close to my heart and that are involved in my books in some way. Visit the Be Kind Love Hard page on my website to learn more about each charity.

A HEARTFELT THANK YOU TO EACH ONE OF YOU
SOPHIA X

A portion of the royalties from the sale of LIVE TO TELL will be donated to Carolina Migrant Network.

For more information on Carolina Migrant Network: https://carolinamigrantnetwork.org/

#BeKindLoveHard

THANK YOU so much for taking the time to read LIVE TO TELL I truly appreciate every single one of you. If you enjoyed reading LIVE TO TELL as much as I enjoyed writing it, it would mean the world to me if you would consider leaving a review on Amazon.

(Really love me? Copy and paste the same review to Bookbub & Goodreads!)

SOPHIA X

PLAYLIST

Complete Playlist on YouTube: Sophia Henry Playlists

Material Girl – Madonna
Live To Tell – Madonna
Caffeine – Foreign Air
oh baby – LCD Soundsystem
Holding Out for a Hero (Cover) – Nothing But Thieves
I Found – Amber Run
Born To Be Yours – Kylo, Imagine Dragons
Fire Escape – Andrew McMahon
Favorite Liar – The Wrecks
She Said – Sundara Karma
Screws - Dreamers
Sit Next To Me – Foster The People
Pray For Me (Kendrick Lamar Cover) - Smallpools
I Can't Stand You Anymore – Sleigh Bells
Troublemaker – Grizfolk
Clumsy – Fergie
Thunder – Mondo Cozmo
Sold – Mondo Cozmo

End of the World – Night Riots
Unconditional – Matt Maeson
Don't Dream it's Over (Cover) – The Head and the Heart
Quarter Past Midnight – Bastille
The High Road – Broken Bells
Do I Have to Talk You Into It – Spoon
I Can Change – LCD Soundsystem
Fast Talk – Houses
This Town – Niall Horan

ALSO BY SOPHIA HENRY

MATERIAL GIRLS SERIES

DEVIL IN DISGUISE (Prequel)

OPEN YOUR HEART

LIVE TO TELL

CRAZY FOR YOU

SAINTS AND SINNERS SERIES

SAINTS

SINNERS

EVEN STRENGTH: Companion to BLUE LINES Aviators 4

DEVIL IN DISGUISE: Prequel to Material Girls Series

AVIATORS HOCKEY SERIES

DELAYED PENALTY

POWER PLAY

UNSPORTSMANLIKE CONDUCT

BLUE LINES

FOREIGN EDITIONS

FRENCH

SAGA MATERIAL GIRLS

DEVIL IN DISGUISE

OPEN YOUR HEART

LIVE TO TELL

CRAZY FOR YOU

DUO SAINTS AND SINNERS

SAINTS

SINNERS

ROMANS AUTONOMES LIÉS AUX SAGAS

EVEN STRENGTH

Saints & Sinners/Aviators Hockey Crossover Novel

SAGA AVIATORS HOCKEY

JINGLE BALL BENDER

BLUE LINES

GERMAN

MATERIAL GIRLS SERIES

OPEN YOUR HEART

LIVE TO TELL

CRAZY FOR YOU

RUSSIAN

SAINTS AND SINNERS SERIES

SAINTS

SINNERS

DON'T MISS OUT!

Get ALL the Sophia Henry news!

Sophia Henry's mailing list is the place to be if you like steamy romance novels that tug at your heart strings. Stay notified of new releases, sales, exclusive content. sophiahenry.com

MERCH STORE

Choose kindness and love with everything you've got. It's not just a motto. It's a way of life. Grab some motivational or bookish merch today! shopkrasivo.com

ABOUT THE AUTHOR

USA Today Bestselling Author Sophia Henry fell in love with reading, writing, and hockey all before she became a teenager. After graduating with a Creative Writing degree from Central Michigan University, she moved to warm and sunny North Carolina to enjoy the remainder of her winters.

She spends her days writing steamy, heartfelt contemporary romance novels hoping they resonate with and encourage others. When Sophia's not writing, she's hanging out with her two high-energy sons, an equally high-energy Plott Hound, and two cats who want nothing to do with any of them. She can also be found watching her beloved Detroit Red Wings and rocking out at as many concerts as she can possibly attend.

Sophia Henry's mailing list is the place to be if you like steamy romance novels that tug at your heart strings. Sign up at sophiahenry.com.

www.ingramcontent.com/pod-product-compliance
Lightning Source LLC
Chambersburg PA
CBHW031958240626
47153CB00003B/1021